THE WATCHER

BOOK ONE OF THE NIGHT REALM SERIES

K.R. BOWMAN

FOREWORD

This is a work of fiction. Names, characters, places, and incidents either are the product of the author's imagination or are used fictitiously. Any resemblance to actual persons, living or dead, events, or locales is entirely coincidental.

❋ Created with Vellum

PROLOGUE

The Realms first defense against the Nightlins are called Watchers.

The Dark

Taut, heavy chains held the prisoner's arms and legs, weighing him to the ground. Blood had pooled underneath him and soaked into what remained of his tattered clothes. The years he had been shut in the darkened room had melded together. His bloodshot eyes could not remember the last time they had seen the sun.

A figure stopped in front of the closed door. Its shadow eclipsed the soft light seeping through the cracks. A key inserted into the lock disrupted the silence. As the door labored to open, pale light spilled across the dirt floor, but it stopped short of the man as if the tendrils of light were teasing him. An ink-black creature stepped through the doorway, blotting out the light as the door closed. The creature made no sound as it made its way toward the prisoner.

"Are you ready?" whispered the raspy voice. The words tangled and barely understood. Its breath pushed out on a wheeze, as it brushed against the man's face—the air foul, like the acrid smell of burning flesh. Poking the gaunt prisoner's chest with its long nails, the creature sliced through the prisoner's paper-thin skin. Despite the excruciating pain, the prisoner made no sound. His mind had left him long ago. His body only remained. His vacant eyes never acknowledged the creature before him.

"I will take that to be a yes." The creature rose. It flicked its wrist, the chains fell away, and the prisoner crumpled to the ground. A dry, scaly hand wrapped around the man's wrist, and the creature dragged him out of the room.

1

I WAS A GROWN-ASS WOMAN, and yet, here I was being carted around, like a baby, because some dick head doctor said I might be a danger to others and/or myself. Blackouts kept knocking me out. We hadn't been able to figure out what was happening, so I had been relegated to the passenger seat for now.

Mariah jammed out next to me as she drove us to college. Her tiny 2005 Chevy Cavalier smelled like lasagna and had rust rings on everything. I cracked the window to let in some fresh air. I had known Mariah since high school, but we didn't become friends until we realized we were going to the same college. Then we clung to each other like life rafts, so we wouldn't have to fend for ourselves.

The moment my ass hit the seat, she launched into everything that happened to her over the summer. I tried to listen to her stories. I nodded my head or said the expected, "Oh really," when I was supposed to, but my mind kept going back to the crazy dreams I'd been having lately.

Anytime, my eyes closed, I caught glimpses of honey gold eyes and pale skin. Sometimes, I swear the smell of evergreens and earth filled my room. Even now, with me being sleepy, if my eyes closed, I might be able to hear strange noises or get a whiff of trees. A couple of mornings, I thought I had seen dirt under my fingernails.

"Sloane! Earth to Sloane!" Mariah practically yelled.

I turned, "Yeah? Sorry."

She shook her head. Her red curls beat her face. "Sloane, you're always in another world." She smirked.

She rounded the corner and drove into the college's parking lot. I tumbled out, practically dragging my bag behind me. The sun's warm rays nearly blinded me. Mariah seemed to leap out of the car. The amount of energy she had really astounded me sometimes.

As we strode down the sidewalk to class, Mariah asked, "Hey, isn't your birthday tomorrow?"

"What? Oh, yeah, it is." It's just another dull day for me.

"Oh, come on, Sloane. Eighteen is kind of a big number," she said.

I replied, "Yeah, but all I can do is vote. It's not like I can buy alcohol yet."

Mariah laughed. "Girl, who cares! That's why we have my older brother!"

I rolled my eyes. I wasn't a party girl. We snuck into a club once, and that was a disaster. I took a tumble, completely sober, thanks to my borrowed high heels and landed face-first into some guy's crotch at the bar. My barely-there dress left my granny panty covered ass up in the air in view for everyone. Without a word, I grabbed Mariah and left. That marked the end of my party days.

We climbed the steep stairs leading us to our class. My heart thumped faster with every step, and sweat beaded on my upper lip. The stairs definitely counted as my weekly exercise. Upon opening the building's door, we were greeted with a welcomed cold blast of air conditioning.

The building had a long hall in the center, with rooms attached to either side. Towering pine trees outside at the opposite ends of the hall seemed to wave through the windows. It was as though they deliberately made the building that way to punish us, showing us the outdoors moments before locking us away.

Obviously distracted, Mariah yanked me through our classroom door.

"Hurry up." She whispered fiercely.

Our teacher nodded at us as we passed. We scurried toward the back. A guy, with dark hair, green eyes, and glasses, sat in the second to last chair. He looked up as I walked toward him.

He smiled. "Hey."

I stumbled for a response, as my foot caught on the leg of the desk, and I nearly fell into the seat next to him. Pain shot through my arm and leg in the process. Heat crawled up my neck, about to stain my cheeks. I smiled briefly, looking away and pretended to study the room.

Our classroom was your standard boring room: beige walls, green chalkboard and dry erase board, and forty desks facing the front. A teacher several years ago had placed signs above the boards that read: 'Reading is fun!' 'Explore the world through a book.' Or my personal favorite, 'It's cool to be a bookworm,' with a book open and a worm eating through the pages. *Why did someone think those were for college students?*

The teacher stood from behind his desk. "Afternoon, everyone. Please turn to page twenty-five. We are starting in the 1800s, covering Europe and the Industrial Revolution." He flicked off the lights and powered up the projector, opening up the first PowerPoint slide.

I took my book out and flipped to the appropriate page, skimming the words, and studying the pictures. A war scene depicted across the page in bright colors. My light brown hair fell across my face as I leaned my head against my fist. It was practically bone meeting bone. I lacked all baby fat and curves for that matter. People always made fun of me for being too skinny. My body didn't want to hang onto fat at all, no matter what I ate. As I rubbed my knuckles against my skin, I couldn't help but be annoyed. My poor skin always had blemishes. I had given up hope on my facade a while ago. After scanning over my pale arm, I peeked back over at the cute guy.

His attention fixed on the teacher at the front of the class, but he glanced at me and smiled again. I smiled back a little steadier. Pretty sure my entire face burned red. It seemed guys rarely took an interest in me, and when they did, I reverted into a thirteen-year-old girl.

The teacher's voice droned on. As I turned my attention back to my book, the colors dissolved, and a tugging sensation pounded behind my eyes. Crap.

"No. Not now. Please, not now." I said through clenched teeth. I massaged my temples, which sometimes helped, but not today. Tingling started at my toes and traveled up my legs. I was on fire. Sweat ran in rivulets down my neck and back. My heart pounded in my ears and pulsated behind my eyes.

I had to get out of this room. *Why did this keep happening?*

Mariah arched a brow, as I tried to stand. I took a step toward the back door and swayed. My legs became mush, and I melted into the floor.

The people around me moved toward me. Their voices sounded far away.

Mariah's worried face appeared above me. Her mouth was saying my name. She frantically looked around and shouted. I tried not to panic but my heart pounded as if it would burst from my chest. The smell of Cedars rushed into the room. Iciness settled over my bones.

Everything closed in. The shape of the windows, doors, and even the hideous tile flooring became indistinct, as everything melted together in a gray blob. Mariah's face melted before my eyes. The lights above me were bright. Pain hammered at my skull. I laid my head on the floor and gave in to the darkness, hoping to see my dream world again.

———

A TANNED leathery face gazed into mine. His fireman's helmet sat precariously on his head.

I blinked a few times. Oh no. Why me? I closed my eyes again.

"Miss?" The fireman asked.

I cracked my eyes open. Embarrassment filled me to the brim. One of these days I'd be a normal girl.

I let out a big sigh and took in my surroundings. The classroom had pretty much vacated except for three other firemen and my teacher. Mariah stood in the farthest corner. I sat up.

"I'm alright. Nothing's wrong." My head swam for a moment. Fuck.

The fireman studied me, "Did you take any drugs or anything?"

I jumped, "What? No. I would never." Oh my gosh is that what they think?

He looked me over, then leaned in slightly and dropped his voice, "Are you pregnant?"

"What?!" I scurried up off the floor, banging into the desks around me. My face heated and I took several steps back. "No, god no." I shook my head to solidify my point. My stomach churned like it would empty everything in the floor.

He held his hands up and backed away, "Sorry, I have to ask. Some women pass out when they're expecting."

Oh my god. I was going to die from embarrassment. My heart was in my throat again.

He nodded, "Do you want to go to the hospital?"

I shook my head again rubbing my arms. Trying to comfort myself. "No, I'm fine. This happens sometimes."

He nodded again, his eyes measuring me then turned to speak to our teacher.

Mariah rushed to me, "Are you okay?" Mariah's eyes filled with concern as she held my bag out to me.

The tension eased. I nodded.

"I'm okay. I hope we figure this out soon."

She searched my eyes then nodded. "I'll take you home."

"Thanks."

We gathered up our things, and I thanked the firemen and my teacher. They asked one more time if I wanted to go to the hospital, but I assured them I was okay. The embarrassment of that moment would haunt me for days.

As Mariah and I walked to her car she asked, "Sloane, you're okay right? You aren't sick or anything?"

"I'm fine, just a migraine. Nothing to worry about." I smiled reassuringly at her. I squinted because the sun hurt my blue eyes so much. I dug in my bag, grabbing my dollar sunglasses. Cheap, but they worked fine. Hastily, I yanked on my jacket to block the sun from scorching my pale skin.

Her eyes studied me; she didn't quite believe me. Mariah didn't say anything, but I could feel her mind going a mile a minute.

"You know you can tell me anything, right?"

"Yeah, I know." I smiled slightly but focused my eyes back to the sidewalk. "Listen, don't worry. I just need some aspirin."

She studied me for a moment then nodded.

We piled back into her car and Mariah pulled onto the road heading to my house. She cranked the radio up. I rolled the window all the way down. The warm air whipped through my hair, I hung my arm out the window and moved my hand up and down to the rhythm of the music.

I felt normal again.

She pulled into my driveway and stopped with the car still running.

Mariah turned to me, "Are we still doing something for your birthday tomorrow?"

I took a deep breath, "Sure."

She shook her head, "One day we will get you excited about it." I only smiled slightly in answer.

"We've got History again and Biology tomorrow, don't forget. I'll be by to pick you up at one-thirty. Maybe we can eat after class?"

"Sure."

"You promise you're okay?"

"Yes, I'm fine." I rolled my eyes at her. "Have a good night."

I climbed out, shutting the car door behind me. Mariah waved as she drove away. I was going to have to tell her more of what had been happening soon. After today, I knew she wouldn't take such lame excuses much longer. Even I knew how lame they were.

It was almost supper time. When I opened the front door, it smelled like my mom had actually cooked. *Oh no.*

"Look what the cat dragged in!" She yelled. Her long, black hair was a mess, and she had some unknown substance on her shirt. That's my mom for you. She gave me a tight hug, as I came in the door. I love my mom, but she's a little too much sometimes, but I think that's how moms are supposed to be, suffocating so you'll want to leave home faster.

My mom was a little more petite than me with delicate features. Her dad's Asian ancestry dominated her features more than her German mother's. I didn't inherit any of mom's beautiful Asian characteristics. Some friends called her a fairy. All she needed were the wings.

"Hi, Mom," I felt like a giant as I hugged her. "What are you making?"

"Some baked chicken with potatoes, and corn, then a surprise for dessert." Her large, brown almond-shaped eyes sparkled with excitement.

"Oh, well, that sounds great." If only, she was known for her cooking. I gave her my best smile while secretly wishing for pizza.

She had the table all set and started laying food out. I sat at the table and watched as she flitted back and forth. Our house was pretty small. It was an older house built in the seventies. It looked like the house never left the seventies with all of its wood paneling everywhere. We only needed shag carpeting to make it complete. Although, if someone came along and wanted to update our house, I wouldn't stop them.

After a few minutes, she sat in front of me. She intently watched as I filled my plate and picked up my fork. The peas were probably the safest, so I tentatively skewered a few and raised them to my mouth. They weren't bad, a little salty for me, but overall, not bad.

"Very good mom," I cleaned each pea off my plate.

Mom let out a sigh of relief. I prodded the somewhat charred chicken, trying not to show my distaste.

"So, how was your first day back?"

"Oh, you know the usual. People being awkward. Our teacher

actually made us take out our books, and he lectured." I really didn't want to tell her about another episode.

"What? No one lectures on the first day! I'm not even that cruel to my students."

"Mom. Kindergartners don't count as students." I rolled my eyes.

"Rude." She eyed me, "Did you learn anything? See any cute boys? Any Leo's walking around?" she wiggled her eyebrows.

"Mom, of course, I didn't learn anything, and I definitely didn't see any cute boys." Anytime I say anything about a guy, she goes off about love and relationships, so I've learned not to say anything about the opposite sex.

"Honey, you're so smart and cute. You should have some love-struck fool following you around." She patted my arm.

"Mom," I said through slightly gritted teeth. I wanted to go off about not being as beautiful as her, also no one likes being called cute, but I didn't feel like having that conversation. So, I took a breath. I inwardly sighed and outwardly smiled, "Zero Leos today. No Brads or Chrises either."

"Chris?" She perked up.

"Yes, mom, Chris Hemsworth? You know, the Aussie? Played Thor, God of Thunder, muscles everywhere." My eyes closed. I may have sighed audibly.

"Well, I'm sure he's no Harrison Ford." A rare sad smile crossed her face. Ugh, I'm such a fucking idiot. I took her mind off of me but made her think of him... I rolled my eyes and took my plate to the sink. "So, dessert?"

Shaking herself out of her memories, she jumped up, "Ohh, it's exciting. Hang on, hang on." She hurried to the fridge. "I saw this at the store, and I just had to get it. Doesn't it look great?" Her eyes widened with excitement.

She held out a plastic container of what looked like, at one point, had been a chocolate cake.

The cake kind of sat up straight, but the icing had run down the sides and coated the container. It looked tasty.

"Wow! Mom, that does look good."

She smiled sheepishly and shrugged a shoulder, "It was on sale. That's why it looks like this."

I chuckled, "You've always said, a messy cake is better."

She brightened more and popped off the plastic lid. Grabbing a knife, she cut out a generous piece and flopped it onto a plate and handed it to me.

"You know my birthday is tomorrow, right?" I said jokingly.

"You know me, always a reason to get more cake. Besides, I know the cake is the only thing you've ever liked about your birthday."

Why did this make me feel guilty? She tried so hard. I owed her the truth.

She cut a piece for herself and licked the knife before putting the lid back.

I glanced at my mom, "Sooo, I had a small episode today."

She dropped her fork, "Shoot. I was afraid something like that happened. You let me talk about guys without rolling your eyes. Sloane, it's been weeks since your last one." She shook her head. "What were you doing?"

"I was in class." I studied her expression. A weight settled around her.

"Oh, Sloane, I'm sorry." She patted my arm.

I pushed the icing around on my plate, "It's okay. It wasn't too bad."

She frowned, "I wish we could figure this out. There doesn't seem to be any triggers. I hoped they had stopped." She pointed her fork at me, "I still think those doctors are idiots. I don't think they checked everything or took us seriously."

I shrugged, "I'm kind of okay with not going to more doctors. Besides, it's not like we can afford it."

"Sloane, you matter way more than money. I'll save up some more, and we will find the right doc."

"Alright, I guess. I'm just tired of getting poked so much and no answers."

She nodded, "I know." She squeezed my arm.

My now empty plate beckoned me, and I licked it clean.

Mom laughed. "Go relax and rest up. I've got more surprises tomorrow." She winked and started cleaning off the table.

Pictures of me and my mom that were never straight and hung in old, weathered frames, decorated the narrow hallway to my room. The diminishing light from the sunset cast abstract shadows across the walls and floors. Once in my room, the setting sun peeked through the trees.

Three walls in my room were painted a warm amber-gold so, when the sun shined in, my room glowed. The one white wall had two equally spaced windows with my bed centered in between. It's my golden sanctuary. I'm usually a neat freak except when I enter my room.

I went to my computer and punched it on. My TV didn't have the internet and watching shows on my phone sucks, so the trusty old computer won. Stacks of paper littered the area. Finally, my computer made that wondrous welcome sound, and I sat in front of the screen, ready to watch some *Lord of the Rings*. Ready to dream of Legolas. Mmmm.

I'm so pathetic.

Hours drifted by; it was almost midnight by the time Gandalf the Grey appeared. I turned the computer off. I dragged myself into the bathroom to brush my teeth and wash my face.

My heavy eyes were stale from staring at the computer screen for so long. I glanced at mom's closed door and padded softly back into my room, climbing under the dark blue sheets. I snuggled deeper under the covers, in search of warmth. The mattress molded to my body, the thick comforter encasing the warmth close to me. The arms of sleep tugged me deeper into rest until a popping noise sounded beside my ear.

My eyes cracked open. I cautiously sat up and studied the room. *What had caused the noise?* Trepidation set in, as the air around me became still and suffocating. The clock in the hall chimed midnight. Ding. Ding. Ding. Ding.

I waited for the final chime, but it never came.

The walls of my room began to vibrate and blur. I clutched the sheets to my chest, as I frantically tried to figure out what was happening. What the heck?

"Mom?" I called out, hoping she would rescue me.

I had to be dreaming. Each wall crumbled before my eyes, opening to the night. As everything evaporated into thin air, the stars grew brighter. The moon grew bigger. I swear I could have touched it.

My bed was gone. My house had vanished. I sat on a patch of dried ground; large trees surrounded me in every direction. They towered over me, maybe fifty-feet tall and ten-feet wide. I was in the middle of a dense forest, wearing my sleep shorts, an old Nike t-shirt, no bra, and no shoes.

Fuck. Shit. What the hell?? What happened?

My legs shook. I pushed my hair back and succeeded in getting dirt on my face and in my hair. I remained on the ground, listening for any sound. I picked up wood chips and some dead leaves. They felt real, so I couldn't be dreaming... right? I could even smell the wet earth, and hear nothing but silence. The darkness surrounding me seemed to absorb the moonlight as if this world was a black hole. Don't animals make noises at night? I stood; thankful, my legs held me. I stepped forward, stopped, and listened again. Nope, nothing. Okay... I took another step.

"This cannot be happening. Hello?" My voice sounded weird in this strange place. I pinched my arm and raked my nails down both arms. I accomplished making red lines on my arms. Yeah, that didn't help. I stopped and leaned over, placing my hands on my knees, trying to breathe. A panic attack was on the way. I squeezed my eyes shut.

"NO, no, no, no. I'm dreaming. This is a dream."

Taking a deep breath, I pushed forward, every now and then, stopping to nurse my feet because of twigs and sharp rocks. My poor feet were going to be shredded by the time I found someone or, by the time something found me or, maybe, I would wake up and not have to worry about it. I really hoped for the latter.

The eerie stillness of the night made my anxiety double. The moon looked like a large, round light bulb. It was easily three times larger than normal. It guided me through the tall, tall trees making my progress much easier. The trees and earth surrounding me drank in the moonlight. Hours drifted by as I roamed. *Why did this place feel oddly familiar?*

The wind picked up, rustling the leaves and branches. A bird called out, and something hit my head. Claws scraped my scalp. I screamed and ran. I dove behind a tree and crouched against the base. Birds of every shape and small animals were running from something in pure terror.

The wind blew harder. The branches creaked and swayed, but I couldn't feel the wind on my skin. I looked upward, trying to focus my eyes. They pieced together what I saw, but I hoped they were wrong. Large animals raced through the treetops, leaping from limb to limb or flying through the foliage. What I assumed were birds were bigger than any bird I had ever laid eyes upon – they almost appeared to be... dragons?

Are you freaking kidding me? No more J.R.R Tolkien before bed!

My dream had just changed into a freaking nightmare. Shit. This has to be my dream.

My eyes transfixed on the birds above me. The body of the bird was thicker than a full-grown man with a wingspan even greater. A long-tail trailed behind it. Its razor-sharp claws clenched together, gleaming in the moonlight. I stayed rooted by that tree for a long time after the dragons or whatever the hell that was had left. I couldn't make up my mind if I should follow them or go in the opposite direction. Blood ran from my head, a surface scratch, but man, it hurt.

In case the dragons came back (my mind boggled at the thought of real dragons), I picked my way through the forest, trying to keep to the direction of the moon, the giant trees loomed over me as I walked in their shadows. I had gone maybe a mile when I heard music playing. Was that Bon Jovi? The notes of "Livin' on a Prayer" drifted through the forest. *This might be my best dream yet.* My heart leapt with joy, and I picked up my pace, as fast as my hurt feet would let me, toward the noise.

A pinprick of light began to be distinguishable through the trees, and the music grew louder. I hid behind a tree and peered out at the scene before me.

There were indeed people who were dancing and laughing. A bonfire was in the middle of a group of people. They all had varying tints of white skin, porcelain, and almost translucent compared to mine, that seemed to glow from within. They were throwing things into the fire, making it climb higher into the night sky and crackle. Sparks flew and scattered with the breeze.

"What are you doing out here alone?"

2

Sloane

I spun to face a tall, intimidating man. His face partly shadowed, which made the angles of his face sharp and hard. His cold, angry eyes glared. He may have been a soldier, with thick leather boots, fitted pants, and a loosely belted shirt, all in black.

"Uh," I took a quick unsteady step backwards, pressing my back tightly to the tree. I dug my fingers into the rough bark, trying to steady myself.

He stared at me, not moving.

"You're a groundling, aren't you?" His voice was deep, and a bit rough, as if he might have been shouting commands all day. It was a pleasant voice, although, by his appearance, I didn't want him addressing me. "How did you get through the barrier?"

What was he talking about? I didn't respond right away. I couldn't keep my eyes off of him. Tall, shadowed, menacing, but from what I could see in the dark, he was kind of handsome. Maybe it was just because he was huge and had a commanding presence? I came looking for people, found one, and now I couldn't help but think, *I wish he wasn't here.* Even more, I wished I wasn't *here.*

He took a step toward me, and I moved behind the tree. He stopped abruptly and watched me.

His eyes traveled down my legs to my bare feet and back to the top of my tousled and blood matted hair. My subconscious chose this time to remind me of how unattractive I was at the moment, even more than usual.

He retreated the step he had taken and placed his hands out palm up, showing he wasn't carrying anything. My brain registered his large hands and how easily they would fit around my small neck.

"Listen, I'm not going to hurt you. All the groundlings are supposed to be at the camp, not up here. You need to go back to the camp and stay there." He commanded me. He expected me to follow his orders. Some sort of machete hung from his belt, and something was strapped across his large, muscular back. I tried not to think about either of them.

I nodded and took a deep breath, "Sorry, you scared me. You came out of nowhere." I giggled nervously, quickly turned, and walked down the hill. *Had I giggled? What an idiot.* I shook my head. I didn't look back, but I could feel his eyes on me the whole time.

When I reached the bottom, people parted like the Red Sea, giving a wide berth, and watching me. No one said anything; they only stared. Everyone was dressed in black. Their pale skin was a stark contrast to the bold color.

I was the only one in my pajamas.

"Hi?" I weakly waved a hand, trying to bridge the gap between alien and species.

The group parted to where an older man stood. His eyes crinkled with amusement and curiosity. His clothes were made simple, again all black. The only thing sticking out amongst the dark was the big, shiny buckles on his boots.

"Well, hallo. I thought all the groundlings had gotten 'ere by now, but suppose not. I'm Brand Bowman." His voice was deep, gentle, and had a slight Scottish accent. He held his hand out to me. His thick hands were rough from hard work and dwarfed mine. His eyes were bright as he smiled at me. "What's your name, lass?"

"Sloane Norwood."

"Nice to meet you, Sloane. Glad ye made it."

"Made it? Where? Uh, what's a groundling?" I asked. I glanced around at the people staring. What was going on? How the hell had I fallen into this place? Was I dreaming about being in a cult? That would be a first for me.

Brand studied me for a moment, glancing at the crowd. "It's what we call newcomers."

"Oh." I scanned the crowd, noticed several whispering, and pointing at me. My shoulders rolled inward, and my head dipped down, somehow hoping that would help hide me. Heat crawled up my neck again. I needed to get out of there.

Small and large canvas tents surrounded the fire. People meandered between each tent. Some held small metal cups or bowls. Tall, cylindrical lights were positioned at each tent opening. The lights gave off a white almost blue hue, making the surrounding darkness feel more alien.

"Yous know what? Why don't ye follow me?" He held his arm out, indicating the path for me to follow. "Let's go into the striped tent over there."

The crowd of about 50 people parted, forming the path to the tent. An oil lamp hung from the middle pole. A cot stood in a corner, along with a washbasin. The tent was surprisingly clean, including the smooth dirt floor. Brand pulled out two stools and sat on one.

"Now isn't this better? Away from prying eyes." He winked. "What happened to ye head? Yous have blood running down your face."

I patted my scalp. "Oh, a bird or something scratched me earlier, but it's fine." The scrape was tender and a little raw.

Brand cleared his throat, "I guess I should ask if ye ken where ye are?" He watched my reaction. I shook my head.

"This," he gestured with his hands around him, "has always been known as the Night Realm. For most of us, we live and die here. It's our job to keep watch of the world from this side." He studied me for a second, "Ye came from the other side, right?"

"Other side?" I asked.

He looked confused for a moment before answering, "I'm sorry, lass, what part of the world are you from?"

"The U.S., Colorado, to be exact."

He smiled, "I t'ought yous were American."

"Are you sure this isn't a dream? This seems pretty outrageous." My voice squeaked and I immediately felt self-conscious.

"Sorry, lassie, it's not a dream."

"But honestly, if it is a dream, you wouldn't know it, and you wouldn't be able to tell me... Listen, I need to get home. My mom will be wondering where I am. My birthday is tomorrow, and we're supposed to have cake. Cake is my favorite part of my birthday." Tears welled in my eyes, threatening to fall. I breathed deep through my nose and out my mouth. "I need to get back home."

"Lass, it'll work out, you'll see. Dinna fash your head about it. We'll take care of ye."

"But if this is a dream, how can you help?"

He frowned, "Well, if it were a dream, I would know, and the people outside would know."

"But, this could all be a construct of my mind." I watched him waiting for the moment he would agree.

He only shook his head, "Lassie, if this was your dream, I'd say you'd have a pretty great imagination."

I glanced around the small tent, at each piece of mismatched furniture, each with history attached to it, from the small wooden cot circa American Civil War times or before, to the oil lamps swinging from the wood brace in the center of the tent. The oil from the burning wick filled the air with a sweet scent. The music outside still pumped through the campsite. People laughed and talked as they passed us. I looked back at Brand, studying his face and clothing. His hair was thin, with varying shades of grey. His thick arms and legs were heavy with muscle from heavy labor. His portly stomach made his black tunic stretch tight.

"I have a question for you."

"Aye, ask away." He leaned forward in anticipation.

"Are there dragons?" My voice nearly squeaked again.

Brand peered at me, "What makes ye ask lass?"

I played with the edge of my shirt, crinkling it in my hands,

"Things I saw when I first arrived, flying through the air." My heart pounded in my ears, remembering what I had seen. "Please, help me get home." My brain felt like it was on the brink of imploding with all the information and overstimulation. My brain had finally turned to mush. Pretty sure, I had stopped thinking and analyzing so much because of it.

"I probably won't believe it until I go to sleep and wake up here."

He nodded and smiled again, but this time there was a hint of sadness in his eyes. "Frankly, you shouldn't be 'ere, but I'm glad ye came. I need to ask some of the others if they have heard of such a thing." He paused; his eyebrows scrunched in concentration. He ran his hand through his sparse hair and rubbed his meaty hands together. He brought his eyes to meet mine, "Well, let's find yous a place to stay the night. Ye won't be goin' 'ome t'night. We'll figure this out on the morrow."

He stood and held the tent flap open for me, where I followed his lead to a larger tent. Muffled voices drifted outside. We walked inside, and the talking halted. Fifteen pairs of eyes stared back at us. *Oh, isn't this wonderful!*

"Everyone, meet Sloane Norwood. She's going to be staying with us for a little while until we can get her home. If someone could show her around and give her a bed for the night, it would be greatly appreciated." Brand glanced at me and winked, then pushed me further into the room.

"You'll be fine." Smiling, he turned away, letting the tent flap close behind him.

Everyone stared at me and didn't say a thing—nothing like leading a lamb to the slaughter.

"Hi. I'm Ashlen Tatum." A perky girl with long wavy dark hair and light green eyes held out her hand. She wore a long-sleeved grey shirt with the ends frayed and a pair of once black jeans that had more of a grey coloring. Thick black boots that she could use to kick in doors protected her feet.

I shook her hand. "Hi," I muttered sheepishly.

She smiled. "There's an empty bed over here by me." She led me to a small bed with the covers pulled tight. Everything reminded me of a military bunkhouse; all the beds were lined up along the brown cloth walls, very tidy and neat. Oil lamps hung from the cross beams casting an eerie yellow glow. I almost expected there to be black well-buffed shoes at the end of each bed and a loud talking officer to come stomping through issuing orders. I sat on the bed corner. My toes brushed the dirt floor, while Ashlen sat across from me.

"So, how are you doing so far?"

"Uh, I'm definitely overloaded right now with information."

She laughed. "I bet! We've never had a new groundling drop in alone before. You are quite the talk of the camp. I'm so jealous," she shook her head in wonder, "every guy will be wondering your name and story. So, where are you from?"

"Oh, Colorado Springs. You?" What did she mean by every guy?

"L.A." She had this very confident air about her. She stood straight and tall. Her chin slightly lifted. Her big hazel eyes met mine with openness and excitement.Very self-assured, which I didn't mind, maybe it would rub off on me.

"Considering how you got here, you might have a choice about this life. Will you stay or leave?"

"I need to get home. My mom is probably losing her mind."

"There's a portal that can take you back, but the Leader is about the only one who knows where it is. I'm sure Brand will take you to him in the morning, then you can get home." Ashlen said assuredly.

"A portal?" I asked.

Ashlen nodded, "Yeah, we use it to go between the two realms."

I felt like I was going to have permanent wrinkles on my face from all the frowning. I leaned forward and put my hands on my head, gripping my hair, and pulled on my scalp, hoping to ease some tension. "I really hope I wake up in my bed."

"Hey, listen, just breathe. Now you know there is more out there. More than just the world you went to sleep in. It's a lot, but you have to admit it's pretty exciting and it's cool. I'll try to explain as much as I can." She took a deep breath, "Where to start? Okay, let me think." She slapped her hands together. "All of us here are eighteen. On the day you turn eighteen, you are transferred to one of the campsites in the Night Realm to finish your training. Back in the Norm at the Realm Department, there are portals connected to this world. That's how we all came here. I believe there might be a few more portals sprinkled around the globe, but those are all mandated by the Norm Defense. My parents work there now." She looked to make sure I was still following. I nodded my head as I took it all in.

"Usually, your parents teach you about our history and mission to get you prepared. My father, who wasn't one for books, began my teachings with weapons." She smiled, her eyes looking past me remembering. "But we all begin true training together. The training goes for about six months. Then we go through the field test. The field test is a beast. They discovered when we were tested that our abilities appear, so by the end of it, we can officially call ourselves Watchers."

So far, I gathered that I would be wielding weapons, killing things, putting myself in danger, while living in the stinky woods so in six months they can test my powers, and I would be whatever she had called them. Are these people insane? Poor Ashlen. She certainly drank the Kool-Aid. I sure as Hell wasn't about to do that! My mind was spinning. I stared at her. My hands shook. I tried to hide my anxiety, but I've never been good at hiding emotions. My chest tightened.

She started speaking again, "See if this sounds familiar before you completely write me off as crazy. A few months before I turned eighteen, I would get these colossal headaches, and my eyes would cross, blurring my vision." She paused, taking my silence as an answer. "I don't know why it happens like that. I don't know if it's because our bodies are preparing us to move to another world or maybe because our abilities are coming to their full potential, but once we come here, the headaches stop. Not everyone becomes a Realmer. My brother works at the Defense Department in the Norm. Not to be judge-y, and it's not like I'm going to report them for doing a shit job at preparing you, but who are your parents?" She asked.

"My mom's name is Anna. She's a teacher, and I'm pretty sure I would know if she was some sort of warrior." I frowned and rested my chin on my palm. "I never met my dad. He left before I was born." I sat straighter and looked at Ashlen.

"Hmm, well, he must be the key to you being here, but I still don't understand." She looked off in space. "You see, your parents bring you to the headquarters so you can travel to the Night Realm. We can't come here by ourselves. You have to have a key to get in. Groundlings don't have keys."

"Umm... so what if you didn't use a key?"

She cocked an eyebrow and shrugged, "I have no idea. I'm sure Brand will figure this out tomorrow. Come on. I'm going to get ready for bed. The bathrooms are this way if you want to follow me. There should be extra toothbrushes and toothpaste for you."

"Thanks." I followed her. The bathroom area was in a smaller tent about ten feet from where we slept. The bathroom had buckets of water for sinks, a leveled dirt floor, and empty buckets to use for our 'special' business with a shovel propped in the corner. Another white-blue bulb emitted light from the corner.

"What's with the weird lights?" I gestured to the bulb.

Ashlen stopped and glanced at it. "Oh, it's for vitamin D since we don't have sunlight here. You know we don't want scurvy. That would suck."

I nodded and frowned, never having heard of bulbs that gave you vitamins. I wasn't quite sure what scurvy was either but with a name like that I didn't think I wanted to find out.

"I guess you're wondering why the primitive lifestyle?" Ashlen asked.

I eyed the shovel and mounds of dirt. Gross.

She chuckled, "This is one of our temporary campsites for our training. We have to move every few weeks so the Nightlins won't find us so easily. The barriers they put up are supposed to keep us undetected, but it's an extra precaution."

Hmm, okay, made sense. My mind was in creative mode tonight to dream this place up. I picked a strange place to get stuck in.

"Anywaysssss, when our powers transcend, we will be able to protect ourselves."

I froze, "Like superpowers?"

She glanced over her shoulder and nodded, "Yeah." She smiled, "Oh, I should have said we get powers."

My mouth hung slightly open, "Superpowers are for comic books or movies – not real life."

She laughed and shook her head, "It's going to be fun, watching you discover everything. Where do you think the people who wrote comics or movies got the ideas? The creators were all Realmers. I guess it's kind of cheating because they didn't use their imaginations, but with the money they've made, we are able to supply the Night Realm and protect the Norm. Granted, it's not like living at the Hilton, but it helps."

I stared at her. "I could wield fire?"

"Ha, no, you probably won't. Usually, it's only the guys who get fire, so lame. There aren't many who've been lucky enough to get that ability." She scrubbed her face with a cloth, she leaned down to the bucket and wrung the water out, laying it over a piece of string stretched across the tent. She turned back with one hand on her hip, "I would love that skill." Her other hand clenched in front of her, "It would be amazing. Can you imagine?" She wriggled her fingers as if fire danced across them.

I shook my head because I couldn't imagine anyone with super-human powers. Not in real life. Trying not to disturb the gash on my scalp, I wrung out my washcloth and patted my face. Most of the blood wiped away.

"I've had my whole life to wrap my brain around everything, and you've only had a few hours." She tied her hair back.

I pulled a stool over and sat to tend to my feet. Small bruises were appearing and cuts dotted across every inch. I tried to wipe them but ended up sticking my feet in the buckets of water.

"Dang, girl. You really weren't prepared." She frowned.

I grimaced as I touched a tender spot.

"Come on, I'm spent, so I'm sure you are. I'll find you something to sleep in." She peered closer at my head, "I'll grab some ointment too."

Surprisingly, they had extra pajamas. The clothes fit with the military motif, starting with dark green cotton pants and a short-sleeve grey cotton shirt. They fit pretty well. They even had some slippers.

The trees loomed over us as we walked between the tents. Everyone acted like they wanted to ignore me, which was better than them staring at me, so I wasn't going to complain. The beds were surprisingly comfortable. The mattress was thin, but it molded to my body. The brown and sticky ointment she gave me had a pleasant herbal aroma, like lavender, which soothed my mind as well.

Information overloaded my mind and body. I was already exhausted from my day in the Norm, that I couldn't rummage through my brain with these new events. Before I knew it, I was asleep.

3

Sloane

"HAPPY BIRTHDAY TO YOU, happy birthday dear Sloooane, happy birthday to yoooooouuuuuu!!!"

With my eyes crusted with sleep, and my mind not attached to my body yet, I didn't know what to expect. Why would someone be singing to me? The light overhead flicked on, and I was blinded for a moment.

"Sloane! Wakey, wakey eggs, and bakey! Get up! You need to blow out these candles before I burn the house down." A short pause, "Sloane?"

"What are you talking about? How'd you know...? Mom?" I came fully awake. I sat straight in my bed and examined my surroundings. My mom, as our yearly custom, had come in at the asscrack of dawn to give me my birthday cake. The candles were lit, while the wax dripped, mixing into the icing. I rubbed my eyes, trying to wake up.

That had to have been the most convincing dream I had ever had.

"Mom... you really outdid yourself this time." I gazed around my room, double-checking for creatures and that my walls were intact. Everything looked normal. I leaned over to blow out the candles.

"For a second, I wasn't so sure you were on this planet with me." Mom set the cake on my desk, cut out two pieces, and placed them on a couple of plates. She handed the biggest to me. "So, how does it feel being a grownup now?"

"Yeah, I think I'm ready to retire and start collecting my social security check." My mom rolled her eyes and ate her piece.

"Don't wish your life away just yet," she said.

The cake had two layers of chocolate sponge with raspberry filling, and fudge drizzled on top, so awesome. "Mmmm. This is amazing." I licked my plate and fork several times, then asked for another slice.

"Mom, you will never guess what I had a dream about last night..." A piece of cake fell onto my pants, that's when I noticed my pajamas. My hand stopped with the fork halfway to my mouth. I still had on the grey cotton shirt and green pants like the ones I had fallen asleep in at the camp. My fingers played along the bottom edge of the shirt. I quickly ran my hand across my scalp. The skin was smooth. Weird. No scrape.

"Really? Hmm... tell me." She hadn't noticed I had stopped. She sat perched on the edge of my bed, dressed in her pajamas. Her pajamas consisted of a faded pair of plaid flannel pants with colors of blue, red, green, and pale yellow. She does change her shirt, though. Sometimes, it's an old high school shirt, hockey playoff shirt, or a shirt she and her friends from school had made in the old days. Today, it was a shirt from high school that read, 'Class of '85! So excited to be alive!'

"It was so... strange. I was transported to another world, no realm, where it's always night. There were these terrifying dragon-like beasts, and I met some fascinating, but different people. A Scotsman named Brand helped me. Everyone called me a groundling. Although I thought I had been dreaming, I'm wearing different pj's than when I went to bed." I glanced up to see my mom's face frozen. Her eyes were so wide. I could see the white all around her eyes.

"Mom?"

"You went there?" she whispered.

"Yeah... wait. You know?"

She dropped her head. She lifted her hand to the spot between her brows, and her arms shook.

"Mom? What is it?"

"Sloane, you can't go back there." Fear held her. "Promise me you won't go back."

"I. Mom, I can't promise. I... don't even know how I got there in the first place. I won't know how to stop from going back." I set my plate on the nightstand and pulled the covers up around me. "Are you telling me that place is real? How would you know? Wait, are you secretly a kick-ass warrior?" Did I really not know my mother at all?

My mom took a deep breath, letting the air out slowly, and stood wearily, "Follow me." She led me down the hall to her room and to the back of her closet. She lowered to her knees, pulling out a dark wooden box hidden under a pile of clothes. The wood had intricate carvings etched along the sides and topped with gold inlaid into the carvings. A tiny latch kept the top secured. She undid the latch and carefully lifted the lid.

I sat on the floor next to her and peered in the box. A beautiful gold necklace and dagger were nestled in plush red velvet. The chain was thin and delicate. At the end of the chain was what appeared to be a compass, it was round but came to a point at the top and bottom. An intricate design decorated the gold metal that encompassed the needle. The needle spun frantically around and around. Mom reached in, pulled the necklace out, and handed it to me. The moment it settled in my hands; the needle slowed then stilled. I glanced at mom, but she had her eyes fixated onto the now resting compass.

"Well, there's my answer." She peered up at me, fear and sadness pouring out of her. She had aged twenty years within the last ten minutes.

"What?" Stirrings of a headache threatened to take over. "What is that supposed to mean? You can't go all Yoda on me, 'There's my answer' and just stop." My temper rose. I didn't feel like controlling it.

"Honestly, I was hoping it wouldn't do anything for you." Her now sad eyes were soft as she watched me. "I found this after your father disappeared. I don't think he meant to leave it, but I thought it might be meaningful since you came along." The corners of her mouth tugged up slightly, but the strain around her eyes stayed.

"So, what exactly are you saying? Dad was some kind of mercenary or...." I waved my hands in the air trying to come up with some sort of word, "Ugh, I don't know. All these years, you've been keeping this from me?"

"I wanted to wait for the right time... I wasn't sure if I was supposed to show it to someone, but I had a feeling I would know when I needed to show you. And well, it worked out that way. Listen, I would have told you before I died."

"Wow. Thanks, mom. It makes me feel so much better."

"Yeah, I know it was awful for me to keep it from you, but I'm not going to just pull out a knife for my *child* to play with." By now, she was glaring at me.

I merely rolled my eyes. "I just want to know what's going on. Okay?"

She shrugged, her eyes remaining focused on the dagger, "Sure."

"So, did dad say anything about a separate night realm with creatures?"

"Ha. No."

"He never mentioned another world or realm? At all?"

"Of course not. He had secrets like everyone does..."

"No, mom, he didn't keep a normal secret from you. Those are like you paid off a stack of parking tickets, or you hate the only food your wife knows how to cook. Not, I work in a secret, dangerous night realm."

Exasperated, she continued, "Are you finished? Obviously, he wasn't going to tell me about some other world. He would have known my reaction. I would have thought he was crazy. I do remember him talking on the phone a few times and mentioning Watchers, Hunters, and Protectors, though. Those are words someone cannot forget especially, in the context he would use them, but he never said anything about a separate world. It's not like we had a lot of time together."

True. Six months isn't very long for a relationship. Then again, she wouldn't have been very focused on those little details, especially if she found out she was pregnant, right after her love disappeared. I slipped the necklace over my head and stood. Mom closed the lid to the box and handed it to me. I ran my hands over the smooth wooden box. My fingertips delicately traced the gold designs; it hummed softly, but I think I was the only one who could hear it. Mom was silent as she watched me. I turned around to see the clock on my mom's dresser. I was going to have to leave for school soon.

"I'm not going to get any real answers while I'm here, so I might as well go to class and try to think about this later. You know, while I was there, I only wanted to get home to you. I never wanted to go back to that hole in the woods. I was scared, but more importantly, I was so worried about how you would feel if I was missing. Now, mom, there is so much I need to know, and you can't, or won't tell me. Hopefully, I can go back tonight, and they'll give me the answers I need."

"I can't tell you because I don't know, Sloane. Do you think I spent all that time pregnant and looking for your father if I knew there was a chance he would be in another world? No, I've mourned him for nearly nineteen years. Or what is almost worse than mourning is the fear that he made the choice to leave. That he left me because I wasn't enough."

Shit. She was pissed and hurt. It was kind of my fault, but I'm not letting her completely off for this one.

"And now you're telling me you are planning on going back?"

"Mom, I have to. At least, I'll try…" I decided anger was not the route to go right now, "I have to. I need to find out what this stuff means, and I want to know what happened to dad too. Don't you? Don't you want to know for sure, beyond a shadow of a doubt, he didn't leave us because he wanted to?"

She continued to stare up at me from the floor. Her eyes were scared and tired. She nodded once. "You know I looked for him, but there was no evidence of him even being alive. It's like he never existed. I don't even have any pictures, so the cops couldn't help me. I knew he had a brother but had no way of contacting him. I was stuck. Then you came along shortly after, and you became my world."

I knelt and squeezed her hand, "Mom, if I have the power to find him or the truth of what happened to him, then I'm going to do it."

She only nodded.

I stood and trudged back to my room, laying the box on my bed. I ambled over to the cake, grabbed a fork, and started eating again. I'm an emotional eater that loves food who can't gain weight, so not the worst combination.

Thoughts of last night's actions swirled through my head. *It was all real... Brand, Ashlen, the dragons, and that insufferable soldier... they were all real. Shit. Was the Night Realm the place I've been dreaming about for years?*

Mom shuffled in and started eating a piece of the cake too. Emotional eating runs in our family. We simply sat on the bed, staring off into space, putting food in our mouths, a robotic yet glorious cycle.

"Is that the time?!" Mom jumped up and raced out of the room. I could hear her bumping around in her room and turning on the water in the bathroom.

I still had a couple of hours before my class, so I gobbled down some more cake. Mom yelled bye as she ran out the door.

I sat curled up on my bed, eating the delicious birthday cake and thinking.

4

MARIAH PULLED into the drive on two wheels. The passenger side window rolled down, and some pop diva was belting out a tune on the radio, "Yo, bitch! Happy birthday!"

I laughed. Opening the door, I slid into the seat.

She took off down the road toward school, singing away at the top of her lungs. I leaned my head against the headrest, letting the sounds reverberate through me. I closed my eyes. The bright sunlight warmed me up. Soon, I drifted away in a cloud.

A flash of gold hair filled my mind. Golden eyes faced me. Coolness settled over me, then another flash of black leathery skin and hollowed eyes pierced through me.

I jolted awake. My breath was shallow and rattled my chest. Gooseflesh prickled across my skin.

Mariah parked the car.

"Come on, birthday girl!" Mariah yelled.

Ugh. I grabbed my bag and grudgingly got out.

Mariah looped her arm through mine and pulled me down the sidewalk.

"We're going to be late on the second day!" She pulled me up the stairs. The air in my chest burned. My thighs worked in overdrive. *I have to get in shape, especially if I am going to be running for my life and fighting dragons.*

Sweating sucks.

The teacher immediately began reciting the *Gettysburg Address*. My mind quickly drifted off into another world full of night creatures, with daring heroines, and most of all - magic. My imagination ran unencumbered.

The hour passed by without me taking notice. People packing up their things, and walking by me brought my consciousness back into the real world. I had subconsciously pulled the chain of the necklace out and was winding it around my fingers.

"So, are we having a party tonight?" Mariah asked as we made our way down the sidewalk toward the biology building.

"Um... no, not tonight. I can't. My mom decided to cook dinner." I made sure to give her my sad yet, exasperated face as I looked at her except I had last night's events pushing to the forefront of my mind, so it was kind of hard to look truly distraught.

"Well... okay, maybe this weekend would be better?"

"Yes, absolutely. I can do something this weekend." Maybe. But probably not. "I'll call and let you know."

She smiled, "Alright, good."

Sitting through Biology class was kind of like torture. I couldn't stop thinking about last night. My fear transformed into excitement. My body practically called out for the other world. Is this why I never seemed to belong? Mariah was my only friend, and she had been great, but she didn't even know me all the years we went to school together. I wanted to get back to the Night Realm as soon as possible. By the time we left, I was the one pulling Mariah down the sidewalk to the car. I'm always a sucker for a good mystery.

"Gosh, girl, what's gotten into you?"

"I'm ready to get home is all."

She laughed. "Girl, you are a conundrum, even if it is your birthday."

We drove home, singing away to Britney Spears and Mariah Carey. When Mariah pulled into the drive, my mom was already

home. I turned to get out of the car. *When would I see her again?* I
leaned over, hugging her. I squeezed her tight. "Thank you for being
my friend."

"Since when did you go all soft on me?" She pulled back so she
could look me in the eyes.

"I've never told you, so I thought 'Hey, why not now?'" I aimed a
goofy smile at her and heaved myself out of the car.

"Thanks for being my bitch too!" She yelled. Lord, she was a crazy
person.

I waved to her and walked inside. The smell of food wafted from
the kitchen, warning me that mom had started cooking. I dropped
my bags by the door and kicked off my shoes. Mom peeked around
the corner of the kitchen and smiled softly.

"Hi."

"Hello."

She turned back into the kitchen. I sat at our small breakfast table
and waited. She dropped a plate, full of every kind of food imagin-
able, in front of me. I jerked my head up to look at her.

"I thought since this is probably your last night here for a while, I
would make your favorites." Her voice was steady, but only I could
hear the slight shake in it. She was putting on her brave face for me. I
didn't want to make my mom go through being left behind again, but
we both knew I had to do this. At least this time, she knew I was leaving. She knew why. She knew where. I tried not to let the guilt eat my
insides.

My plate had waffles, grilled chicken, spaghetti covered with
sauce and cheese, blueberries, watermelon, corn, sweet potatoes, and
black-eyed peas. Oh. My. Gosh. My eyes were huge as saucers, and my
mouth had gone slack.

"Whoa."

"Yep. You need to be good and healthy, where you're going."

"I don't think I'm going to be able to eat all of this."

"Just try." She smiled and sat her plate down, which wasn't much
different from mine.

"Where are you going?"

"Nowhere."

"Then why is your plate the same as mine?"

"Well, it all seemed great to me." She winked and began eating. We talked about the day like it was any other. We even contemplated future trips we had planned.

Around nine o'clock, I padded into my bedroom, tossing my bag onto the floor. The necklace around my neck felt heavy on its chain. I tugged the knife out of the box. It was as long as my forearm, with intricate designs along the handle and sheath. I pulled the knife out of the sheath, the metal gleamed brightly under the lights, and what looked like some kind of ancient writing was written along the middle of the blade. Mom walked in and sat on the bed beside me.

"Not a day will pass that I won't think about you." She wrapped an arm around my shoulders, pressing my face against her. "Are you sure you'll be going back tonight?"

I sighed, "I'm not completely sure. Half of me still thinks it was a dream. But with this around my neck and this in my hand, it feels too real. That place pulls me."

She nodded slowly, her head brushing against the top of mine. She pushed my hair back.

I squeezed my eyes shut, trying not to cry, knowing it was inevitable, "You know I'll miss you a lot, even though you drive me crazy." She tightened her arms around me and kissed the top of my head.

"Please, be safe. When you come back, I want you to have all your appendages and limbs in working order."

"Great, mom, thanks for reminding me."

"I love you and happy birthday. I have always prepared myself for the day you would leave for a big university, but nothing like traveling to another realm." She half-heartedly chuckled. "At least, when I knew you were going to leave me one day, I could call you every minute of every day, but now I won't even get a postcard."

"I love you, mom. Mariah will wonder what happened. Will you tell her?"

She nodded, "You bet, don't worry." She took my hand in hers.

The clock down the hall began to chime. A tingling sensation traveled from my toes and up to my head. "I think it's happening." Mom squeezed my hand with desperation, and her eyes shimmered with tears.

"Be safe."

My vision blurred. The walls shivered, becoming thin. The drywall became tree limbs and branches. The carpet turned into dirt and leaves. Slowly, the bed and my mom dissolved away in pieces. Tears tumbled down her cheeks. She squeezed her eyes shut, making the corners of her eyes crinkle. She grew more transparent with each passing second. Her absent hand in mine left a cold mark as my world dissolved into the Night Realm.

5

THE CRISP, night air filled my lungs. I stood. This time I was smart enough to wear sneakers, jeans, and a jacket over my t-shirt. I slipped the knife into my back pocket, pushing it through the bottom seam of the pocket. My hair blew across my face. The breeze dried my tears cool on my cheeks. The stark white moon shone brightly, giving light to the dark forest floor to guide my journey to camp.

It didn't take me long to find the camp again. Apparently, when I came back, it transported me closer, which was kind of whoever is over that sort of thing. The campfires glinted through the trees, and people flitted from one fire to another.

I made my way toward the camp when something knocked me flat to the ground. My adrenaline pumped, and I panicked. I tried to shove off the ground, but someone or something kept me pressed into the ground. A warm breath brushed my neck.

"Be still. They're coming," said a low, protective voice.

"What?" Shit, it was the man from the night before.

"Be quiet." He stayed on top of me, covering my head with his arms. He smelled like dirt and trees; he surprisingly smelled wonderful, or maybe it was because my face was smashed into the ground.

A horn sounded throughout the camp. People immediately stopped what they were doing and moved into action.

"Would you get the fuck off of..." A loud, screeching noise erupted through the night, making my ears ring. The flapping of wings beat in the air. People screamed. Fires were extinguished. Utter chaos ensued. People set up barricades and drew their weapons. More screeching and sparks erupted from the flying creatures above. They flew over us, down the hill to dive toward the people around the tents. The man yanked me up and jerked me up the hill.

"Would you move it, so we won't get killed?" he bellowed at me.

I picked up my pace and sprinted after him, only staggering a few times. My heart hammered against my ribs, and my body was sore from being squashed into the ground. He led me to a small hole, where five other guys sat crouched against the dirt walls.

"Who's that?" A scruffy guy, with shoulder-length hair, turned angry black eyes to glare at me.

I gasped. My mouth fell open, and I pushed my back against the dirt wall, trying to get away from him. His eyes were solid black, making his eyes look like twin holes in his face. I just stared at him. What hell had I dropped into?

"Some girl, who keeps getting in the way. Why haven't you taken off yet?" My captor asked them.

"We were waiting for you." A scrawny guy, with hands too big to be on his body, began pulling weapons from his back and tossed a couple onto the dirt floor. He held out a small sword to me. For some reason, I took it from him. His eyes were completely black too. He looked like a demon. My mouth hung open in horror.

My captor gaped at me incredulously, reached over, and snatched the weapon back. "Don't give her any weapons. She's a groundling; she doesn't know how to use it." He put the sword through a slip of leather tied around his hips. "Guys, just go. I'll babysit her." He turned toward me, and I wanted to scream. His eyes slowly changed to black. The whites of his eyes disappeared in seconds.

The black holes, where his eyes were supposed to be, were more menacing when he was annoyed and angry. Part of me wanted to run from him, while another part wanted to cling to him for protection. I shook my head, trying to clear it.

The guys looked at me, then climbed out of the hole. The darkness swallowed them whole. One moment they were there, the next, gone. I stood in the pit, staring up with my mouth hanging wide.

"Where did they go? What's wrong with your eyes?" I blurted. I turned to the guy. He was watching the camp, and the sight caught my breath. How was this possible? Winged creatures swooped down and grabbed people, taking them up into the air and dropping them. I sank next to him and watched the scene unfold; it was utterly surreal. Unchecked tears spilled down my cheeks.

A loud, whistling noise sounded over our heads. The wind whipped my hair across my eyes. Another creature slammed into the other darker ones. The screeching grew louder and louder. I had to cover my ears with my hands. The creature that had attacked the others tore them apart and ate them. Black liquid sprayed from the creatures and dripped from the dragon's pointed snout. It was a light brown color with gold streaks flecked throughout its feathers, a cross between a large eagle and maybe a dragon. It looked somehow ethereal and strangely translucent. The dark creatures took off as fast as they could, quickly disappearing into the night.

The guy beside me watched everything intently and silently. I think he had forgotten I was there because when my arm brushed his, he nearly jumped on me. Instead, he grabbed my arm, yanking me up and over the lip of the hole. He dragged me toward camp.

"Wait! Wait! Where are you taking me?" My heels dragged through the dirt, my body leaning backward, trying to pull my arm from his grip.

Anger etched his face. I blanched when he turned those black eyes on me. I shrank back. Again, I tried pulling my arm from his grip. He let go, and I stumbled. He kept walking. I stood out in the open, watching him. He stooped and picked up someone injured and kept striding through camp. Who was this guy? I slowly ambled toward the camp. I had no clue where I needed to be or what I had gotten myself into.

People wandered aimlessly around, with the same black eyes as my irritating protector. Some stopped to help others, and some seemed to be in shock. The ones in shock were younger, and some I recognized from the tent where I had stayed last night.

As people rushed or pushed past me, I caught movement out of the corner of my eye. A man with long blond hair that fell past his shoulders strode toward the forest away from all of the commotion. He wasn't wearing a shirt, so I could see scars of all kinds etched across his shoulders and back. He had three thick black tattooed rings encircling his bicep. He seemed to know someone was looking at him because he stopped in mid-stride at the edge of the forest and turned back.

His eyes found mine; I couldn't tear my eyes away from him. His eyes were the same black as everyone else, but as he stared at me, they changed to a bright amber. His long hair was filled with different shades of gold that somehow reminded me of my dreams. The corners of his mouth lifted ever so slightly, his gaze turning from mine, as he stepped into the shadows of the trees and disappeared.

No fucking way... Was he the guy from my dreams?

I tried to find Ashlen among the people rushing past. I spotted Brand. He was having the injured gathered into one of the tents located in the middle of the camp.

"Sloane!" Brand pushed through the crowd of people, making his way toward me. "Where have you been?" Brand's face was full of concern and looked as if he had aged since the last time I saw him. With the added stress, his Scottish accent became thicker. His eyes were also the jet-black color that made me think twice before talking to him.

"I, uh, went home." I swallowed hard, trying not to notice the black eyes.

"Home?" His face changed to puzzlement. He ran a hand across his eyes. The black slowly receded from the whites of his eyes and pushed back into the containment of his pupil. "Could ye help us with the injured? I need to go check on more."

I blinked, then nodded, "Sure. What do I need to do?"

"Just go 'round and ask each of 'em what's wrong and give 'em either a red tag or yellow tag. Red is an emergency. Yellow is they need regular 'elp." He shoved the stack of cards into my hands. I scrambled to keep them from falling onto the ground. He patted my shoulder and turned out the doorway of the tent.

I rotated in a circle looking at nearly twenty people who laid on makeshift beds. I shuffled through the tags and started working. There weren't as many emergencies as I thought there would be; most were in shock and needed to have a conversation with a sane person. I told them they would be fine, and we were going to get them help. Honestly, I barely remember anything I said to anyone. Whatever I said, seemed to calm them some.

But there were casualties and even more with extensive injuries. The people, who seemed qualified to handle those types of injuries, immediately took over the situation from me, which I was thankful. Everything was a mess. People rushed around. The air was full of tension. It was complete chaos. I tried my best to stay out of the way.

Several hours passed as I checked on each patient. More were carried in, and I had to make room. Gradually, people were checked by a more qualified person. Brand came in and sat on a stool in a corner. His shoulders were drooping; he laid his elbows on his legs and put his head in his hands. I maneuvered around the patients and sat on the floor beside him. I kept quiet, waiting.

"Sloane, you did really well tonight. Thank you, lass, for helping."

"Absolutely, I'm glad to help." I was exhausted but grateful that I was able to do something to help these people.

Brand sat quietly on the stool for a few minutes. His face contorted into concentration. The lines on his face appeared deeper. I rose slowly and as quietly as I could. I left him sitting by himself. I didn't want to intrude on his thoughts.

I sat outside the patient area until things quieted a bit. Brand eventually came outside to check on the survivors. Most of the people had gone to their sleeping quarters and were in bed. There were a few roaming the campsite trying to be useful. A group of women talked about Hunters that were patrolling around the camp to keep watch. I'm guessing Hunters were a good thing.

"Why don't you go on and find your bed?" Brand stood beside me; he bent down and put his hand on my arm and gently helped me to my feet. He nudged me toward the girl's sleeping quarters.

My feet were like lead as I wound my way toward the huge tent. I hadn't realized how tired I was. Being surrounded by darkness didn't help my sleep schedule either. A shadow to my left moved, and a massive figure blocked my path.

"Well, you did survive." My captor stood before the opening of the tent with his arms crossed over his broad chest and stared me down. His eyes had returned to the rich dark green color that matched the realm's vegetation.

Exhaustion was setting in, and when it takes residence, I get cranky. "Yes... Thank you for your concern." I was fed up with his moodiness and lack of empathy.

His eyebrow arched then he took a step toward me. I stood my ground. "It's going to be interesting to see how long you'll last," with that snide remark, he sauntered off into the center of camp.

Jackass. Ugh, boys.

I stomped into the tent. The majority of the beds were empty, including Ashlen's. Most of the occupants were asleep, except a small group gathered in the corner of the tent, whispering. I sat on the bed's edge, tugging off my Vans. I placed my shoes under the bed. Climbing in with my clothes on, I pulled the sheets over my head, letting the whispers lull me to sleep.

————

THE NEXT MORNING, we woke up to the smell of bacon, at least, that's what it smelled like to me. Ashlen still wasn't in her bunk. When we went outside, the moon still shone unwavering in the morning as a small hint of light could be seen from the horizon. My watch displayed at nine o'clock. It was going to take some time to get used to not seeing the sun anymore. My heart twinged a little with the realization. The cool, morning air and dew-covered ground welcomed me.

The tiniest bit of light broke the horizon and touched the plants around me. The plants lit from within, which made me stop in my tracks. My mouth fell open like a fish out of water. The trees and each piece of grass took a deep breath, absorbing as much light as possible in those moments. It was like I had stepped into James Cameron's *Avatar* world Pandora. Tendrils of steam rose from the heated earth, making the Night Realm more like a hazy dream. Maybe ten minutes passed, then the small amount of light blinked out. Darkness enveloped us once again, with only the moon as light. The Realmers continued by, not paying any attention.

Unbelievable. I shook my head and followed everyone to the food.

Whatever they had cooked didn't look anything like bacon, but I ate it up; to me, it tasted more like chicken. I found out later it was part of the creature that had attacked us. These particular Nightlins were called Aeroes.

I surveyed the wreckage from the night before. The campfire had been strewn across the middle of the camp, and several tents had been knocked over or torn to pieces. The people around me had hollow eyes and vacant expressions. We ate, hardly talking at all. A few voices carried across the camp, but most were hushed. We grabbed food, brought it to our mouths. Chew. Chew. Swallow. Grab more food. Repeat.

I needed to do something useful. I went in search of Ashlen and Brand. I found Brand first. He had walked out of the survivor tent. His face and clothes were completely covered with soot and dirt. He was a mess.

"Brand, how is everything?"

Brand stopped, running a hand through his dirty hair. His Scottish accent was more pronounced with his tiredness. "Sloane, there ya are I was coming to find ya. In all the commotion, ma head's mush. Last night, yous said ya had gone home, what da ya mean?"

"Well, exactly that. I went home the night before. I went to sleep in the tent, and then, I woke up in the Norm world."

"Hmm, I dinna ken what to say..." He scrubbed his face. "If ever there was a time when something weird was going to happen, it would be now."

"I wish I could help explain, but I'm probably more lost than you."

"Eh, don't worry, lass, it'll all be revealed. I'm sure of it. But we need to figure out how to get you home to stay, or have ya decided to stay with us?" His eyes twinkled as he slowly smiled.

"Despite everything that happened last night, I think I'm going to stay. I have so many questions, and I know the only place with answers is here." I pulled the necklace up from under my shirt and held it out to him. "When I went back, my mother gave this to me and told me it was my father's. She also gave me a knife with writing on it."

Brand came closer and lifted the necklace to his face. "Well, I'll be." He looked at me with amusement. "If I'm correct, this necklace will lead you to wherever you want."

I took the necklace from him and studied it closely, trying to see the magic behind it. No way could I have something this cool. It was worn and even had rust around the edges. I shook my head back and forth.

Brand smiled and placed his hands on his hips. "Ya said ya had a knife too?"

I nodded and drew the knife out, holding it out to show him. He carefully took it.

"Hmmm..." He turned his eyes toward me; his eyes traveled down to my shoes and back up to my face. "Yous keep surprising me. These artifacts haven't been seen in years, and the only reason why I ken about them is because my mum and da told me story after story about 'em." He shook his head in awe.

I liked him immensely. Maybe my father resembled him, minus the accent, sadly. He handed the knife back to me. I placed it in my pocket.

"That dagger will kill any and all Nightlin it touches. You have some pretty prizes you're carrying." He crossed his arms over his barrel chest and surveyed the camp.

"Do these attacks happen a lot?"

"Aye, they 'appen a good bit. This last one, though." He shook his head. "We had the barriers in place, so they shouldn't have found us. At least, we weren't attacked by so many this time."He turned back to me, "We're gonna need to set up some time so that we can train you."

6

Sloane

ASHLEN WAS in the survivor tent with minor scrapes and bruises all over. She had a terrible headache, but other than that, she was fine.

"What took you so long?" she croaked.

I slipped my arm around her shoulders to help her up. She sat on the edge of the bed and stood - very slowly.

"I feel as if someone slammed a two by four across my whole body and maybe ran me over." Her face twisted in pain, and she placed her free hand at the base of her back.

"I'm sorry it took me forever to find you."

"It's alright. I'm glad you came back. We had no idea where you had gone. Callum led the guys and searched the whole outskirts of the forest for you."

"Callum?" I asked.

She nodded. Her face contorting into pain from the movement, "I'm sure you've seen him. He's the dark-headed brooding guy with a limited vocabulary of maybe five words. He's the type that can get by with his looks?" Even in pain, her animated face winked.

"Oh. Right. Yeah, I know who you're talking about now. He's moody and rude, but I'm pretty sure he said about ten different words to me."

"Really?" She said with surprise.

"Yep."

"Wow. Aren't you lucky." She continued to watch the ground, concentrating on moving her feet. "Just be careful around him. He likes to use his temper to his advantage."

"Don't worry. Red flags erupted the moment I ran into him, literally."

"Alright, don't ever say I didn't warn you."

I rolled my eyes, "Okay, okay, moving on."

The corner of her mouth twitched, "Okay."

We traveled slowly across the camp. Sometimes we stopped so she could catch her breath or let her rest. People dragged debris and wood to large piles for burning. She had a hard time lifting her feet, so we took baby steps. We reached the sleeping quarters with some ease, though. Only a couple of people were in bed. I helped her to lie down on her bed, and she tentatively laid back.

"When does training start?"

Ashlen turned her head so she could see me. "It already started about a month ago. I guess you'll have to catch up. I don't think it should take you too long."

"Sure, except, I'm the only one who hasn't had the history lesson."

"Oh, I wouldn't worry too much about that. We can help you." She stared back up at the ceiling. "I think they said we would start training again in a few weeks."

"Good. We need some sort of order and something that everyone can look forward to." I laid on my bed to take a short nap. I was more than ready to begin training.

"Ashlen?"

"Yeah?" she croaked.

"Can you tell me why people's eyes turn black?"

Ashlen shifted in her bed and chuckled, "I bet seeing that almost made you faint." She chuckled again, "It happens whenever the Nightlins get close. Warning us, they're near. It's our first mark as Watchers."

I settled back into bed, "Oh, okay." I paused, letting that information sink in, "You said something about marks before. What other marks appear?"

Ashlen yawned deeply, "If we're lucky to become Protectors, you get a second mark, where you use a force field for protection." I looked around to see if anyone else was paying attention, but nothing.

"As a Hunter, you get your final mark. That's when you change the force field into one of those gigantic dragon-like creatures, your Czar, and use it for travel and, more importantly, attacking the Nightlins. It's all straight from a sci-fi movie." She yawned again.

"What about tattoos?"

"Hmm?" She had her eyes closed. She would be asleep in a few minutes.

"I saw a guy with bands tattooed on his arm." I whispered.

Ashlen shifted some in her bed. "Oh, that. Yeah, some people like to mark which level they're at."

Ashlen sighed softly then, and her breathing grew deeper as she fell asleep. I laid my head back and shut my eyes, welcoming the darkness.

Later that night, we had a memorial. Four people had died during and after the fight due to injuries, and three were missing. The pyre stood in the center of the camp. We gathered around with our heads bowed and eyes closed. The faces surrounding me were filled with sadness, fear, and anger. Only a handful had masked their feelings behind a calm façade.

One pair of eyes stared fixedly at me from underneath his dark hair. The fire reflected in his dark green eyes casting shadows across his face, making him seem younger and poignant. I met his stare for a moment then back at the fire as the ashes flew off into the sky.

———

THE NEXT FEW weeks passed quite slowly. I met with Brand every single day to catch up on the history of the Night Realm. Brand had me reading a 100-year-old small paper book bound in leather;

someone had had the bright idea to write down the full history of the realm. It had drawings and other people's notes that had been passed down from each family and comprised the book for the one day when someone, like me, needed it.

JANUARY 1901 – Our History

   Age of the Night Realm has always been since the Night was born. The first to cross over was given as a sacrifice so that the creatures would be sustained and not attack the people as each year passed, more and more crossed over. Sometimes the tradition would carry from family to family, and sometimes the tradition would end.

   No one is really sure how the Nightlins first crossed over into the Norm, but we know that the moment one of the creatures crossed over the threshold of this world, it gave free reign to all Nightlins. The punishment belongs to us to guard the portals until this world ends.

   Our days are filled with the regular twenty-four, except that we only have a few minutes of daylight each day - 8 minutes to be exact. We never truly see the sun, only a haze of light.

   The first recorded leader of the Night Realm was Kane. He is said to have been cruel and cunning. Each leader is given a key so they can cross to both worlds freely. A magnificent sword, with gold inlaid and intricate designs across the hilt and scabbard of the sword, is passed down to each leader. The only way that someone can become the next leader is if the current leader freely gives over their leadership. If the leader dies in war, then his second takes the responsibility of the Leadership. Whoever holds that leadership lives an immortal life, keeping their bodies frozen in time. They do not age as long as they hold the key.

   The main portals between the two realms are spread throughout the world. Each is guarded by realmers in that region.

   Nightlins are creatures that scavenge and kill. Their main goal is to take over this realm and the other. There are Nightlin creatures that can fly. Others swim, some are large, others small, most with razor-sharp teeth, and gigantic claws. They ravage and tear with no cognitive thought. They want blood. In the other world, the feeling that makes the hairs on your arms stand up or turns the air colder, are the creatures that have slipped through from this realm. They are the cause of the feelings of despair and tragedies. Nightlins live to destroy. There is still so much more that we need to learn about them.

The "Normal World" or "Norm" is directly affected by the Nightlins. Each time someone crosses over to the Realm, and however long the portal stays open, Nightlins are able to crossover as well. In the "Norm," the Nightlins feed on death and fear, so that's what they create. We know when more Nightlins have crossed over because of the increase in death and crime. Over the past few years, the numbers have slowly escalated.

Our first defense against the Nightlins are called Watchers. Watchers seem to acquire different specialties from gravity-defying acts to night vision. The first mark of a Watcher is their eyes changing to black, whenever Nightlins appear. The Watchers are trained in weaponry and do exactly what their title entails; they keep watch over our camps and the world beyond ours. As the years pass by, their aging slows.

The second is the Protector. Protectors' powers evolve to shielding and more extensive weaponry. Not everyone will become a Protector. Some will remain Watchers. We have no knowledge as to why some are promoted to Protectors and some stay as Watchers, but it has been like this always. When someone is chosen to be a Protector, white light falls from their fingertips, forming a shield that is indestructible. I have even seen a Protector that can exude a light from within that repels the Nightlins.

Hunters are the final defense, and like the Protector, not all become Hunters; only the finest and most worthy. A Hunter's third mark is absorbing the energy around them, and shifting that energy to form a large dragon-like bird with wingspans stretching to fifty feet wide and large mouths filled with razor-sharp teeth; they are called Czars. The Hunters use the Czars as an extension of themselves. They are the greatest of all the defenders.

Many in the Norm have forgotten or denied the Night Realms existence and the warriors who bravely fight for their lives, so we continue in silence —watching, protecting, and hunting the creatures that would gladly take each of their lives. The constant duel between good and evil will always exist in both of our worlds since Adam ate the fruit.

We live to keep the dark from engulfing the light.

THE TEXT CONSISTED of more stories about fights between the Nightlins and Realmers. Stories about the leaders, their families, and their untimely deaths were printed on those pages with rigorous description. Every event and feeling recorded. I learned a lot in those first two weeks about our history. At least, it was interesting and new history that hadn't been hammered into my head since the beginning of first grade.

By the third week, Brand began teaching me how to fight. We used sticks at first, then graduated to sharper slats of wood. Those weeks I was so sore and bruised. So many times, I was afraid I would permanently be purple. As Brand instructed me, people stopped and watched us, including the tall, dark-haired man that would prop against a post and just watch for hours, Callum. Our eyes would meet briefly, and a shiver would slide down my back. I could never tell if he was laughing at me or if he thoroughly disapproved of my fighting skills.

As the weeks progressed, surprisingly, I improved. I was able to defend myself and attack efficiently. A couple of times, I whacked Brand's arms. When I did, I was so happy with myself that I stopped defending. Therefore, I gave him the opportunity to knock me into the ground.

I arrived in the camp with a soft body, and through those tough weeks, my body was getting muscle definition. I hadn't known my body was capable of muscles. My hair grew longer, shinier, and thicker. I used leather strips to tie it back. I've always been uncomfortable with my body and dressed modestly to hide it. So, my new wardrobe of sleeveless tops and painted on pants made me more than a little uncomfortable. They were made of thin, soft leather and tough leather boots that came to my knees. All in black, of course. I never removed the compass from my neck, and Brand gave me a leather holder that fitted around my thigh for the dagger.

I gradually became a decent fighter. At least, I was able to think and plan my strategy while swinging a sword. I sparred with other groundlings. We still used the wooden swords, but those hits left some nasty bruises.

One afternoon, I was sparring with Ashlen. Neither of us had shields, but we had hardened leather armor covering our arms, shins, back, and chests. We danced around each other on a square patch of grass jabbing and shielding, jabbing, and shielding. White light poles were positioned around the fighting circle. Other groundlings crowded around us, yells, and the sound of the wood against wood striking resounded throughout the camp.

"Come on, girly. Hit me with your best shot," Ashlen smirked, brandishing her sword in front of my face.

"Hey, I love that song." I lunged at her, swiftly deflecting her blows and swiping her legs out from under her. She landed heavily on her back with her sword flying out of her hands. I bent over her, smiling, "How does that song go again?" I held my hand out and helped her to her feet.

Ashlen got up, smiling, and dusted her back off.

"I think it's time for you to try fighting someone with a little more punch." Callum stood to the side, leaning against that post again. His arms crossed over his chest, with a cocky smile plastered on his face. He wore a black sleeveless shirt, pants, and leather boots that came almost to his knees. Two black bands, marking him as a Protector, were cut into his left forearm. The sleeveless shirt emphasized his muscular shoulders and arms. Not that I noticed.

My eyebrow arched, "Uh, I'm not so sure..." I glanced at Ashlen to see her reaction. She still had a smirk on her face, but this one was reflected at Callum.

He strolled over to Ashlen and took the sword from her. He shrugged his shoulders, "Come on, hit me with your best shot." He took his stance, one corner of his mouth pulled back, and he circled me. It felt like a lion circling his prey.

I watched him. My shoulders tightened as I lifted my sword and took my defensive position. Our eyes locked, his deep green eyes taking in my every movement. With lightning reflexes, he lunged at me, aiming for my middle. I barely had time to block him and ended up staggering back a few steps. Man, he hit hard. I quickly rallied, planting my feet and centering my body over my legs. He lunged again toward my shoulder. I swung the wood sword upward, spiraling around his sword and turning my back and elbow into his body, making him have to find better footing. I spun in a circle, knowing he would be right on top of me. As I turned, he was already in mid-swing at my legs.

The motions began to slow, and small details became more prominent, like how the veins in his arms were a faint blue and pulsing with the blood surging through his body. This fight felt different. I easily jumped over his swing, but as I did, he cut the swing short and jabbed with his arm outstretched, knocking me straight to the ground. As if he could sense my new moves and strength, he didn't stop his attack. His sword came down straight on my head. The splinters from the wooden sword stood out from the end as it came toward my face. I rolled into his legs taking him down. *I just took Callum down!* I hit his chest with every ounce that my elbow could carry. The smug ass, he actually laughed. What did I just do? How?

I rolled over on my side to look at him. His face filled with total delight. His sword laid by his side, forgotten, and his hand pressed to his chest. My face contorted into confusion.

"Wow, that was the most fun I have had in a long time." He smiled a big toothy grin at me. It changed his handsome hard features into an almost breath-taking beauty.

"I - I'm so glad I could amuse you." I tentatively got up and shook my head at him. He watched me from his position on the ground. "You are a strange man." His smile dimmed. He sat up, linking his arms around his knees. I wiped the dirt off of me as best I could and found about thirty or more people watching us. Oh, great.

"Wait." Callum jumped up and grabbed my arm, making me look at him.

"Ow." I tried to pull away from him, but his grip tightened.

"No, wait. There's something wrong with your eyes." He stepped toward me.

"What do you mean?" I ran my fingertips across my eyes to see if I could feel something. They felt normal. I could see fine.

"Here, let me see," When I didn't jump away, he slowly lifted his hand and cupped my face, lifting my face toward his. My breathing grew shallower, being so close to him and in this position. His eyes delved deep into mine, studying me. "I don't believe it."

"What don't you believe?"

"The whites of your eyes were bleeding into the iris."

"What?" I jerked my arm from his grip.

"It's almost like you have the beginning markings of a Watcher." He spoke low and hesitantly. His expression was blank. He turned from me, pushing his way through the people. I stared after him.

Ashlen walked up to me slowly, her voice low and soft as she spoke, "Hey, let me see?"

I only nodded. I met her eyes. She studied them.

"He's right. The white was taking over the rest of your eyes, but they're back to normal now." She half-smiled and squeezed my arm, "So nothing to worry about."

I couldn't meet her gaze. I felt like some kind of experiment that had gone horribly wrong.

The group of people that had been around us kept a wide berth. I felt like a fish in a bowl. Way too many people surrounded me, most of them I barely knew or hadn't even spoken to. I felt claustrophobic. I kept my gaze focused on the ground and tried to make my escape.

"Let me through. Please..." I didn't have to ask twice. The people parted, giving me plenty of breathing space. They held uncertainty on their faces. Tears slid down my cheeks. I ran. Ashlen called after me, but I didn't stop.

"Brand!" He was going into his tent when I saw him. A tall, muscular guy with light brown hair was talking with him. He stopped and waited for me to catch up.

"Aye?" he seemed to register that something was wrong. He addressed the younger guy, "Harris, would you mind giving me a few minutes?"

"Sure, Brand, no problem." Ah, Harris, a good ole southern boy.

The syllables were extra-long and drawn out. He smiled really big, the expression engulfing his entire face. Winking at me, he walked away.

Brand's smile faded around the edges, and he held the flap to his tent back for me to go through. "Have a seat. What's happened now."

I couldn't sit down. I ended up pacing in front of him.

He watched me for a moment then cleared his throat. "If yous dinna tell me what's going on, I can't help lassie."

I stopped in the middle of the floor, keeping my eyes on the floor like I was afraid he might see them.

"Something happened to my eyes when I was sparring." Silence followed, and I peeked at him. He studied me.

"So, you're getting your Watcher marks this early? Well, that's great! You should be proud." He smiled brightly.

I shook my head slowly, "My eyes didn't change to black they turned white." It felt like the air sucked from my lungs. I took the seat beside him, folding my hands into my lap.

"You said they turned white?"

I nodded.

"Tell me what happened." His face was solemn.

"I was sparring with Callum, and when we finished, my eyes had changed colors." His eyebrows rose when I mentioned Callum.

"Callum?"

"Yes."

"Hmm, why would he do that? That doesn't sound like him."

"Uh... I have no idea. Ashlen and I were fighting, and he was judging us. He came up to me at the end, took Ashlen's weapon, then started attacking."

"How'd you do?" His eyes twinkled with a smile.

"Well, not too bad. I, uh, unarmed him." I barely shrugged.

He sat up straighter, "Did ye now? Well, good for ye!" He slapped my back. "I bet he enjoyed that."

I looked at him with more than confusion on my face, "Well, yeah, he laughed for a while. I don't see what this has to do with my eyes?"

"Right. Sorry, but I can't really explain it to yous. I've never heard of someone's eyes changing to white." He paused, and I could tell he was trying to sort out something to say.

"Granted, your markings are different, but being different isn't always a bad thing. I'll do my best to get in contact with the Leader as quickly as I can. I'm sure he will figure something out or have a way to discern the meaning behind your eyes. I think the best we can do is wait and see if they turn white, who knows what really happened. It's not something you should be worrying over right now, concentrate on your studies, and we will find the answer as soon as we can." He studied me and patted my back gently.

"Most of the kids will get the beginning markings within the next few weeks. You are different, that much is obvious in the way you arrived here. It's like when some people grow faster than others. You're one of those people that excel a little faster. These markings are something that should make yous happy. The first mark usually needs a catalyst of some sort. You need something that pushes you to the next limit. It can be emotional or physical..." He watched me with a grin on his old leathered face. "Yous are doing mighty well for someone who had no clue about this world a few weeks ago." This time his face was filled with pride and admiration like I was his own child.

My smile widened, and I leaned over to hug him. He didn't react right away. I guess I thoroughly surprised him, but then he wrapped his arms around me, giving me a good bear hug. I pulled away, laughing.

"I guess if you aren't too worried about these early marks, I can *try* not to worry about them either. But why did Callum react the way he did?"

"Well, Callum is a hard one to figure out. He mostly keeps to himself, scouts on his own, and from what I know, he hasn't had the easiest life. I guess because ye haven't truly worked hard for those marks, he might think that ye dinna really deserve them... since he has been here, he works nonstop to be the best." He spread his hands out in front of him as a way of explanation. He patted my knee, "Listen, dinna fash about it. Ye just keep working hard, and he'll come around." He winked at me.

"I'm trying to stay away from him, Brand. Which is usually easy since he's never here," I rose. "I don't need to be around someone with a scary temper and brooding issues."

He smiled and shook his head, "He chooses duty, to be alone. He needs a friend, that's all I'm saying." He gently pushed me outside. "Come on. I think it's time to eat."

We headed to the center of the camp, where the fire grew bigger by the minute with smells of meat being spiced and sautéed, and fresh vegetables getting thrown into a stew wafted through the camp. I found a seat by Ashlen and grabbed whatever I could get my hands on.

———

THE NEXT COUPLE of weeks progressed as slow as a snail race. My eyes had stayed their natural color the whole time, which made me breathe a sigh of relief. The only thing that the groundlings did during those weeks was fighting, learning more history, fighting some more, learning about weapons, and more fighting. I learned about archery, which I became very fond of and somewhat accomplished. By the end of those weeks, I had a couple more friends.

William Harrison or "Harris" as he likes to be called, the same guy who had winked at me playfully, actually became a fast friend. He's tall, over six feet with light shaggy brown hair, and big mischievous blue eyes. I have yet to see a serious look come across his features. Harris is from good ole Alabama, so his deep southern twang warms you from your toes to the tip of your nose. He also loves to play pranks, which he persuaded Ashlen and me to be conspirators with him a couple of times. Personally, I think Ashlen has a small crush on him, and that's why she tolerates his antics, but who knows for sure.

A petite girl with a big voice and fierce strength rounded out our little group so far. Her name is Raleigh Kirkland. She has short dark brown hair that touches the top of her shoulders, big brown eyes, and a kilowatt smile. She's either running, fighting, climbing trees, or swimming; anything that will keep her going. Colorful tattoos trail down her left arm and right bicep. Her deep brown skin had a milky tint without the sunlight, contrasting with the bright colors of the ink. You wouldn't think she would be much of a warrior, but she is fearless and super-fast. I have trouble sparring with her because she moves so quickly, I can barely keep up, but she makes me better.

We usually found ourselves sitting by a small fire telling jokes or stories about the normal world and our past lives. I loved being around them because we almost always had something to laugh about, and when it came to team exercises, we always came out on top.

The night was unusually cold. The four of us lounged around the fire, enjoying stories. Harris told a hysterical story about when he was a boy, and he had been caught running away from home. He was in the middle of describing his trek through the woods when screeching noises erupted through the dark.

At first, I didn't think anything about the noises until I heard screams. Fire lit up the sky coming from the center of camp. Groundlings scattered everywhere. It was mass hysteria. The Watchers tried to keep control of everyone, but no one paid attention.

Protectors ran from the trees to the camp's center, forming a large circle. Tendrils of white light ran down their arms forming shields in front of them. Brand stood in the middle of the camp. Light erupted from the ground, wrapping around him. I spotted Callum sprinting toward us. A shield already alighted on his forearm, while he held a crossbow in the other.

A girl stumbled toward us. Claw marks marred her face, and blood stained the front of her shirt. She grabbed me and slid to the ground.

"They're coming. Nightlins. You have... to... get out. Run." She gasped. Her eyes rolled into the back of her head. I clutched her hands in mine; someone yelled in my ear, yanking on my arm. I watched as life drained from her body. Her blood covered my clothes and hands. Any noise around me became garbled. My eyes weren't able to connect the scene before me. I vaguely remember someone picking me up. At one point, my body shut down, and the lights went out.

———

The Dark

THE AGONY that pumped through his body nearly made him pass out. Numerous dark figures surrounded and moved around him. They were doing something to his body. It felt like thousands of needles had been jammed into his skin, with tourniquets tightening on his joints. At any moment, his blood would stream out of his pores.

His eyes roamed across the entirety of the space he could see, but he was mostly in the dark. Only the light from the moon could be seen from narrow windows at the top of the walls. He remembered what it felt like to be in the light; remembered its warmth and calming reassurance. Yet, here he was on the dark side.

His mind tried to hold onto the good things; the light. He remembered her beautiful face and soft skin. He missed her, just the thought of her tore through his soul. Maybe he would die quickly. Hopefully, it would be over soon. Then he could float away in a dream.

Pain pulsed behind his eyes. He turned away from the moonlight, letting the darkness take over. Hoping for the end.

7

SMOKE AND FOOD assailed my senses. The rustle of clothing and murmuring of voices were dim. My eyes fluttered open. All at once, my senses rushed back. Four shapes surrounded a fire. The closest shape to me patted my head.

"Hey, you okay?" It was Ashlen. I could barely recognize her features. Her face was covered with soot and dirt.

"What?" I propped up on my elbow and peered at her.

"Are you okay? You kind of passed out, which I don't blame you. I would have done the same if I had gotten the chance." She smiled reassuringly.

"Fainted?" I raised my hand to my forehead, except I noticed that my hand was covered with brown stains—dried blood. My head started to get woozy again. "Shit. I've got to get over this."

"Don't worry about it. I have trouble with blood. Sometimes," Harris winked. He held out a rag for me to use.

I laid back onto the dry leaves, trying to wipe the stains off. I spotted Raleigh propped against a tree not too far away. The small fire crackled and spat out tiny embers. Smoke drifted off into the night. Footsteps approached crunching through the dry leaves and sticks announcing their arrival, but I couldn't see anyone. A man came through the trees toward our small group. The man, who I had seen at the camp, with the golden eyes, stepped into the circle near the fire. He knelt in front of me, gentle hands held my face, as he checked me for injuries. I was in awe of his gold hair falling across his bare shoulders. *Was this the guy from my dreams?*

"You're awake, finally." He grinned, moving, and extended his hand to me, "I'm Graham."

I was totally taken aback by him. I was an idiot who couldn't say a thing. I slipped my hand into his and nodded. His perfect smile broadened, creating small dimples on either side of his full lips. *What the hell was wrong with me? Get all loopy when a cute guy smiles at me.*

He sat with his back against a log and addressed us, "It seems that the majority of the camp has fallen or is in hiding. The creatures are running all over the grounds. It's not just the Aeroes, but also the Inklings, the Raptors, several Spirits, and I saw one Skeleton. I'm the only Hunter within fifty miles. I could attack them, but I probably wouldn't do very well trying to avenge the fallen, and then you would be left alone." He looked around our small circle at each of us.

"What can we do?" I asked through clenched teeth. My head was killing me, and my stomach demanded food.

Graham met my eyes with something that felt like admiration, "Right now, I think our best bet is to get all of you to the capitol, to Kingston. There we can meet with the leader and gather more Hunters. The Nightlins are greedy, of course, but this is their biggest attack in a long while. I don't understand why they chose now, but I think that Leader Stevenson can give us the best counsel."

"How far is Kingston?" Ashlen asked.

"Maybe a day, you should be fine, since you've got Callum and me here."

My head jerked, and I scanned the edges of the fire. Callum propped against a tree facing away. Only a third of his face and the top of his arm could be seen. He only acknowledged Graham using his name with a slight nod.

Only six survivors...

———

WHEN THE FIRST tease of light appeared, we were already on our way to the capitol. No trail or path for us to follow, so we only had Graham and Callum to trust. Harris kept us entertained, but everyone was tired. Thankfully, we had five bags between the six of us filled with extra clothes and meager food rations. We stopped in the middle of a large field to eat and rest for only thirty minutes. Then we were on our way again.

Graham led the way, and Callum kept watch at the rear of the group. Callum had been his usual quiet self since Graham joined our little soiree, but something seemed different about his silence. I could tell he didn't approve of Graham. His eyes hadn't even met mine since I woke up. Usually, I could feel him watching me, and now it was like he wasn't there at all. The only time I knew exactly where he was, was when Graham would address him, and he would speak.

Callum kept silent the whole time of our journey.

That night we found a small area in the midst of tightly woven trees that could give us a sense of protection. Harris started the fire and set out food to cook.

Pulling a small box from his pack, Graham set it on the ground. It was a simple black cube from what I could tell. He pressed something in the middle, and the cube lit up with a faint white glow. Light shot up from the middle and disappeared. A small dome fell around us.

"I was lucky to find one of the barriers during the chaos. This should help shield us from any Nightlins, and keep the firelight from announcing our presence." Graham smiled at me as he stood. He disappeared through the trees again.

Callum stood just within the light of the fire, facing the forest like he was watching for something or someone. Raleigh rolled her bed out by the fire. Ashlen and I sat across from Raleigh and Harris. Ashlen smiled like a schoolgirl, as Harris rambled about the food.

I leaned over to Ashlen, "Hey, when I... fainted earlier, who picked me up?"

She smirked, "Callum, of course."

I frowned slightly, "of course." I should have thanked him. I looked in his direction. One side of his face could be seen. He acted like he was listening to something. He was still for a moment then focused his attention back to the black forest.

I hate being in someone's debt. I pushed myself up and made my way to him. He glanced at me, but then focused his attention back to the pitch-black darkness.

"So, thank you," I paused, trying to think of something else to say, "for you know, picking me up and carrying my lame ass here."

He chuckled and looked at me from the corner of his eye. One broad shoulder lifted in a type of shrug. He shifted somewhat uncomfortably.

"It's nothing."

"Hopefully, I didn't weigh too much." What was I saying? Why can't I talk like a normal person around him?

He glanced at me again. A small smile played on his lips. "No, I could barely tell you were on my shoulder."

I nodded. "Thanks again."

He turned fully toward me, looking me square in the eyes. I felt self-conscious again.

"You're welcome."

"Tonight, we are havin' us some more stew. How 'bout I put some extra spices in this one, just to change it up a bit?" Harris leaned across the small fire where the tiny pot sat perched on the embers. He poured in the leftover stew and grabbed something from one of the bags, and tossed it in. The smells that wafted over made my stomach beg for it and made my nose want to run, but we ate it and wanted more after. Harris seemed to be talking to himself.

I was grateful for the distraction. I escaped from Callum and sat at the base of a large tree near Ashlen.

"Harris, can you be quiet for two minutes? You're grinding a headache into my skull." Raleigh narrowed her eyes at him, and Harris mumbled under his breath.

"I'll give ya two minutes," He sat counting out the seconds. "Alright, times up. So, did I ever tell y'all that story about my Papa, when he was in the navy during WWII, and his boat got shot up?" He turned to each of us.

"No," I leaned against the base of the tree with my arms folded across my stomach.

Harris immediately dove straight into the story waving his arms around and getting more animated as the story progressed.

"Ashlen?"

She focused her attention away from Harris, "Yeah?"

"What's Graham's story?"

She smiled like she knew I'd ask. Her smile became sad. "I heard that a few years ago, his fiancée disappeared."

I know my face turned shocked. She nodded, "Yeah, I only remember people talking about it. I wasn't here when it happened, I just heard from others. Apparently, it was during another attack by the Nightlins. One of the Aeros snatched her up. She was a Protector at the time."

"Oh, wow." I scanned the area to make sure he hadn't come back yet.

"Guys loved talking about her. You know them, only care about the hot girls." She rolled her eyes. "But they said she was super sweet and a great fighter too. Graham took it pretty badly, obviously. He was crazy in love with her. He was in the battle too, but couldn't get to her in time. I heard he's struggled with major survivor's guilt."

"That's awful." Poor guy. I don't know how I would be if that had happened to me.

She nodded again. She studied me for a moment, "But, maybe he is ready to move on and start living... and loving again?" She nudged me with her elbow.

I chuckled and shook my head. I decided to make my confession to Ashlen.

"Before I came here, I would have dreams. At least, that's what I thought they were." She nodded her head, encouraging me to continue. "I would see these gold eyes and smell the trees."

One of her eyebrows rose. "You think it was him in your dreams?"

"That's what I've been trying to figure out." I could feel the embarrassment creeping over my cheeks.

She smiled and shrugged her shoulders. "Well, I'm hoping it was him. How romantic would that be?"

I laughed and snuggled back against the tree. My eyes grew heavy, and I knew I would be sound asleep in the next few moments.

Graham appeared out of the darkness and called Callum to him.

"I'll take the first watch if you take the second?" Graham asked.

"Yeah, sure. How long will we rest here?" Callum had his face averted from Graham's eyes, searching beyond the light of the fire.

"I say three hours and then head out."

Callum nodded and walked to the other side of the fire, which was across from me. He gave me the briefest of glances that made me question if it even happened. He curled up on the ground with a bag under his head and his back to the fire. With his face to the forest, he still guarded us in his sleep. If he ever really slept. He was our fierce Protector. Even in the darkest part of the forest, he made me feel safe.

Graham disappeared behind a tree. The night wrapped around him, swallowing him whole. Out of exhaustion, the heat of the fire instantly lulled me to sleep and forced me to stop thinking about the golden-eyed man and the dark protector.

———

"SLOANE. SLOANE. WAKE UP," someone shook my arm roughly and spoke in my ear yell-whispering. "Get up. We're leaving." My eyes fluttered open to the face of Graham towering over me. His hands gripped my arms, lifting me gently into a sitting position, making us almost nose to nose. How did he look so good this early?

"Yeah, yeah I'm awake," I pushed his hands away and pulled my back up straight. His lips twitched up as I grumbled to myself. I examined the small camp. My eyes had to adjust to the dark. Callum woke the others. Raleigh already had her things stuffed in her bag and seemed anxious to go. Harris was about the same as me; it took

Callum a lot of effort to get him up. Ashlen was strapping her backpack on and tightening her shoes, but her eyes were filled with sleep.

"How do you guys do this?" I asked Graham. He stood next to me, strapping on various weapons. Different blades were belted down his worn leather pants and stuck along the side of his boots. He had on a tunic with his bow and arrows strapped across his back, and something like a crossbow was slung across his shoulders. Legolas popped into my head, and my heart quickened. *I really needed a love life outside of fiction.*

He held out a hand to help me up. As I took his hand and he pulled up, he said, "We've had to do this for a while, so we know what to do. It won't take you long to grow accustomed too. If you don't, you'll die, so you tend to learn pretty quickly." Blunt, to the point, and honest. His hand lingered in mine for a moment; his eyes fixed on mine.

"Okay, they're ready." Callum stepped up beside us, but his gaze went from our hands then turned away, searching the woods.

Graham released my hand. He nodded at the others and hiked on into the trees. For the first few hours, everyone was silent. The night was quiet and still. No wind played through the trees. Sometimes, little animals scampered through the treetops or underbrush.

Harris seemed to come out of his groggy state and started humming the Indiana Jones' theme song, which had all of us smiling except for Callum, who was his brooding self.

I found myself behind Graham with Ashlen behind me, next was Harris, then Raleigh, and Callum bringing up the rear. I couldn't take the silence any longer, which was unusual for me. I wanted to know more about my possible dream man who was leading us. Literally. Easy question first.

"Graham, where are you from?"

He glanced over his shoulder at me, "I'm originally from Australia, but then my family moved to California for my dad's job."

"Oh, ok, that makes sense. You have that surfer guy look," I said, teasing him.

He laughed, "Really? Hmm... thanks?"

I found myself laughing, "Yes, that was a compliment." The sky lightened as we walked through the trees. They were making it seem eerie, as the light filtered through the trees and then blinked out again. The trees and grass around us took a deep inhale of the light, then settled back into darkness. Fog settled over the ground and dew collected on the grass. My hair was getting curlier and frizzier by each passing second.

Graham smiled and continued walking on, "What about you? Where are you from?"

"Colorado."

He nodded, "Do you miss it?"

The question took me by surprise. I was shocked how quickly time passed, and in two months, I rarely thought of home. "Yes. Not so much the place. I didn't ski or run with a huge crowd, but I miss home. I hope my mom is okay." I wondered what she was doing. What did she tell Mariah? Wow, I had completely forgotten about her. I'm such a terrible friend. I hoped mom was handling me being away okay. I would have been going off to a university soon, so she would have had to deal with my absence sooner or later, but I had been hoping for it to be later. Besides, universities weren't life or death like the Nightrealm.

He glanced back at me, "I'm sure she is. I'm not much of a big group person either. Life here is difficult. You need people to lean on." A sad smile graced his lips.

I nodded. My awkwardness was ready to change the subject. "So, how old are you, oh, wise one?"

"Twenty-three."

My eyes grew slightly bigger, "Really? Wow. So how long have you been a Hunter?"

He turned his eyes toward me, "Only a year. I was a Protector for two years, then something happened, and I changed." His eyes held that same sadness again. I wonder if his fiancé's death made his mark come?

Hmm... interesting, "Earlier, you said something about different Nightlins?"

"Yeah, there are several different kinds. You know what Aeroes are, right?"

"Yep, those are the ones that can fly."

"Yeah, next would be... Inklings. Those can be nasty buggers. They can change parts of their bodies into a mist, so if you strike one, they can move their bodies around the blow and not be hurt or incapacitated. In order to kill them, you have to strike them twice. First, hit the heart and then take off their head."

I gulped.

He chuckled, "Raptors make up the majority of the Nightlins. They are usually the smallest, but they are just as mean if not meaner. They have the black rubbery skin, and you can see the bones trying to push through. Those are the easiest to kill. All you have to do is run your sword through them, and you usually hit a vital organ." He made a jabbing motion with his hand and chuckled.

"Spirits look exactly as their name says. They are made up of a black mist, and yet if you do pierce the mist with a weapon, you can kill them. I think the mist is a kind of camouflage; it looks like you can see through it, and they glide like they are real spirits, but I think underneath the mist are real tangible organs. If you think you see a shadow move, then it's probably one of them... You keeping up so far?" I nodded.

"Now," he paused dramatically, "the worst—the Skeleton. Skeletons are the biggest of any of the Nightlins. They are made up of bones and ligaments, just like the name. Our ancestors weren't very creative with naming them, but with the Skeleton, it usually takes several of us to take one of them down. It's a combination of hacking their limbs off, which sometimes have a mind of their own, and ripping off their heads. Oh, and they can practically fly. Just remember, these creatures don't care about anything except killing. They won't stop or hesitate."

The more he talked about the Nightlins, the faster my heartbeat, and my anxiety rose.

"Well, thank you, I am officially more scared of being here, out in the open, than I was a few minutes ago."

He flashed a grin, "Well, at least now you know what you're up against and what to expect."

I nodded, "Yes, that's true." My stomach was starting to hurt, either from nerves or hunger, I couldn't tell.

"So, can you answer one more thing for me?"

"Sure, I can try."

"Okay, well, if you can make a gorgeously huge bird appear out of thin air, then why don't you pick us up and fly us to Kingston, instead of us having to walk there?"

He kind of chuckled and glanced back at me, "I certainly wish it was that simple. Because I would gladly get us there faster," he then began talking while ticking off his fingers. "Firstly, I like walking, but most important is I can only carry about two to three people maximum. Second, it drains a lot out of me. I don't want to be dozing off to the side where I could be killed, or you all could be killed easier without me, so things will remain as they are unless there's an emergency."

I smiled, "Oh, alright, makes sense." I quietly filed the Nightlin information away for later usage.

Ashlen, Harris, and Raleigh were laughing about something behind me. Raleigh was laughing wildly, and Harris was hee-hawing. They could have been three friends laughing on their way to a house party. I checked back to see what Callum was up to, but his attention was focused to the side, sweeping his eyes across the wooded area. He reminded me of a soldier, keeping track of everyone and the surroundings. His eyes didn't find mine, and for some reason, I felt disappointed.

When we came to a small shallow creek, the moon was high in the sky. The creek was ten feet or more below the ground level. Graham slid down the bank and hopped carefully across the rocks with his arms stretched out for balance. He crossed over, grabbed a root, and pulled himself up the bank. We all followed his lead.

I was less graceful than he was; therefore, I had mud smeared all over me, and my shoes were filled with water. He turned back to help me climb up the bank. He reached down, taking my arm and pulling me up. Like the klutz that I am, when I got to the top, my foot slipped, and I all but fell into his arms. His arms locked tight around me with my cheek pressed into his chiseled chest.

"Whoa, you okay?" His face filled with concern.

I giggled nervously, "Yep, I'm just perfect." I eased away from him; my hands pressed against him. I quickly backed away, smoothing down my shirt, and promptly turned to help Ashlen. Fucking hell, I hated it when I acted like a little girl. The one time, I wouldn't mind if a Nightlin swooped down and carried me away from my embarrassment. I mentally eye-rolled.

Ashlen was a lot more graceful in coming up the bank side. Her long legs gracefully scaled the banks. She gave me a funny look and a smirk all at once. I rolled my eyes at her. Graham began helping Raleigh and Harris. Callum simply took hold of a branch, swinging effortlessly up beside us.

"Show off," I glared at him.

Callum glanced at me. I think I saw the hint of a smile.

8

WE WERE STANDING on an outcrop perched above a deep valley. The moon was so big. It seemed to fill up the vastness of the sky. Mammoth sized mountain ranges stood in the north—Nightlin territory. A small thin river ran through the valley, disappearing into the smaller mountain range in the east. The water glistened like silver thread under the moonlight.

Graham sighed with relief and rested his large firm hand on my shoulder, "Always good to be home."

He turned to me. I nearly jumped back. It was going to take a while before I grew used to seeing black holes where a person's eyes should be and moved his hand.

He chuckled, "Shame, you can't see it, groundlings."

Ashlen only shrugged.

Harris stood on the very edge of the cliff and peered down. "So, are we jumpin' or flyin' down? Purdy sure, I could roll and tumble on down with no problem." He laughed to himself.

Raleigh rolled her eyes, "What's the plan people?"

Graham smiled, "Don't worry, we're just going to climb down. It's pretty easy."

We took a small path, like the ones mountain goats would make, and carefully tread down the mountainside. I refrained from tripping the best that I could. I only smacked into Graham a couple of times. *Most* of the time, it wasn't intentional. By the time we reached the bottom of the mountain, I was drenched in sweat, and my legs felt like Jell-O.

I couldn't tell where we were going, but Graham led us to the opposite side of the valley. We came to the river and hidden away in the brush was a small platform with a rope running across to the opposite side.

"Alright, load up. We haven't got all night," he said somewhat jokingly. Graham stood on the platform and grabbed the rope to hold it steady.

Raleigh hopped on first, and Callum last like usual, he's always ready to watch our backs. Graham easily pulled us across to the other bank. Thankfully the river wasn't moving fast, nor was it very wide.

Somewhere a bell tolled.

Graham looked up as he tied the rope off, "Shit, we've got to get moving. They're about to close the gates."

Instead of stepping off onto the bank, Graham stood at the edge of the platform that jutted out into the river. He motioned to Callum, "Show them how it's done."

Callum nodded, "Sure." He shouldered his pack, walked to the edge of the platform, turned to face us, then fell backward with a stupid smirk on his face.

We barely registered what had happened.

Ashlen lunged toward him, but it was too late. He disappeared. We rushed to the edge and stared into the black water. The water only reflected our stunned faces.

Graham laughed out loud, "You should have seen your faces! Got to give it to Callum." He laughed again.

I stared at him, "What the hell just happened?"

Harris looked up and down the river.

Graham smiled, "There's a portal into the city right where Callum fell. Remember, we hide portals for safety." He gazed up at the sky like he was checking a clock, "Okay, guys, you've got to jump in now before they lock it."

The four of us looked at each other. Raleigh conceded first and stepped up. She grabbed her bag, running to the edge and leapt off. Ashlen, Harris, and I peered over the edge. Nothing appeared in the water.

Harris turned to us, "Hum, not about to let a lil girl show me up. I'm goin' next! See you on the other side, gorgeous." With a wink, he grabbed both of his bags, stood at the edge, and stepped off. He disappeared instantly—no sound or splash.

"Alright girl, let's go before they lock us out." Ashlen tightened her backpack and took my hand. She smiled, "Ready, Freddie?"

I frowned at the black water and sighed, "As ready as I'll ever be."

She nodded, "One, two, jump!"

My skin instinctually waited for cold water to rush over, but instead; I felt the ice-cold air rush by us. The air acted like a vacuum, seemingly trying to suck us down at the same time. Within five seconds, my feet hit a dirt floor. It took a moment to pry my eyes open. Someone grabbed my arm and yanked me forward. I glared. Callum smirked and said, "You'll thank me." A second later, Graham landed in the same spot I had been, where I likely would have been squashed.

I stuck my tongue out at Callum's already turned back.

Graham said, "So glad you all made it." Something popped above him, and we gazed up. From this side, an oval sized black hole was right above us. The popping noise issued from it, it crackled and popped again, then blinked out.

"Whoa, that was a close call. Next time, everyone needs to move faster."

I shook my head, "Hopefully, there won't be a next time."

We were now inside of the mountain. Rows of crops led to the city gate. Large sun lamps were positioned above the plants, encouraging them to grow. Rows of corn, beans, potatoes, and fruit vines littered the area. A handful of men and women were picking the produce. The city had thick rock walls around the main entrance, but the rest of the city disappeared into the inner mountain. People steadily proceeded toward the entrance. Lanterns hung on each side of the gates, with guards fanned out. Guards scattered everywhere. Graham nodded to each we passed.

We trekked up the path to the main building where the Leader supposedly stayed. At the iron gates, we had to trudge up numerous steep steps. My thighs were on fire by the time we reached the top, and I was breathing heavily. I refused to bend over to catch my breath, though no one would see. Everyone was in front of me, except Callum. Before I knew it, I felt lighter. My bag was quickly being removed from my shoulder. I couldn't help but stop and smile at the man now in front of me. "I can carry my own bag. I'm not weak."

"I know," was all he said and kept going. I stood there, dumb-founded as he walked away. Then I hurried to catch up. How could one man be so infuriating? Rude, grumpy one minute, and then protective and sweet the next.

The castle-like structure was not as big as pictures of castles like the ones that I had seen in books, but it was still overwhelming. It wasn't Gothic style -- with flying buttresses or medieval; it was square, with rounded edges. It was built to withstand heavy fighting. Graham spoke to one of the guards, who then turned to lead us into the structure, disappearing into the rock. We were walking into the belly of the mountain now. I half expected to see dwarves mining mithril or for Legolas to round a corner.

More *Lord of the Rings*. Heavy large wooden doors opened to allow us entry. As we went inside, a big living area was the central gathering spot of the building. A fire was lit in the middle with tables and chairs surrounding. Oil lamps and oblong white-blue bulbs hung from the rafters. The interior was rustic. People used rocks to help build and mold it, so there wasn't much steel or metal used.

A group of maybe twenty people came in from a side door. They were laughing and seemed to be close-knit. One man moved away from the group to make his way toward us. The rest of the people settled around the fire and at the tables.

"Hello, welcome to Kingston. I'm the Leader of these rabble-rousers," he held his hand out to everyone and shook our hands, "you can all call me Chuck."

He was tall and lean with simple dark brown pants tucked into black boots and a beige shirt with long sleeves. He looked like the average Joe; medium brown hair a little long that curled over the tops of his ears and chestnut-colored eyes. A medallion hung from his neck that oddly resembled my necklace. I subconsciously touched the necklace hidden under my shirt.

Chuck led us to the tables where the others had assembled and sat at the head of the table so that he could see everyone.

He motioned to a man standing by a door in the far corner of the room, "Tom, can we get some drinks and food for our guests." The man nodded and disappeared behind the door.

Chuck addressed Graham, "I heard about the attack at Brand's Camp. Are you sure you are the only survivors?"

Graham leaned on the table, setting his hands on top and cracking his knuckles. His hair fell across his shoulders, "I can't be completely sure, but when I went back and searched through the wreckage, there were no traces of anyone. Some may have run off into hiding, but I can't be sure." He shook his head with a grimace on his face. Without a doubt, Graham's pain was evident. I was sure, at any moment, tears would fall, but he kept it together. Seeing his pain, I simultaneously wanted to comfort him and kill the monsters that started this.

The Leader nodded his head, "Alright, we will hold a vigil for them tomorrow night. I'll send a few Hunters over to see what the Nightlins are doing and hopefully destroy them. Maybe we can find some survivors. Any insight on how they penetrated our barriers?"

Ashlen leaned over and whispered in my ear, "Not a good enough reason to use the word penetrate." She barely contained her snorts.

I fought to keep my giggles under control.

Graham eyed us and shook his head, "Sir, it's hard to say. As you must have heard, we were attacked before, and over half were badly injured. We were sitting ducks. It happened so fast. We just tried to survive."

Chuck nodded his head, "You all did a good job. I'm glad you made it here. I'll get a hunting party for tomorrow."

"If it's fine with you, I'd like to be part of that team," Graham said.

I turned sharply and gaped at Graham. I knew my face was filled with astonishment. Graham glanced at me but focused his attention on the Leader. Callum was staring at me, watching my movements and reactions. His face was void of any emotion. He met my eyes for a few moments, then calmly turned toward the Leader. I clasped my hands in my lap and studied the wood grain of the table, slightly embarrassed that he caught my attention to Graham. *But why should I care what he thinks?*

"Yes, that will be fine with me. I've been getting news from the other side—more reports of accidents and ghost sightings. I'll need to let them know about this last attack. We haven't been able to figure out how they're traveling over. Somehow, they're traveling faster and through portals that we have no information on. I'm afraid the Nightlins may be making new ones."

"Making portals? Can they do that? I thought that was impossible?" Graham asked.

"That's what we are trying to figure out. We have people trying to work out the science on the other side. Since the disappearances of James and Jacob, the Nightlins' power has expanded. I don't know if the brothers have something to do with the powerbase or what, but we've got hundreds of people trying to find the answer. But I don't have much hope since we have been searching for that answer for over twenty years." Chuck rubbed his hand across his face, showing how tired he actually was. He looked around the table and at each of us, "The rest here are either Groundlings or Watchers I'm assuming? Except, of course, Callum."

"Yes, all of them are Groundlings, for the most part. Sloane here," Graham poked me with his elbow, "she is not quite a Groundling or a Watcher. She has some interesting anomalies."

Chuck's chestnut eyes examined me, "How do you mean?"

Graham nodded, encouraging me to speak. My mouth was locked shut.

After an awkward silence, Graham decided to speak for me, "Well, first, she showed up on her own, transported home, and the next day back, and then it seems her eyes can change to solid white," Silence followed that announcement. I was afraid to meet Chuck's eyes, so I glanced at Graham. His golden eyes encouraged me.

Chuck sat for a minute, then replied, "Well, that is something I have never heard. I'll talk to Patrice, see if she has any idea as to what it means. It sounds as if you are on your way to becoming a Watcher, but I have no way of telling you what the white means."

"You think the white might mean something?" I faced him. My curiosity was overriding my shyness.

"I'm not completely sure, but usually these things have a bigger meaning than what we initially think. We will go see Patrice, she's a kind of historian, and she should be able to decipher the meaning or should at least be able to give you some kind of direction." Chuck smiled encouragingly at me. I had a good feeling about him.

Tom came through the door, laden with lots of food and drinks. Several other servers filed out behind with even more food on platters ranging from bread, fruit, veggies, and several kinds of meat. Plates were passed around, and silverware placed in our palms. People talked amongst themselves, but I was busy thinking over how things kept changing for me.

———

LIGHTS FLICKERED as we trudged up the stairs. The flames inside the lamps danced side to side, casting long contorted shapes onto the stone walls and steps.The stone steps had seen a lot of use. A path had been worn up the middle. We curved upwards and landed in a small, dimly lit hallway. Callum and Harris had to bend their heads slightly; otherwise, they would have scraped them. The hallway only allowed enough room for two small people to walk side by side. Ashlen's arm kept bumping up against mine. Chuck led the way down the hall to a once blue painted door. Long strips of peeled paint showed the wood grain underneath.

He knocked loudly and waited for a response.

The door creaked open, and a short old lady appeared peeking around the edge of the door. Her white hair was sparse and stuck out in odd directions. Her clothes were rumpled and dirty, and the glasses perched on her nose had a crack in one lens and were held together in the middle with tape. The eyes behind the cracked glasses were sharp and demanding. A scar cracked the right side of her face. Her eyes settled on Chuck and then opened the door further to allow us room to enter.

Chuck went in, taking a seat on a worn wicker chair in the corner, while the rest of us sat on the floor or on stools. The lady closed the door and locked it, which consisted of a large wooden plank that she slid into place across the door, before turning back and taking a seat in a big green upholstered chair. A tall linear bulb was anchored in the corner. My guess was another Vitamin D bulb. The room was sparsely furnished with the fireplace centered in the room. A small kitchenette was to the right, and a small wooden framed bed was to the left of the sitting area. It was kind of creepy to be in a room with no windows.

"Well, why are you all here?" Her voice was gravelly and tired, but her eyes stared pointedly at all of us.

Chuck replied courteously, "We have a girl here that I think you'll find her markings to be of interest, and I was hoping you could shed some light on them?"

She leaned back in her chair and folded her arms across her stomach, "And why did you think I would do that?"

"Patrice, you are the one who knows more about markings than anyone else I know."

"There was a time when you came to see me because you wanted to, not because you needed something." She glared at Chuck. Her stare was accusatory.

I looked from one to the other. I raised my eyebrows in surprise.

Chuck leaned forward on his elbows, "Patrice, you know why I can't come to see you anymore." He glanced at all of us and then back to her, "We can discuss this later."

She waved her hand as in dismissal and straightened up in her chair, "Which one of these girls?"

"Sloane, could you come over here?" Chuck waved me over to stand next to them.

I got up from my seat on the floor by Ashlen and went over to Chuck and Patrice. I brushed my hair across my shoulders, tugging on the ends, a nervous habit of mine. Everyone had their eyes on me, except for Callum, who thought something more interesting was happening outside the door. Graham met my eyes and smiled with the yellow flames of the fire, dancing in his golden eyes.

Chuck said, "You won't be able to see now, but her eyes had begun to change white when she was challenged. We are hoping you might be able to share some knowledge on the cause."

Patrice's chair squeaked as she got up. Her rough hands pulled my face down closer to her. I had to stop the urge to jerk away. She stared into my eyes, unflinchingly. I couldn't keep the helpless fearful look off my face, so I just stared back. She jerked away, then grabbed my hands. She turned my palms face-up so she could study them. She traced the lines on my hands, murmuring as she did. I wanted to see Chuck's reaction, but he was steadily watching Patrice.

"Hmm... for once you're right, these markings may be of interest."

"How do you know?" I asked.

She traced a line that ran from my thumb to the other side of my hand, "This marking I have seen before, it usually means a continuance. Fate decided you will become a Hunter, but not without a price. Who are your parents?"

I pulled my hands from her. *I'll be a Hunter?* "My mom isn't part of this realm, and my father, I don't know who he is or what he was. You're sure I will be a Hunter?"

Patrice slowly nodded, staring at the floor as if the answer might be there, and turned back to sit in her chair. "Yes, I am sure." She waved her hand like she was dismissing my question and settled back into her chair, "Your father must be the key. When did he disappear?"

I quickly glanced around the room. Everyone had their eyes fixed on me, waiting for my response. I wasn't used to talking about my dad in front of so many people. Even at home, mom and I were the only ones that talked about it. If someone ever asked, I would say he wasn't around and never elaborated.

I took a deep calming breath and replied, "It was when he and my mom were in college together. They had planned on getting married then, one night he was gone. It was a year after they had met. The only thing my mom had of him was this necklace and dagger." I lifted the necklace from under my shirt and over my head to hand to her then took the dagger out from its holder on my leg.

She took the necklace from me carefully. Her eyes enlarged, filling with astonishment. She examined the necklace then at me and back to the necklace again. Chuck sat on the edge of his seat and stared. It was like they were both suddenly entranced.

"Your father... must have been one of the Sullivan twins. That's the only explanation as to why you would have this." Patrice carefully turned the necklace over to study the designs. She addressed Chuck, "Is that not what you think as well?"

Chuck slowly nodded, "How could this be?" His eyes bore into me.

"Wait, my mom said my father's name was Jacob Sloane. That's why she named me Sloane. Why would he give her a different name?"

Patrice was nodding as I spoke, "Jacob was the older brother, by a few minutes. Most of the Realmers are encouraged to give fake names in the Norm to try and keep the Norms far from the Realm."

"Great, so everything I know about my father is a lie." Anger bubbled up inside of me.

"He only lied about his name, not about everything else. He lied because we are all made to, so don't blame him. Remember, he had no knowledge of you. Otherwise, your story would have turned out differently. If he was here now, he would ask you to forgive him, and he would have loved telling you his family's history," Chuck's eyes were pleading with me.

I had nothing to say, just a blank expression. It's not that I didn't understand. It was that I was angry that I would never get to have the chance for him to tell me his history. I was going to have to learn from someone else what my family had done, I had lost that moment, and I would never get it back.

Patrice still examined the necklace and dagger.

"With these pieces, you have to know the name to activate the magic within. There is a library below that might be able to help with that. These objects only work for those who share the same bloodline. Your father always had these items with him. If it is the same man, his father's blood is in these objects, and so is yours."

Blood. "Someone's blood is in that thing?" I couldn't help the queasiness that spiked through me.

She nodded, "It's how these objects are able to work, and how they are entrusted to only family members. It keeps others safe. If these objects were to get into the wrong hands, they would not be able to wield them." She carefully handed me the necklace and dagger back. "You must keep them safe from harm and hidden. Not everyone should know that you have these."

My eyes widened with unease. I nodded and placed the dagger back in the holder on my thigh and the necklace around my neck. I took my seat by Ashlen.

She studied me, "Would you like to know what your palms told me?"

I examined my hands, really studying the lines on my palms like they might hold some kind of secrets. "Uh... I think I'll just be surprised unless it's something bad? Like when you said it would come for a price?"

She smiled knowingly and nodded, "Well, it doesn't say what the price will be just that you will have to pay one, and your heart will break. These lines are only a general outline of what will happen in your life, so keep living your life, don't stop because of some warning that may or may not have a heavy bearing on the outcome. These lines only give us hints of what is to come. Of course, like your life, your lines are not yet finished, so more has yet to be revealed. The tide will shift either for good or bad, but we will not know until it happens."

Oh, great. I'm going to have to pay a price? What kind of price? I don't have anything to give. My heart is going to break? Physically or emotionally? How is my heart going to break?

This is too much. I can feel the stress building and layering. What does she mean? Does it only hint to my future? Why in the world should I trust palm reading? I mean, really, who believes in those kinds of things? Will my future end good or bad? I hope my mom is okay and Mariah too. They would not believe what I'm going through right now. I'm fighting demons and night creatures; this is ridiculous. Where's a guide book?

"Sloane?"

I jerked my head up to Ashlen, "Yeah, sorry?"

She smiled and held her hand out to help me up, "Come on, we're leaving."

Everyone else was either at the door or already in the hall. I grasped her hand and stood. She put her arm around my shoulder and squeezed me against her side.

"They're going to show us to our rooms, so we, meaning you, can get some rest."

"I'm not all that tired." I stifled a yawn.

Chuck led the way down the hall with Patrice by his side. They were bent toward each other and whispering about who knows what. Graham was right behind them with his hands clasped behind his back. Harris and Raleigh followed. Callum was behind us trailing by about ten feet. Ashlen had her arm looped through mine.

Ashlen moved closer and whispered, "So, who are you going to fall in love with?"

I glanced at her and turned toward down the hall then quickly glanced back at Callum.

"I'm not planning on falling in love with anyone. It's ridiculous, especially right now, with everything going on." I glared at her and lowered my voice using my best self-righteous tone. "Is all you think about, boys? Do you know how insane that is, especially right now, with our futures in the balance? Monsters keep trying to kill us. My priority is finding out what happened to my dad and keeping the Nightlins from taking over that is it. My plate is full."

She made an exasperated noise, "Oh, come on! I just want a tiny little normalcy in my life. I need it, or I'm going to go cray-cray. We haven't been able to talk about boys, and now you are ruining it for me. If your heart is going to break, you might as well enjoy one of them thoroughly before then. Personally, I think Graham would be a great choice."

For a moment, I let myself fantasize. Those golden eyes and long hair. His biceps and lackadaisical smile.

"He is attractive. I'll give you that."

Ashlen giggled and pulled on my arm, "Of course, he is! Every girl thinks so! I think he might like you, though."

My heart stuttered. Nope. Not going to think about it anymore.

"And you're so lucky if you'll be a Hunter, I wonder what your Czar will look like, something dangerous so people will take you seriously." She gripped my arm tighter and, with one hand, made clawing motions. "Like black with dark purple highlights and long needle-like talons. But you do have blue eyes, so maybe it'll be a gorgeous sapphire color."

I swatted her hand away and rolled my eyes, "You're full of it - it being ridiculousness. Besides, have you forgotten these guys have superpowers? They can probably hear everything we're saying."

"Oh, who cares? I'm sure they're used to hearing girls talking about them. There are more guys than girls in this place, so we have choices. Anyways," she lifted her chin up, "I don't think I'm into Harris anymore..."

I stared at her, "Ha. Yeah, right. You," I poked her arm, "are the one that has fallen in love, not me."

She glared at me then haughtily said, "Have not. There's a difference between fun and love." She stared down the hall and, in an indirect way, undoubtedly making sure he hadn't heard that.

We continued on in silence. She eventually dropped her arm to swing at her side. Chuck showed us to our rooms. The three of us girls shared a rather large room, with a fireplace, three beds, one window, and a small kitchen. The window had two boards positioned on either side that acted as shutters. The same long bulbs from downstairs hung from the ceiling. They seemed pretty serious about this vitamin stuff.

The guys were in a room next to us that I hoped was identical to ours. No reason for them to have a better room than us girls.

As we walked into our room, I watched the guys make their way down to theirs. Callum's eyes locked onto mine as he passed. The corner of his mouth twitched like he was trying not to smile. Graham stopped at the doorway. He winked at me, then sauntered in. Callum's face changed to annoyance. He glanced at me and walked through the door, shutting it heavily.

Chuck and Patrice continued down the hallway picking up their whispered conversation. I drifted to the bed closest to the door, crawled under the covers, and fell asleep within a matter of seconds.

9

THE FLASH OF LIGHT, signaling morning, interrupted my sleep. No shades were on the windows, so the light had unobstructed freedom to shine. I rolled over. Mumbling noises came from the kitchen area. I opened one eye to see Harris standing against the counter with his back to me, and Ashlen stood in front of the makeshift stove, which consisted of a fire with a metal stand sitting over it. The cabinets were just planks of wood set up as shelving and were built around the make-shift stove. Ashlen was moving something around on the oven top. I searched for Raleigh, but she wasn't in either bed. The heat from the stove made it hard to breathe. I threw the covers off and kicked my shoes off. I stretched as far as I could and slowly sat up. Ashlen and Harris watched me.

"Mornin'."

"Hi, Harris," my throat croaked as I spoke.

I stood and shuffled across the room to sit on a stool by them propping my elbows on the counter. Eggs were frying in the skillet along with some vegetables. I scrunched my nose and got up to get closer to the food. I grabbed some bread and peanut butter from off the shelf that ran along the perimeter of the wall and set them on the counter.

Harris ended up spending all morning in our area. For someone who wasn't in love, Ashlen could have fooled me. She gave Harris every dazzling smile and laugh she had. They both beamed as they talked in a secretive manner. I didn't mind since I was still exhausted. Someone rapped on the door, and Harris sauntered over to open the door. A young girl came in with clothes draped over her arms. She carried the garments to a chair and set them down.

"These are for the feast this afternoon. The Leader said you had no dress clothes, so I brought some for you to try. I have some pins in case we need to hem them or make them fit better. Just let me know." She bowed her head and strolled out the door closing it softly behind her.

Ashlen and I immediately looked at each other. I'm pretty sure we were thinking the same thing... this whole situation was straight out of a movie. I stuffed some of the bread into my mouth and strode to the garments.

One was a simple blue dress with long sleeves and a small sheer train. Another was a deep red wine color made just like the blue one. Two were different shades of green with scoop necks, and the length hit the top of the floor. I opted for the wine-colored dress just because I wanted something different than the usual blues and blacks I wore. Ashlen chose one of the green dresses that showed off her beautiful green eyes and dark hair.

Harris went back to his room to see if he had gotten some new clothes while we got baths and fixed our hair. Long luxurious baths were something I missed while at the training camp. I could tell Ashlen had too. We both seemed happier and refreshed.

I stood in front of the dingy mirror and tried to make sure I was presentable. The girl came back and made some slight modifications, so the dresses would be more tailored.

Once I slipped the dress on, I didn't realize how much it would stick to my body and how low the scoop of the neck was. I knew what to expect before even looking in the mirror, my boobs were barely there. I figured with me training every day and already being rail-thin the mirror would reflect that, but somehow, I looked different. This dress gave me an hourglass figure. My breasts were a little fuller along with my hips. It looked like I had gained weight, and in all the right places. *Wow.* I stood there somewhat dumbfounded, even noticing the color of my hair. It must be a trick of the light or the color of the dress, but my light brown hue was lighter. *I was turning blonde?* I tugged at the low neck and at the silky fabric on my hips.

Ashlen swatted my hands. "Stop picking at it. You're beautiful."

I frowned slightly. I wrapped my hair up into a side chignon. I wasn't too sure about so much skin showing, but I thought to hell with it. I've got to learn to show off what my momma gave me. No matter how little that was. I'll probably regret it later if I get lots of stares but oh well. I turned in the mirror. Even the back was low, a first for me. What was I thinking?

Ashlen cleaned up very nicely. Her green dress had one thigh-high slit, showing off her long legs. She wore her hair down, but it twisted on one side, giving more view of her perfectly symmetrical face. Her huge boobs had been smashed into her dress, threatening to rip the seams. She came to stand beside me in the mirror.

"We look pretty damn great if I do say so myself." Ashlen nodded her head and smiled the biggest I had ever seen her smile. She linked her arm through mine.

I turned my head to the side to get one last glimpse at my hair and smiled, "Yes, we do. I'm sure Harris's mouth will gape when he sees you." I winked at her.

She pinched my arm, "I'm sure Graham will stop dead in his tracks when he sees you and maybe Callum as well."

I made a face at her and dragged her toward the door, "Whatever, let's go." The truth was I couldn't wait to see what Graham's reaction was, and I wanted to see how well he spruced up too, but I wasn't about to admit it out loud, especially to Ashlen. I knew she would have something silly to say.

We walked out the door and down the hallway to the stairs that would carry us to the dining hall. I hardly tripped and kept Ashlen from stepping on the train of my dress. As we walked, other people fell in line with us; all were dressed in their finest clothes. We greeted each person we passed, like old friends. We glided into the dining hall through double wooden doors that had beautiful carvings etched across. Large candelabras hung from the rafters, and the fire was aglow in the center of the room. Giant wooden rectangular tables were spread throughout the room. In front of the room, I could see Graham sitting by Chuck both in deep conversation. Harris sat by Graham with an empty chair beside him. On the other side of Chuck was another empty chair, then Callum, and then Raleigh. How is it that I'm always by Callum? While everyone was dressed in their finest, he was dressed simply. Despite his gorgeous body and face, his expression was sour. It's like he's always sucking on one of those lemon heads.

Graham cleaned up nicely, just as I had thought. He wore a jade green tailored shirt, a dark coffee brown vest, with dark brown pants, and his regular tan boots. He had combed his hair and pulled it back, tying it off with a leather strip. His gold eyes weren't unobstructed since his hair wasn't in his face and reflected handsomely next to the jade color of his shirt. His skin even had a more honey hue to it.

"Hey, don't worry, I'll make Graham and Callum switch seats so you can be by Graham." Ashlen winked at me.

I grabbed her arm, "No, no, don't do that. I don't want people to notice." My heart jumped with fear.

"Sloane, no one will notice."

I tightened my grip, "Please, don't. Please?"

Her lips flattened into a thin line as she thought. She crossed her eyes. "Ugh, fine. But don't whine to me later about having to sit next to close-mouthed Cal."

I nodded.

We split up, Ashlen went to her seat by Harris, who indeed dropped his mouth when he saw her, and I walked to my seat between Chuck and Callum. My eyes drifted over to Graham, who watched me, I smiled at him, and he smiled. As I made my way to my seat, Callum rose and pulled my chair out. I stopped in shock for a moment. He kept his eyes turned away from me until I stepped forward. His eyes met mine for a tiny second then he helped scoot my chair in.

"Thank you."

"You are very welcome." He scooted his chair in and didn't attempt any further conversation with me. I glanced at Ashlen, who made an I-told-you face.

Chuck asked me, "How are you today? Did you sleep well?"

"Alright, and yes. Thanks for letting us borrow the clothes and hosting us, and really for everything."

"Absolutely, you can have anything you want. You are one of us, and we take care of each other. Now, if you'll excuse me for a moment." He stood to address the rest of the crowd, "Good afternoon, everyone, we are here today to welcome our visitors and celebrate their wellness. We also need to take a moment of silence to remember those fallen in the recent battle." He bowed his head, and everyone in the room did the same. Reverent silence filled the hall.

When the minute was over, he sat. "Let's celebrate life. Let the festivities begin."

Everyone through the room began clapping, the music swelled, and with the sounds of instruments, the festivities commenced. The food came out on large steaming platters that contained favorite dishes from around the world. Some began to eat while others needed to move. People started dancing around and between the tables. Chuck and Graham started their conversation back up, while Harris and Ashlen headed to the dance floor. A tall, dark, and handsome man asked Raleigh to dance. I loved watching everyone. A smile began to slide across my face. A large and lined hand appeared in front of me. I turned thinking it was Graham, but it was Callum. I'm pretty sure my features didn't hide my disappointment, because his face hardened slightly.

"May I have this dance?"

"Oh, well, I don't know if you want to dance with me. You know how *graceful* I am."

His eyes and mouth softened, "I'll take my chances."

I nodded and slowly stood. He pulled my chair out for me as I stood and helped me slide between the chairs. His hand slid into mine as we made our way toward the other dancers. I glanced back at the table. Both Graham and Chuck watched our progression. Graham didn't seem very happy at first, but then smiled when he noticed me looking at him.

Callum gently pulled me around, so I faced him. He placed one hand on my waist and lifted our linked hands. We swayed to the music slowly getting used to the rhythm, then Callum began taking small steps backwards and forwards. I tried not to stare at our feet. I was trying so hard not to step on his feet.

"Sloane, it'll be easier if you look at me."

I glanced up at him for a moment, "Um, I don't think so."

"You haven't stepped on me yet. Just trust me." His eyes were more alive in that moment than I had ever seen them, even more than when we had fought that first time.

"Okay," I managed to squeak out.

I kept my eyes on him and noticed, more closely, that he too cleaned up well. His hair was combed, and he had shaved, which somehow made his face seem softer and more attractive. Instead of his thick black boots, he had on shoes that resembled loafers or moccasins, which was a surprise. I never thought I would see him wearing something like loafers. His pants were a light tan coupled with a dark blue shirt that had a small silver stripe running through it. Every piece of clothing fit him well like it had been made just for him.

We traveled around the dance floor, easily waltzing past other couples. He held me carefully like he thought I might break. His hand was pressed against my bare back, giving me a slight direction as we moved. I tried not to overthink it. I tried not to think about his massive warm hand on my back. He brought his head closer to mine.

"See? You're doing great," he whispered.

I felt like I was on air. Every now and then, he twirled me around, which made me laugh, and my smile grew. The tightness in my body lessened. His eyes seemed brighter, and a real smile tugged at his mouth. The more I took him in, the more our bodies synced and swayed. I did not step on his feet once.

"So, Callum, what's your favorite movie?"

A full smile threatened his lips, "What made you ask that?"

I shrugged a shoulder, "Humor me. I barely know anything about you."

He smirked as we made a turn, "I haven't seen that many movies. Every now and then, they have movie nights, but I usually miss them." He glanced at me. The usual hard lines of his face were soft and carefree. "I would probably have to say *The Princess Bride*."

"Inconceivable!" I laughed. "I love that movie."

Callum smiled wide, showing one dimple.

"May I cut in?"

We halted. Callum stiffened. Graham smiled at us. Callum's face had closed off once again. Callum glanced at Graham then back at me. I opened my mouth to say something, not sure what, but Callum spoke first, "Go ahead." He dropped his arms from around me and turned away without looking back. A hole formed between us. It felt like a cavern had opened wide. Why was it so easy for him to walk away? It shouldn't matter, but it did hurt a little every time.

Graham took my hand into his, sliding his arm around my waist and immediately led me into the dance. He smiled widely and winked like we were sharing a secret. We waltzed around and around the room together. He tried to talk to me over the music, but I could barely hear. I took a wrong step and smashed his foot with mine.

I grimaced and mouthed, sorry. He laughed and shook his head, but tightened his hold on me. I couldn't quite keep up with him. He always seemed to be one step ahead of me. I stepped on his feet several times, but each time Graham seemed to think it was funny, and we would swing around the floor a little faster.

Strange, how I thought that with him everything would glide more smoothly.

Our song ended, and I gave an excuse about my feet being tired so

I could return to the table. Graham smiled and tucked my hand into the crook of his arm. He led me back to the table and helped me to sit in my chair. Callum was gone. Graham took Raleigh's seat next to me. Everyone else was either on the dance floor, talking, or eating.

"So, are you enjoying yourself?" Graham leaned back in his chair with one arm stretched across the back of mine.

"Yes, I am. Are you?"

His mouth rose slightly at the corner, "Yes, I am, except I can tell something is bothering you."

I raised an eyebrow and watched the dancers. My fingers played with the folds of my dress, and I watched curiously as I tangled the cloth around my fingers. What was bothering me? Graham stilled my fingers. His thumb stroked back and forth across my hand. I gave a small smile, smoothing my dress in the process.

I took a deep breath, "I'm just trying to figure out people and what my role is in this world." I smiled more brightly, which didn't help me be more at ease.

Graham nodded and scanned over the crowd, "I know what you mean. Of course, I think you have it a little harder than I did." His eyes bored straight into me, "Listen, I know everyone says this, but it will all work out just be patient. I'll help you figure this out, okay? I'll be with you until the end."

"Except, you're leaving in like," I glanced at my wrist like I had a watch on, "oh, two hours to go fight Nightlins."

He shook his head and smiled, "I have to go, you know that. Besides, I'll be back before you even realize I was gone."

I rested my elbows on the table. Resting my chin in my hands, I turned and looked at him. "Hmm... maybe. Just make sure you come back in one piece, please." I folded my hands in my lap, "I don't think I could stand it right now if I lost one of my friends. I don't know if you've noticed, but I don't have that many."

He squeezed my arm, "I won't let anything happen to me, I promise. And you're wrong, you have more friends than you realize." He smiled warmly at me and stood. "I'm going to go say bye to some others."

"Alright, see you in a bit." I scanned over the crowd again, picking out Harris and Ashlen slow dancing and very much in their own world. There was no space between them. Raleigh was with a different guy, but she seemed very cozy with a new guy. I continued peeking around the room, secretly hoping that I would spot the dark blue shirt and dark hair; that he would be against the wall somewhere keeping watch like usual.

I felt content and the happiest I had been since I had traveled to this strange world. Taking in the rustic style of the room and all the smiling faces, funny, how this place seems more like home than the one in the Norm.

———

THE PARTY ENDED ALL TOO SOON. About twenty Hunters and Protectors began the descent down to the main gate. We congregated around the large gates waving, hugging, and kissing the warriors goodbye, telling them to be safe and that we could not wait till they were home again. Graham was fitted with numerous amounts of weapons, which he assured he would use accordingly.

Tears ran down my face. I don't know if it was because I was afraid for Graham or for all the warriors or just the realization of having to say goodbye to people that had begun to feel like family. All around me, men and women hugged and kissed goodbye. Relatives gave lucky charms to help keep their loved ones safe.

Graham spoke to a man who patted his back and gave him a warm hug. He saw me standing to the side and released the man. He walked over and stopped in front of me. He brushed his fingers across my face wiping up my tears.

"Hey, don't cry. I told you everything will be fine. We'll be back before you know it." His palm rested on my cheek, bringing his other hand to the other side of my face, he cupped my face. Fuck, is he about to do what I think he's about to do? He leaned down; our faces were centimeters away from each other. I closed my eyes. His breath tickled my nose. His lips landed on my right cheek by my ear, far from my lips.

My eyes popped open, and I breathed out. *Relief* flooded through me. His hands slid to my shoulders. He pulled back slowly and winked.

"I'm going to miss seeing your sweet face for the next few weeks."

I crossed my arms over my chest and glanced around. Callum stood between some people; his eyes fixed on us. I looked away quickly. Heat rose to my cheeks. I took a steadying deep breath to keep my face from burning. I'm sure he wasn't thrilled about staying here to protect the capitol. I'm sure he would rather be off fighting Nightlins.

"You will? Huh? I guess I'll miss you too." I smiled.

His smile broadened, "You guess?" He laughed, squeezed my shoulders, and dropped his hands to his side. His eyes studied me for a few seconds. "Make sure you take care of yourself. Remember, I won't be here to catch you when you fall." He winked at me again. My face flushed again. He reached out and wrapped his arms around me. He pulled me up against him, his chin rested on my shoulder. My arms slowly slid around his back. He gave one last hard squeeze and joined the warriors marching out the gates.

We all gathered at the edge of the road watching the warriors. They gathered next to the portals along the mountain wall. A portal in the middle glowed a soft white. One at a time, they stepped through, disappearing immediately. Graham looked back one more time and waved as he stepped through the shimmering skin of the portal wall.

I headed back toward the main building with everyone else. My arms dropped to my side. My eyes focused on the ground before me, as my legs propelled me forward. I gathered the bottom of my dress up, so it wouldn't drag on the ground. As I followed the path, people went inside their homes. Food wafted out, and laughter erupted from open windows.

A crunch sounded behind me. I turned, thinking it was some more people heading to the main building, but it was Callum. He stopped in mid-stride. Our eyes locked. My mouth slowly spread into a smile. He ran his hand through his hair and looked away. When he looked back at me, a ghost of a smile was on his face and shining from his eyes. He walked toward me and stopped an arm's length from me.

"Caught you," my smile grew even bigger.

"You did." He shook his head, gave a crooked smile, and shrugged, "I just wanted to make sure you were okay." His eyes examined every line of my face.

"I'm fine." I tried waving off my emotions.

He glanced over my shoulder and up to the main house. "Well, do you mind if I keep you company or I could go back to stalking you in the shadows?" He smiled coyly at me.

"Oh, my goodness, did you just make a joke? Or do my ears deceive me?"

He narrowed his eyes and walked around me. I watched him for a moment then jogged to keep up with him. The night breeze blew in our faces swirling strands of my hair around my shoulders. We continued on in silence, but it was a comfortable silence between two friends.

"Your hair is longer." He tugged on a long strand that had escaped from the pins. I felt a rush.

My head jerked up to look at his face. I pulled a few strands across my shoulders to play with the ends. The ends just met the inside of the bend in my arm. "Yeah, it has. I mean, I haven't had a hair cut in over two months, which I'm sure isn't a good thing." I flipped my hair back over my shoulder, trying to stick the fallen strands back into the chignon and glanced at him. He was staring straight ahead at the path in front of us. "Your hair hasn't grown at all it seems, why is that?"

"I use my knife to keep it short."

"Oh, how very manly of you. Have you not heard of scissors?"

He glanced at me and shook his head again. "You're awfully sassy tonight."

"And you don't like it?" I baited him, and I had no idea why.

Maybe it was the mixture of emotions that coursed through me. I don't know. But I was trying to get him to react. To something.

He shoved his hands into his pockets, "I didn't say I didn't like it." His voice was low and gentle. It reminded me of the voice he had used the first night we had met.

The anger that, for some reason, was building up deflated. I brushed my fingers down his arm, "Hey, I'm sorry. I don't know why I'm acting all snippy."

His eyes traveled down his arm to where I had touched him. The corners of his mouth pulled slightly. "I wasn't taking your snippiness as bad. You've had a hard couple of months. I would be a little snippy too." He glanced at me, and his stride got faster. "And then well tonight having to say goodbye to..." He didn't finish the sentence, and the unsaid words were left floating in the open air.

I tried to study his face, but I couldn't read his expression. I grabbed his arm to slow him down, "I tend to have trouble with good-byes. I've never had many people in my life, so it's hard for me to just let them go, especially if there is a chance that they will be in danger."

He finally turned to me. His expression was a mixture of confusion, thoughtfulness, and maybe amusement. He walked straight to the door and held it open for me.

When we got inside, people were cleaning up from the party. We took the hall to our rooms and continued on in silence. I wasn't exactly sure what to say or if what I did say had upset him in some way. So, I kept my mouth shut. My eyes would sneak a peek at him in my peripheral vision, but his attention was focused down the hallway. His hands clenched at his side.

We reached my door, and I stopped, preparing to say goodnight.

He stopped and studied me. His eyes roved from my head to my toes. My heart thundered in my chest. Sweat threatened to appear.

Was he going to kiss me? *I wished he would.*

His hands were shoved in his pockets again. His shoulders rounded, he leaned in a tiny bit, and his head bent forward. "I'll see you later."

He turned on his heel and continued down the hall to his room. He opened the door and shut it behind him, without looking back at me.

I stood in the hall outside my door for a good minute, just staring at the closed door to his room. Fucking Men.

10

THE NEXT MORNING, I went to find the library. It was quiet and still in the main building. I guess people were still resting from the late-night festivities. I had to travel to the very back of the building through the rough stone hallways using light from torches to find my way. Tall skinny windows lined the whole room of the library. Large wooden bookcases were lined up in the middle of the space with ten rows and numerous columns. As I strolled through the bookcases, I came to a big heavy wooden table with several large candles sitting around the edge; the melted wax pooled all around the candles. A small, frail man with huge glasses bent over the table. Papers and books were spread out all over the table, and some chairs were stacked on the floor. He was so close to the table that his nose almost touched the paper that was laid out on the surface.

My shoes scuffed the stones as I walked toward him. He jerked his head up. His eyes were magnified through his thick glasses.

"Can I help you?" His voice was gravelly and quiet; it made me think of my grandfather.

"Yes, that would be great if you could. I'm searching for papers about my father, my family, and maybe do some research on some of my... anomalies?"

He tilted his head and scratched behind his ear. He shuffled around the table to stand in front of me. "Who is your father?"

I hesitated for a moment, about to respond with Jacob Sloane, but corrected myself, "Jacob Sullivan."

His eyes grew slightly larger, which I didn't think was possible. His bushy eyebrows disappearing under the worn fedora perched on his head. His eyes fixated on the floor. He scratched his chin then shuffled down one of the aisles of books. I'm guessing that means I'm supposed to follow him.

Surprisingly, I had to rush after him. He disappeared around one of the many corners. I ran around a few of the corners and caught a glimpse of him shuffling by one of the bookcases. I finally caught up with him in the farthest corner of the room. The space had a moldy wet dog smell. My nose immediately wanted to retreat.

He leaned over to examine the row of books and papers near the bottom of the case. He pulled out a dark blue book that was tattered around the top and bottom of the spine. He pushed it into my hands and then started stacking more books, papers, and scrolls into my arms. He turned a toothy grin in my direction and then gestured for me to follow.

We came to a long table that was a few feet from the table that he had been working at. He gingerly took the materials from my arms and set them out on the counter.

"Here are the majority of the materials that are about your father and that may be able to help with your anomalies." He coughed and cleared his throat, "But if you will tell me about what has happened then I may be able to provide some more illumination on the meanings." He smiled sheepishly at me.

I smiled sweetly at him, "Yes, of course, umm, well, my eyes at one point had changed white..."

"Hmm... Come over here to the light so I might see better," he scurried over to the narrow window and waited for me to stand before him.

I walked over and stood in the moonlight for him. He leaned in close so he could examine my eyes.

"Hmmm... let's see what we have here." He stared unblinkingly at me.

"What's your name?" I decided to ask while he was staring intensely into my retinas.

"What?" He blinked several times, trying to recall, "Oh, it's Clifford Robertson."

I inclined my head, "Well, it's nice to meet you, Clifford Robertson. My name is Sloane."

He grunted in, I guessed, what was an acknowledgment. He stayed silent for several minutes and then went over to the table to pick up a green paperback book. He started leafing through the pages.

"Did you see anything?" I asked.

He looked at me for a second, "Err no. What have you learned so far?"

"Patrice said that I'll become a Hunter, but I'll have to pay a price, and my heart will break." My face and my body cringed as I said the words. "Also, she read my palms. She said my story had started already," I held out my hand for him to see. "This long line is supposed to mean a continuance."

"Humph, she did a palm reading, huh?" he set the book down and ambled toward me. "Let me see." He took my hand in his, but instead placed his other hand on top of it, encasing my hand between each of his own. He closed his eyes and bowed his head.

"Well, that is mostly what I have discerned as well." His large eyes looked up at me, and he scratched his chin again, "But you will have powers that have not been seen in a very long time. Your palm says that you will have to overcome abandonment and deceit."

"What? Abandonment? Deceit?"

His eyes looked curiously at me, "Yes... some other meanings are mixed in, but we will have to," he shuffled through the loose pages and books, "find those meanings somehow in these old pages." He picked up one of the books and handed them to me. He tapped the cover of the book, "Why don't you try this one first."

I sat at the stool that was pushed up under the table and pulled the book across so it rested in front of me. I traced the edge of the paper with my fingers, feeling the coarse flakes of wood that had made it. The writing on the page was in long cursive penmanship. The ink was a deep black. The ink was from a quill pen because of the strokes and how specks of ink blotted the page.

The first page I read was from my grandfather, who, in the Norm, would be considered a general in his army. From what I could tell, my grandfather was a very abrasive and stern man. Though, most of the people said that he was a great Leader and enforcer. He was the Leader for fifty-seven years. One of the books was a journal written with his hand. The pages were filled with accounts from different battles against the Nightlins. Every date was recorded, and every detail about each Nightlin was rehashed and examined.

I spent several hours at that table reading each loose piece of paper and noting in each book, something that might reference my odd white eyes. Clifford moved back to study at his table, so I assumed he was studying something because he would read then scribble furiously on a notepad beside him. His thick glasses would slide down his nose every ten seconds, so he was constantly fighting to keep them perched on his nose.

By the time I had gone through maybe an eighth of what had been laid out on the table, it was time to eat; my stomach rumbled in affirmation. I passed by Clifford without him noticing me. His focus was so intent on what was before him.

I trudged through the hallways to find the dining hall. My back and bum were sore from sitting and leaning across the table. The luscious smell of warm bread, meat, and veggies wafted down the hall and straight to my nose, warming my insides. I walked swiftly into the dining hall and scanned the large crowd of people trying to find my friends. I spotted Raleigh in the corner of the room, snuggled up close to a dark-haired stranger. That woman loved a new man every night. I couldn't help but smile and shake my head.

Would I ever be so carefree, and let go of my fears, or would I always be stuck in my head? I continued trying to spot Ashlen.

Fingers wrapped around my elbow and guided me forward. It was Callum.

"Oh, great, my favorite person," I said with a slight smirk. It was meant to be flirty, but it probably came out full of sarcasm, but I wasn't trying to be. Sarcasm is just my way to ease tension. But to be honest, I was still a little pissed over the way he left me last night at my door. I tossed and turned over those feelings for far too long last night.

"All of us are seated over here." He kept his eyes straight forward, but his fingers were gently curled around the bend of my arm. He applied light pressure on my arm to guide me to where we were going. His tone gave nothing away, and that irritated me too.

We threaded our way through the crowd, they parted until we came to a large table where Chuck, Ashlen, Harris, and Patrice sat.

Callum guided me around to an empty chair by Chuck. Callum took his seat at the end of the table by Patrice.

"Sloane, I heard you've been in the library all morning?" Chuck asked.

"Oh, yes."

"Did you learn anything new?" Chuck continued to eat eagerly. I tried not to judge him too harshly by his bad table manners.

"Well, I did learn a little more about my grandfather, but nothing about my eyes, though, maybe a little more about my palm reading."

"And..."

"Apparently," I paused to take a breath. "I will have to overcome abandonment and deceit." Sarcasm took over again, "Isn't that just lovely?"

His eyebrows rose as he spoke, "I think everyone has to overcome abandonment and deceit at some point in their lives, so I do not think you should weigh those words so heavily. The fact that it is a part of you does mean something, of course. Though everyone has words like those in their future and intertwined in their own lives. As harsh and negative as they sound, they are general parts of life. When you came here, you left your mother and friends behind. Is that not a form of loss or abandonment?"

A slight weight lifted from my shoulders, and I nodded my head. Hopefully, those words won't be significant. "So, do you mind telling me what words warned you?"

He placed his elbows on the table and folded his hands together. "My palms told me to be careful of the road before me, to watch those around me, and that some people would try to manipulate me. It did say that I would become *a* leader of my people." He kind of chuckled, "Just not *the* Leader."

"Your palms said all that?" I was somewhat surprised.

He nodded and smiled, "Maybe not in those exact words, but that was the general information given to me."

"Does everyone have their palms read?"

"No, not everyone's story is written on their hands. Some have to find it in their blood, eyes, or even their hair. Of course, not just one reader can read each of those. It takes a special person to read each." He smiled again, "But now I'm making things more complicated for you."

I smiled at him and gazed around the room at all the people dancing and laughing. I was really starting to love it here. If only mom were here.

"Do you mind if I ask you something else?"

He smiled, "No, I guess not. What's the question?"

"How long have you been the Leader?"

He laughed and leaned back in his chair, putting his hands behind his head. "That is an excellent question. I think the best question would be: When?" his eyes sparkled with laughter.

"Okay, when did you become the Leader?"

"Well, I was thirty-seven when I was given the Leadership. Your grandfather handed me the position when your father and uncle disappeared. He was never the same. So, I've been the Leader for almost twenty years." His eyes became serious as he looked at me, "If your father and his brother hadn't disappeared then I wouldn't be where I am today."

"Oh." I stared at my lap. "Will you tell me about my uncle?"

He smiled gently, "Sure, James was seven minutes younger than your dad. He was really funny and outgoing. Almost every girl was in love with him. He lived a pretty carefree life." Chuck ran his rough hands across the tabletop, lost in thought, "Of course, he was when he was ten. He was charming and could almost talk his way out of anything."

"What kind of power did he have?"

"I believe he had Ice."

My eyebrows rose, "Ice? I haven't heard of that one."

Chuck chuckled, "I think you've barely scratched the surface of our world."

I let out a big sigh, "Very true." I paused, thinking again. "James was in the Norm for how long?"

"Oh, he was probably there for about a year, then it was time for him to come back. We are all sent over to the Norm so we can learn more of how our world affects the Norm and so we can see the Norm Defense. The Norm Defense is made up of people from our Realm who fight the last battle. Watchers, Protectors, and Hunters are all represented in the Defense."

"One day, I might be on the other side, fighting?"

"Absolutely. The more people we have over there, the better off the world will be. That has been one of my goals. To get the majority of the Realmers over to the Norm."

I tried to file all the information away for later. Raleigh was making her way across the room to our table with her guy in tow. Patrice was talking to Callum. I smiled slightly at him before I turned away. I spotted Ashlen and Harris dancing. They both had big grins plastered on their faces and were very close.

"Can you tell me more about the disappearance of my father, Jacob?"

Chuck glanced at me quickly. "I'll tell you everything I know, which isn't much." He surveyed the room, "They had gone out with some other Hunters one night to raid a Nightlin camp. Your father had been dispatched to one area of the realm while James was sent to another. The other fighters, with them, said there were a lot more Nightlins than what they had first thought. They attacked the creatures, and more Nightlins surrounded the group of fighters. One of the men, who had been with your father, said it was strange how the Nightlins were able to capture Jacob. The creatures seemed to go straight for him like they knew who he was and overpowered him. Thankfully, most of the warriors survived." He patted my arm.

I nodded, silently thankful to hear that from someone. Callum was still talking to Patrice when I glanced down the table.

"Where are the other fighters that were with my dad when he was taken?"

Chuck studied me for a moment before answering, "Some have died since then but, I know a couple of them left to travel to one of the larger cities, Jamestown, and I think maybe one or two transferred to the Norm defense." Chuck watched me like he was trying to read my mind. "I'm sorry I don't remember all of their names... I'm sure you can find that out from the library."

"What names do you remember?"

He shook his head and scratched at the base of his neck, "I'm pretty sure your father and uncle were a part of a special team, The Dirty Dozen, there were twelve fighters." I couldn't help but smile to myself over the little joke my dad and others seemed to be in on. Clearly, Chuck had not been in the Norm during the 1960s. With all seriousness, he continued, "Out of the twelve, seven of the realmers have passed." He looked at me quickly, and I just nodded, "I'm including James and Jacob in with the seven. I think Christopher Handlin is at the Norm Defense along with a Sarah or Samantha. I'm sure Chris would remember her name if she isn't there anymore. The two that left, one had some J name, and then the other guy had a Spanish name," he shrugged. "I'm sorry I can't remember those two, they left pretty quickly after the incident, and we never heard from them again. And the other one, I have no idea."

"That's okay. You've given me a lot." We sat in silence for a few minutes. My eyes wandered over the crowd of people, not really absorbing anything.

"Listen, I'm going to have the four of you begin training again to be Watchers. I think we are going to set it up for tomorrow."

"Oh? That will be great. I'm anxious to get started." My voice came out monotone. My mind wasn't entirely on the subject at hand. Training was far from my mind at the moment. It was reeling and going on overload with all the information he had given me. I needed to be back in the library. I needed to find out what happened to my father. I needed some sort of balance to all of this... stuff.

I rose from my seat and pushed my way between the chairs. Chuck watched me leave; his face held concern and something else I couldn't quite name. I could feel his eyes watching me as I made my way through the crowd. Words and sentences flowed through my mind. Facts and figures were being calculated. I was trying to put my past and my father's history in order, trying to fill in the blank spaces.

I walked through the crowd in a haze.

11

I FOUND the hall that led back to the library. The flames, in the wooden torches, flickered as I passed by them. The smell of dirt and moist air tickled my nose. Soft footsteps echoed behind me. I didn't have to turn around to know who it was. I was lost in my thoughts. When I got to the library, I went straight to my corner of the room, where the table had all the books piled up. I took my seat and stared at the books and pages.

A chair appeared on the opposite side of the table. Callum sat, his eyes roaming over the books and papers. He slid a red bound book across to sit in front of him. My face betrayed everything I was thinking. Callum wasn't one to talk out feelings. Instead, he was a man of action, and that meant a lot to me. It was also very confusing in figuring out where I stood with him.

"What are you searching for?"

I eyed him, "Anything about my dad and uncle."

"Okay, want some help?"

He always seemed ready to help me. I nodded slowly, "Sure. Anything about Jacob and James Sullivan. Maybe even my grandfather, Charles."

He nodded, "Alright."

His dark hair was a mess. Strands stuck out in odd directions; the product of his knife cutting I assumed. The candles positioned on the tables and hanging from the ceiling barely gave off sufficient light. His eyes began to move across each page, and I followed his example.

We sat at the table for hours, not saying anything to one another. Occasionally, he or I would shift in our chairs, or I would sigh, but other than that, we didn't even acknowledge each other too lost in our research. I was reading loose pages of paper. Most were letters. One, in particular, was from my dad to my grandfather. My back immediately straightened, and I grasped the page, making the paper crinkle. I released the tension in my fingers and started reading.

OCTOBER 10TH,

Dear father,

As you may have noticed, James has not been acting himself. I think something may have happened while he was in the Norm. I ask you to please consider his wishes and mine. I know we have never seen eye to eye, but surely you will see the greater good from these actions that I wish to take.

Your son,

Jacob

I SAT BACK and tried to wrap my head around what I had just read. Callum was watching me. I handed the letter to him, so he could read it. What could my father have been speaking about?

"Hmm, that is strange." Callum placed the letter back in front of me.

"Yeah," I mumbled as I played with the edge of the paper. I couldn't believe I was holding a letter my father had written. I wished I had more things of his. Each was further proof of his existence and that I was now living in his world.

"Were there some more pages with it?" Callum inquired.

I shuffled some pages, "Yeah, there's a few more here."

He took half of the stack, "I'll go through these, while you go through that stack."

I smiled and nodded, "Okay, thank you."

He raised his eyes to mine. A ghost of a smile tugged at his lips and then disappeared. "Not a problem." He began reading.

I mentally rolled my eyes and began sifting through the pages before me. Mostly, what I found were some notes taken from Jacob during their night raids and hunting trips. There were also some journal entries written by James, my uncle. It felt weird saying that and knowing that I had more family.

"Hey," Callum pressed a worn page into my hand, "you should read this." I tried to study his face to get some sort of feeling from him, but he only looked confused.

Taking a breath, I unfolded the faded yellow piece of paper. The bottom half had been ripped, and dark stains covered the edges.

I began to read:

22 OCTOBER, 1990:

Father,

Something has happened to me that I can't explain, just that something did happen. I fell in love. I met this incredible girl while in the Norm. She makes me feel like the most important man in the world. She is caring, giving, and the most exquisite woman I have ever known. I am asking you to let me bring her over here, or I must go back to her. I didn't even get to explain why I left. She is very important to me. I want to build a life with her. Surely, you must know how I feel?

I know you will love her as much as I do. I pray each day that I will be able to see her again. Please don't let my prayers go unanswered. I will do anything you want of me so I can be with her again.

Waiting with hope your son,

James

· · ·

THE PAPER that I held shook. My breathing came out faster. My chest tightened. Tears welled up. They threatened to spill over. What my mom wouldn't do to know that this letter existed. As if sensing my distress, Callum was up and next to me. He gently wrapped his arm around me. His warm body heat, strong muscles, and woodsy scent were beginning to drive away all my good sense.

For the first time in my life, I wanted to be held tightly and just breathe. Confusion was my normal state nowadays. I stopped. I wasn't sure what to think of the signature. Ignoring Callum's presence next to me, I pointed to the letter.

"What the hell does this mean?"

Startled, Callum darted from my eyes to the letter and sighed, "Maybe there are more answers in some of these pages." He began pulling some pages out. I didn't mean to, but I leaned in closer.

Quietly he asked, "Sloane, are you alright?"

"Yes. I'm just so confused. This letter is from James, but my father's name is Jacob."

All I could do was watch him. I looked at the page, trying to decipher its meaning.

Callum watched me for a moment, then went back to his seat and turned his attention back to what he had been reading. I looked back at the letter. There were another few pages beneath it. I quickly pulled the paper out that was directly beneath.

28 November 1990

Leader,

You say it takes love to be a great Leader. You don't show it. You say it takes understanding. You obviously don't understand. You want me to be a Great Leader, but I'm telling you now that I will not be a great Leader because of you. I will be a great Leader because of myself. From this day forward, I will no longer call you my father, you will be just what you want to be, a Leader.

I will tell you this though, I will find a way.

Captain James Sullivan

· · ·

THE HAIR on my arms stood up. Wow, go, James. Just from reading these letters, I learned more about my family than I had in the past month. My uncle definitely had gumption. He most definitely loved my mom. I wasn't sure what to think. Was there some sort of love triangle? Did they fight over mom? That was weird to think about.

The other papers were from other Captains or officers. There was one other letter from James, but he only wrote about the camp and Nightlins. He was direct, efficient with business, and to the point. He did exactly what he said he would do; treated my grandfather like a Leader.

"Look what I found." Callum got up and came around to my side of the table, bringing his chair with him. He sat and flipped to a page in a small butter-yellow book. "This belonged to James at least for a short time. A note was attached to it saying that they found it at the campsite where he had been taken. It isn't even filled." He flipped through the pages in the back of the book showing the blank pages. He glanced at me, "But this is what I wanted to show you."

He held the book out to me. I practically snatched it from him. I grimaced.

He smiled, "It's okay."

The corners of my mouth lifted slightly. I turned my attention back to the small soft leather book in my hands. Gently, I leafed through the first few pages.

"Here," Callum pointed to a yellowed and creased page.

17 FEBRUARY 1991

Another day at the camp. George and Bailey are sitting in the corner of the camp, playing some sort of useless card game. Dorian is at the edge of camp staring off into the bleak distance like always, probably brooding about something or someone. Ava is lying on the ground, snoring softly. I still don't understand how she can fall asleep wherever she lays her head. Patrick and Morgan are out scouting and keeping watch in the forest. I can never see the enemy with my eyes, but I can feel them watching us.

We are out here at the request of the Leader... apparently, there was a Nightlin group spotted over this way, and we are supposed to establish a visual and take them down. I grow tired of his requests and orders. I wish Jacob were here so we could complain about him together. Jacob is, as far as I know, on the opposite side of the Realm searching for Nightlins too.

I think it was more of a ploy to keep Jacob and me apart. He hasn't let us go on a search party together since October. If only I had Artemis with me so I could at least know Jacob's real location. I hope she isn't lost forever. I'm pretty sure I left her in the Norm, and if she is there, she's in safer hands than if she was here. There she can't be used against me or anyone else.

"See?"

I tore my eyes from the page, "See what?"

Callum's mouth became a thin line. "Look, at this part here," he pointed near the end of the page. "Where it says: 'If only I had Artemis with me so I could at least know Jacob's location.'" I could tell he was getting excited. He might be crazy. He let out an exasperated breath. "I thought you were smarter than this."

My eyebrows shot up, "Excuse you?"

He held his hands up, "You aren't giving this your full attention. I'm trying to help you." He pointed at the page again, "Artemis... I think your father was referring to the necklace."

The light bulb clicked on. I snatched the book back and reread the passage. Artemis.

"So, what does this mean? What can I do?"

Callum's face lit up. Somehow, I didn't think it was possible. I really liked how he was interested in all of this. He cracked his knuckles, "Well, why don't you say its name? See if it will work?"

I looked down at the necklace, lifting it to study more closely at the lifeless needles and ornate design. Hmmm... well, why don't I?

I put my mouth closer to the necklace. I cleared my throat and whispered, "Artemis." The needles jerked and twitched. They slowly began moving around and around in clockwise directions. Callum's eyes were glued to the needles.

"Are you thinking of something you want?"

"Umm... I don't know."

"What do you mean, you don't know?"

I let out a frustrated sigh, "Fine, I'll think of food or something." I closed my eyes and thought of... Ashlen. I peered down at the necklace to see the largest needle swing around and point straight out in front of me. I frowned.

"What did you think of?"

"Ashlen."

"Well, let's follow it where it says to go." He grasped my arm, pulling me up from the stool. He leaned over my shoulder to watch the needle. "It says to go straight."

He yanked me around the table and down the aisle of bookcases. I was very aware of his fingers wrapped around my forearm, tugging me gently along behind him. We went down the long hallway and into the dining hall. He released my arm as we entered the dining hall; the absence of the warmth of his hand was noticeable.

I held the necklace flat in the palm of my hand. As we reached the center of the dining hall, the large needle swung to the left and pointed out the main door. I looked up at Callum, and he eagerly pulled me out the door to the outside. As soon as we stepped outside, the needle pushed slightly to the left, pointing to a small red barn.

Callum led me along. My heart thumped faster and faster with every step I took. I couldn't believe it was actually working. Callum opened the door of the barn. We stepped through the doorway and stopped. The needle pointed straight ahead. So, we walked straight down the middle of the barn, passing the stalls lined against each wall. Whispering and giggling came from the last darkened stall.

"Ashlen?" I asked hesitantly.

Moaning emitted from the stall. Callum and I stopped. My face felt red. I glanced at Callum, and my face burned hotter. Callum only smiled with a little twinkle in his eyes.

"Ash?" I called a little bit louder.

Something dropped, and someone gasped, "Ouch." Some indistinct noises were made and then some shuffling. Ashlen popped her head around the stall door.

"Sloane, hey... were you looking for me?" Her hair was disheveled with pieces of straw stuck in it, and dirt was on her face.

I took a step toward her, "Well, yes, I guess. I found the name on my necklace, and we were testing it out. I decided I would find you, and well, it led me straight to you." My voice got more excited as I talked, and I moved closer to her to show her the necklace.

She smiled and nodded and squeezed through the stall door, closing it behind her. She moved closer to see the necklace, tugging her shirt down a little and straightening the rest of her attire.

"Wow, that is totally awesome." The needles were spinning around and around, telling me that I had found what I had been searching for.

A noise sounded behind her. Something rattled the stall door. Ashlen's face had grown noticeably pinker. I smirked at her and put my hand over my mouth to try and hold in my laughter.

Callum's eyes bounced all around the room, except he wouldn't meet my eyes. *Was he embarrassed?*

"Alright, we know you're in there. Come on out." I crossed my arms over my chest to wait.

The door slid back, slowly revealing Harris. He smiled sheepishly at me. "Aw, now you had to go and catch us." He staggered out of the stall jerking his pants up in the process and stood behind Ashlen. "You don't have to worry about her innocence, we were just sharing some sugar."

I literally laughed out loud, while Ashlen swatted at Harris and covered her face. I saw Callum smile slightly, then he turned away from us. I shook my head and smiled at Harris.

"Harris, you do have a way with words."

He grinned and put his arm around Ashlen's shoulders.

"Well, we will leave you two to it. I was just trying out the necklace. Pretend we were never here." I waved my fingers at them, then left down the aisle of the barn and out the door. Callum was waiting outside on a log. He looked up as I came out of the door. I clapped my hands together, "The necklace works!"

Callum rolled his eyes at me and shook his head. "Come on. Let's go back to the library and bury our noses in those books."

12

CALLUM and I stayed at the small library table again, going through books and pages for several more hours. My eyes were dry and could barely stay open by the time we stopped. I kept fingering the necklace, turning it over and tracing the edges. I peeked over the top of the book in my hand to see what Callum was doing. He was bent over the table with a notepad next to him and a pen in his hand. He was taking notes. He would read for a few minutes then jot something down.

His dark hair covered his eyes, and the muscles in his arms flexed with each stroke he made. He stopped writing and moved his eyes up to me. I quickly fixed my attention back to my book.

"So, what have you been reading about?" a slightly smug expression settled on his features. *He totally caught me watching him, crap.*

I tried not to let the heat crawl up my neck, "This was written by my grandfather, who wrote all about the battles they fought against the Nightlins. Nothing has been said about weird abilities, my father, or the dagger."

Callum nodded and pushed the pages into the middle of the table. He stood and stretched, pushing his arms above his head. Several of his vertebrae popped.

"I'm going to get something to eat." He studied me for a moment.

"Alright. I'm going to stay here for a little bit longer."

He nodded then disappeared between the bookcases. I looked down at the papers scattered on the table. A thick dark leather-bound book caught my attention. On the first page, it was dated 1793 and signed by Charles O'Grady. Designs were etched onto the worn page. I flipped to the next page to find more writing. The penmanship was messy and almost illegible. For the first ten pages, the person wrote about the history of the Night Realm, much like what I had read about in my studies with Brand. Unease settled in my stomach as I thought of Brand. I really missed his face and his Scottish accent.

I kept my eyes on the table in front of me, hoping to find some clues within all of the discarded pages. I was surprised when the chair in front of me scooted back and Chuck sat down. He put his elbows on the table and leaned forward, looking over the sheets of paper and the many dusty books.

"Hi," he kept his eyes down, casually scanning everything, "Callum told me you were down here."

I nodded, "Yeah, I was trying to find out any kind of information on my family."

"Which is only natural," Chuck smiled gently.

I handed him the letters from Jacob and James. I watched him read them. He read each carefully, and I could tell by the last letter from James to my grandfather that Chuck was maybe just as confused as I was.

He slightly frowned, "I'm not quite sure what to think about these, except to say that it sounds like your father is James, not Jacob."

"But my mom said my father's name was Jacob."

"I don't doubt that he told her that, but by going by these documents, then it appears that indeed Jacob may very well not be your father." He laid the pages down gently in front of me. "I'll admit when you first said it was Jacob, I was slightly surprised. Jacob always seemed to be more about himself than any other person. Your father changed his last name Norm side, who's to say that he didn't lie about his first name as well?"

My story keeps getting more and more complicated. My head throbbed. The pages before me seemed to take up more space. I felt like pushing them all into the floor. I wanted to cry or scream or eat. All of the above?

"Sloane, I wish there was something I could say to help you. Something that would help clear this all up, but there's nothing I can say, and I'm sorry. I wish I knew what had happened twenty years ago. It makes me almost as frustrated as you. I knew these men, and I have no information I can give you." He took a breath and paused for a minute, "We live in such secrecy that this road before you will be difficult. You won't have a lot of advantages to find the information you are so hungry for." His eyes tried to gauge my emotions.

I smiled slightly and nodded. The panic building up inside me had been extinguished if only for a moment. Chuck was on my side, trying to help me. I took a steadying breath, "Thank you, Chuck, I appreciate all the information you've given me. I want to ask you, though, if I do get to a point where I'm on the other side and need help, what can I do?"

"First, go to the Defense in Oklahoma City. They will be able to help you with any kind of information on the people's names I had given you. The Defense is almost all digital, unlike us. Make sure to tell them, Nightlins fly and birds crow. They have the ability to get you back here or to get in touch with me. Hopefully, I'll be on the other side too, so you won't have to go through it alone, but we can't be sure what might happen next year." Chuck ran his hands across the rough wooden table, "Things are not getting better in the Norm. Crime and death rates are steadily rising. Those are our first indications that Nightlins are making it to the other side, so Sloane, above all, just take care of yourself. Watch out for anything and anyone."

I slowly nodded and spoke quietly, "Okay, I'll do my best."

Chuck nodded, "It's late you should be getting some rest."

"I will. I'm going to go through these for a few more minutes then, head on up."

He smiled, "Okay, good. Take care, Sloane. I'll see you later. Come see me if you need me for anything."

"Thank you."

He studied me for a moment, then rose from his chair and turned away, disappearing among the rows of books.

I continued flipping through the pages of the O'Grady book. Part of the book talked about medicine and advancements in the Realm. Page thirty-three was where the book took a more interesting route. The person had drawn out different hands, showing each line and curve. He gave the meaning behind each or rather what the lines helped to explain. The writer gave the person's history behind each palm and broke down how that person's palms related to the outcome of his or her life. Maybe if we could study my palms, and figure out what has happened to me, then we could see if they correlate.

Looking around the library, I tried to find Clifford, but I didn't spot his little hat poking out from anywhere. Outside, the sky was pitch-black. Only a tiny bit of light from the moon filtered through the windows.

I closed the book, laying my hand on the old leather cover, and stood up from my chair. I grabbed the design book and James's journal, tucking them under my arm on my way out of the library. I nearly ran into Callum as I rounded the corner.

"Oh! Sorry. Were you coming to help some more?" I asked.

Callum seemed slightly embarrassed, "Yeah, I was going to check on you."

My eyebrows rose in surprise. "Thanks. I'm done for the day. I was just heading back to my room."

He nodded, "Alright, I'll go with you."

I immediately got nervous. I smiled tentatively, "Okay."

We walked through the halls in comfortable silence, except my need to fill it overtook.

"Callum? How is it you know this world so well?"

"Oh, I was born here."

My eyebrows rose in surprise, "Oh?"

He studied me for a moment and then seemed to decide to elaborate, "I haven't ever been to the Norm. I was raised here with my sister, so I know most of these woods, even some of the farther ones near Jamestown." He almost sounded proud.

"I didn't know you had a sister?"

Darkness settled around him, "She passed on a long time ago." A muscle twitched in his jaw.

Fuck.

A few seconds passed before I spoke, "I'm so sorry, Callum." I whispered.

He nodded once but said nothing more. We arrived at my door first. He gave a short bow and turned toward his door.

My heart grew heavier with each step.

———

WE WOKE up at five a.m. and lit the candles around the room so we could get ready for our training. Ashlen was less of a morning person than I was, but Raleigh was the exception. She loved mornings. Sometimes I wondered how we became friends. We were all so different. Raleigh sat at the table, stirring her tea and humming to herself. Ashlen moped around with hooded eyes and her hair in a mess, mumbling. I'm pretty sure I looked like her, but I said zilch. I never talk until I've at least had breakfast better yet when I've had lunch.

"Come on, you guys. You've got to wake up." Raleigh said cheerily.

"How can you be awake right now? You barely get sleep." Ashlen said grumpily.

Raleigh chuckled. "I get lots of exercise, so it makes up for my loss of sleep." She giggled again.

Ashlen rolled her eyes, "Ugh. How do you get so much action?"

Raleigh laughed again, "What can I say? I'm very popular."

"Do you see the same guy every night?"

"What? No. Of course not. That's rule number one. They're on rotation." She sipped her tea.

I couldn't help but smile.

Ashlen laughed, "Girl, you better be careful."

"Don't worry, we use protection every single time." She blew on her tea. "Even if we use a pack of condoms a night." Raleigh giggled again.

Ashlen nearly choked on her toast. "A pack?" She coughed.

Raleigh shrugged and smiled. I was just happy; those were a modern necessity the realm had.

We strapped our armor on to our shins, arms, chests, and heads. The first practice session was to be held in a clear space right outside the city gates. The town was still as we wound along the path to the front gates. We reached the gates and nodded tiredly at the guardsmen as we passed. They watched us curiously and barely acknowledged us.

Tendrils of fog hovered above the grass, slithering through the blades. Tall linear lights had been placed around the supposed fighting area in a large oval shape. The white light cast an eerie glow on the ground.

Hunters and Protectors were gathered in the center of the space. Our small group made our way toward them. I spotted Harris on the edge of the group with a huge grin displayed on his face, his eyes locked onto Ashlen. I glanced at Ashlen. She suddenly perked up; her eyes were all for him. I couldn't help but smile.

The Hunters and Protectors spread apart as we approached. Callum was part of the group. He was positioned in the center of the group holding several swords. The others surrounding him were either standing loosely or holding their own swords.

A guy with short-cropped hair, as if he had stepped out of an army ad, which included the tight t-shirt that stretched over large muscles, took several steps toward me, "I'll take this one." He winked at me and smiled boldly.

My eyebrows rose, I smiled because I was surprised by his audacity not because I was interested. I glanced around me at the others to see if they were paying attention. They were. I let out a sigh.

"Sorry, man, but we always work together." Callum held a sword out to me hilt first. I took it from him with a small thankful smile.

The guy looked Callum over, "You turn me down and take a new girl instead? What else am I supposed to do?"

My eyebrows shot up, and I looked between them.

"Rory, cool it. We've been over this." His mouth pulled slightly to the side. Then he addressed the group. "Okay, since there are only four of you in training, each person will have a Hunter and Protector assisting them. Chuck put me in charge because I know all of you, but Jess," he indicated a very tall, lean, and dark-haired man that was standing beside him, "will be the lead Hunter."

Jess nodded at each of us like we were an experiment or puzzle. He folded his arms across his chest and took a step toward us.

"I will give you a brief history of myself," his voice was very smooth with a slight Russian accent. He paced in front of us his long white tunic flowing and moving with his body as he moved with his hands locked behind him, "I have been a Hunter for twenty-two years, and yes that makes me over the age of forty." He couldn't be a day over 25. "I have seen a lot of battles and death. So," he clapped his hands together and stopped to face us, "I am going to give you all the knowledge and experience I have in order for you to survive this realm. The only rule for our fighting practices is no use of Protector or Hunter abilities when training," He looked us squarely in the eyes. "Alright, let's get started."

The Hunters and Protectors immediately split up going to one person or another, where it was an equal number of Hunters and Protectors to the trainees. Callum stood by me along with a tall willowy red-headed girl named Irene.

Our groups spread out across the space. We each had wood swords and a small, lightweight shield. Each of the Hunters and Protectors had on the same kind of armor that we had.

We started doing slow movements with shielding and bracing. We sparred with our partner one at a time, taking turns.

Ashlen sparred with Miranda, a Hunter, first. Miranda's caramel skin was hard with muscle, her eyes determined. She had on tight black leather pants, a dark green sleeveless shirt that emphasized the muscles in her arms, and shiny black combat boots. Her shield sparked with lavender light. I wouldn't want to meet her in a dark alley.

Raleigh began her match with Molly, a Protector. Molly didn't look over the age of eighteen. Molly's short curly brown hair bounced when she moved. Her usually dark skin had a milky tint to it since we never saw the sun. She was about five feet tall. Her face round, making her cheeks full and lips pouty. She looked like the girl who would be a professional babysitter.

The Protector assigned to Harris, Stephen, initiated the fight first. Stephen's raven black hair fell straight across his forehead. His pale skin was a stark contrast to his hair, but his eyes were bright and a deep blue like the ocean depths. He was slightly taller than Harris, which made him about 6'3". Stephen moved gracefully and swiftly.

I started with Irene. She was graceful and easy-going. She moved slowly enough to give me time to move along with her, but then she and Callum switched.

Callum wasn't as slow as Irene had been with me. He seemed to know exactly how fast he could push me. More clinks and bangs of the wood hitting could be heard from my side of the space than from anyone else's. I caught glimpses of the others slowly moving around each other like they were in a dance. The only sounds would be the soft clinks of the swords sliding across each other. I was starting to get frustrated.

Callum did not hold back. But I didn't either. He would gain a few feet on me, then I would push him back those few feet plus some more, then he would push again. In a sudden movement, he lunged at me, swiping his sword at my middle. I raised my sword arm and turned to the side, but my feet got twisted, and I tumbled to the ground. The sword flew from my grasp, and dirt flew into my eyes and open mouth. I pushed up on my arms, coughing out dirt. Callum knelt on the ground, watching me.

"Dirt isn't all that healthy for you."

I glared at him. "Really? Ya think?"

He put his hand under my arm to try and help me up, but me being the stubborn person I am, jerked my arm from him and stood up on my own. I snatched my sword from the ground, facing him again.

His eyebrows arched as he took in my stance. He rolled his shoulders and prepared to attack.

I didn't give him long to get ready. I lunged at him this time. I drove my sword at his legs, though, forcing him to jump. As he jumped, he tried to swing his blade at my head, but I drove the heel of my palm into his chin. This time he stumbled and almost fell to the ground. His knee hit the ground, but he kept blocking my blows. A small trickle of blood ran down his chin.

I aimed my sword for his head again, but this time power and light exuded from Callum's outstretched hand. A large rectangular shield spread out, blocking my attack easily. My wooden sword hit the shield with a thud. White light sparked.

"Not fair!" I yelled, charging again.

"Irene! Now!"

As I attacked Callum, Irene moved in from the side, so I had to deflect her aim. A gust of wind blasted my face, and I coughed, trying to catch my breath. Irene had power over air. Great. Her shield burst to life, a shimmering light blue. A wind cyclone enveloped me. Every few seconds, the wind would break, giving me time to breathe but not much else. I was being suffocated. The air being pulled from my lungs burned. I screamed with everything in me, and the wind stopped.

I gasped in air as quickly as I could.

I had them in front of me, both sharing in defense and offense. My heart beat so fast I could hear it in my ears. My head seemed to get lighter, but my arms and legs moved faster. It was like everything around me slowed. They moved quickly but somehow; I was faster. I popped up behind them. Not knowing how I was doing this. The background became a blur, except for Callum and Irene. My eyes, arms, and feet followed their every move.

"Alright, enough." The words were spoken with a rough accent, and loud enough for us to hear over the clatter of the swords.

Callum's sword and mine met, ringing out into the dark morning.

Our eyes held under the swords raised above our heads. His eyes were filled with amusement and something else I couldn't quite name. Pride? Mine were reflecting fierce obstinance. He lowered his sword first. My sword followed. Our eyes locked together.

"What kind of display was that?" Jess came to stand beside us, looking back and forth between us.

Callum turned to him, "I thought I would push her to her limits. She needs to be pushed every once and awhile." A small smile fell on his lips.

"Oh, really?" One eyebrow arched. I glowered at him. If only I could shoot lasers from my eyes.

"Whatever is going on between the two of you needs to be solved outside of the training circle. Here, we are training for the future. We will not be hosting any hostile feelings toward one another. You, as her Protector, are supposed to be helping her. This," he waved his hands between Callum and me, "is not helping. Irene, I thought better of you."

Irene's face became stone, at the mention of her name.

Callum became more solemn and nodded his head. This time when his eyes met mine, they were silent and steadfast. He held his hand out to me, "Please forgive my rude behavior, and my pushing you to better yourself."

"Callum," Jess's tone warned.

Before Callum could say another word, I spun around and began marching toward the city. Why does he do this to me? Every step brought a new pounding to my head. I didn't even notice the footsteps behind me until I was halfway back.

"Sloane, stop. You're acting like a child." My head whipped back around when I heard those words.

"Callum, look who's talking. You were the one who had to show off. I'm learning, and then you go all Matrix on my ass. You and another Hunter. What the hell, Callum! You could have seriously hurt me, then I'd be of no use, and even further behind on my training."

"I pushed you just enough to make you better. You know what, I am the best because I've earned it. We all walk on eggshells because we feel bad for the girl who doesn't know anything. Who didn't know our world existed and was dropped here by accident one night. But here is the thing Sloane, at this point, you've chosen this life. You chose to stay. You made your choice, and now your abilities affect the rest of us."

"You pitied me," my eyes went wide. If I could have sent fire into him at that moment, I would have.

He studied my face. Silence settled around us. "No, not pity..."

I waited, but he didn't say anything else.

Motherfucking piece of shit. I whipped around and stomped back to the main gate, my boots clomping with each footfall. The fighting replayed through my head, and the words Callum had said were on a cycle. I was more annoyed than mad, with how Callum treated me. I felt like I was being pulled and yanked back and forth. I wanted to like him, but he made it so difficult sometimes. Other times it felt like I more than liked him. As I walked, a tingling sensation traveled from my toes to the top of my head.

Shit.

My feet went numb first, then my legs followed. My legs gave under my weight, and I fell forward, barely catching myself with my hands. I lowered myself slowly to the ground. People yelled, and the ground shook as they ran. My vision blurred, and then my old friend darkness embraced me.

The Dark

POWER. That's all he felt running through his body. He tensed his muscles throughout his body, then slowly let each muscle release. The power surging through his limbs made him want to yell at the top of his lungs with... excitement. He kept swinging his limbs back and forth, stalking around the small room. He had so much energy. Energy. That's what it was. Energy was flowing through him. Every sense was heightened and put into overdrive. His eyes acted as binoculars, zooming in on whatever he focused on. He could smell the bugs and critters racing along the edge of the walls. His hearing could pick up on the tiny unimportant beatings of their hearts as they ran along. His mouth split apart into a wide opening, what is it called? He traced the edges of his mouth, trying to remember the word for this movement. A smile? Yes, that's it, a smile, yet, not one that shows goodness, but happiness for pain and power.

His head seared with pain. He doubled over, pressing his hands to his head. Sharp pain was shooting through his mind like needles puncturing the skin. Pictures of events and places were jumping across his mind, trying to push to the forefront of his senses.

A girl's face popped into his mind as clear as day. Every line of her face shone brightly and was filled with complete happiness. Dark hair framed her pretty face and fell across her shoulders. Her eyes and attention were focused right on him. His heart stopped for a full second. Who was this girl?

The picture disintegrated from his mind; pieces of the image, chipping and falling away.

What was he supposed to be doing?

Power. Energy. That's all he needed. That's what he is supposed to be doing. He rubbed his hands together and turned toward the door.

13

I woke up to the sound of whispering, and a candle flickered on the table beside my bed. Blankets were piled on top of me to my chin. I pushed the blankets off and sat up slowly. The whispering stilled, as everyone noticed that I was awake.

Around the room, everyone was accounted for: Callum, Jess, Ashlen, Raleigh, Harris, Chuck, Irene, and even Patrice. Patrice sat on the bed beside me and patted my arm.

"Dear, are you all right? Everyone was very frightened for you. You should be ashamed of yourself. You've been passed out for five hours. It's past lunchtime."

I pressed my hand to my head, "I what?" I could only stare at her.

"You should be ashamed of yourself for making us fuss over you. Do you know what happened?"

"No, I passed out like usual, but I hadn't done that in this world yet, so I thought I was in the clear. What happened?"

Patrice studied my face for a moment then replied, "We brought you up here to check you for any ailments." She folded her hands in her lap, "I didn't believe it when you had first told me of your white eyes, but when we tried to check your pupils, we couldn't because you had none."

I sat straighter. Callum's face was turned away, while everyone else looked at me with pity.

"Are they still white?" I spotted a smudged mirror propped in the corner and practically bounded off the bed, running toward it.

Patrice addressed everyone, "Everyone out. Leave now." They listened and filed out the door.

I looked back to the mirror and tentatively ran my fingers around my eyes, making sure they were mine. Hot tears ran down my face. Patrice came up to me, her reflection cast in the mirror. She placed her hands on my shoulders.

"You have no reason to cry. This is good, not bad." The wrinkles around her eyes lengthened as she smiled. "Your abilities may be different from everyone else, but different is not always bad."

I nodded slowly and tried to steady my breathing, "What if I mess up?"

"We all mess up. If you do, we will be there to help." She squeezed my shoulders. "Get some rest, and I'll see you tomorrow." She smiled again and left, shutting the door quietly behind her.

Soft knocks sounded a few seconds later. Callum stepped through the doorway with a tray of sandwiches and veggies.

I was so tired I didn't feel like having to deal with him at the moment, except he had food... and food is the key to my heart.

I sat on my bed, "Yes?"

He frowned, "Sloane, I just wanted to apologize to you for my actions and I thought you might be hungry since you missed lunch."

I waited a moment more, eyeing the food.

I pressed my lips together into a thin line. "Okay."

He studied me, "Okay. Get some rest." He set the tray on the edge of the bed and softly closed the door behind him. I felt bad for being mean. I didn't hate him at all. I knew he was trying to help me be better, he just drives me crazy for some reason.

I snatched up a couple of sandwiches and some carrots, then tried to take a nap.

I couldn't go to sleep. My mind was again spinning with everything that had taken place over the course of the past week. I kept going to the mirror to see if my eyes had changed again, but I saw my regular blue irises staring back.

Someone knocked on the door. Ashlen peered around the door frame.

"Hi." She walked in and closed the door. "Listen, here's the thing. I'm busting you out." She leaned forward and formed her hands into a gun. She started moving around like one of Charlie's angels. "You can't be stuck in this room, in this building, because you'll go cray, especially with everything that has been thrown at you. So, here's what we're going to do, I'm taking you out so you can enjoy yourself." She beamed at me. "Come on, get your stuff together. We're going."

"Are you serious?" I asked.

She nodded and picked up my jacket. She held it out to me, "Let's go, come on. What else will you do? Besides, we can get you better food and drinks." She shook the jacket in my face.

I slowly took the jacket from her. She smiled and jogged to the door, opening it with a flourish, she gestured with her arm for me to walk out. I rolled my eyes and walked through the door, expecting nothing but fun.

————

WE ENDED up at a small building at the edge of the city. The atmosphere was loud, with laughter and talking. It was a bar for the most part with men jabbering, or gawking at women was the main attraction. There was a kind of band set up in the corner of the building playing instruments that resembled guitars. Wooden tables and chairs were placed around the whole space with a small bar in the middle.

I didn't recognize a single person. Ashlen led me to a table right next to the bar. She waved to the bartender, "Give me two, uh, beers." She winked at me and sat down.

The bartender came over after a few minutes, and set our beers down a little disapprovingly, sloshing it onto the table. Ashlen rolled her eyes and pushed a glass over to me. We sat in the crowded bar and soaked in the atmosphere watching while people danced in one corner of the room. They had pushed some tables to the side and cleared a space for some room.

My beer tasted awful so I took miniscule sips.

My people-watching skills went into overdrive, which helped to keep my mind off of my problems.

"Hey, there, cutie."

Rory leaned across the table; his hands spread out on the table. The t-shirt he wore read: 'Cock-y.' The letters stretched wide across his muscular chest. I guessed for better emphasis. Wow. How perfect his t-shirt was for him?

"Nice shirt."

He glanced down, "Thanks." He smiled wider and held his hand out, "How about a dance?"

My eyebrows rose, then pinched together. I spent a few moments scrutinizing him and his motives. I decided, what would it hurt? So, I got up (not taking his hand) and went to the dance floor. I turned to face him. He stepped right up in front of me with barely any room between us. I couldn't help but smile nervously. He took it as encouragement though and pulled me closer.

"Dude," I pushed him away slightly and narrowed my eyes.

He smiled again and took a minuscule step back.

We danced and danced. My eyes closed, and my mind drifted off into another dimension, where my mother cooked some disastrous meal and Mariah complained about shopping.

"Well, aren't you two so cute?"

I jerked my head up to see a voluptuous blonde sneering at us. She was dressed head to toe in black latex and showing a lot of cleavage. Kinky much? Isn't she sweating? I'd be wet with sweat in that thing. I was surprised to see she had makeup on. Her white-blonde hair contrasted nicely with her black outfit and blood-red lips. One hand placed on one curvy hip. Her other hand pushed her hair back. Black leather gloves covered her hands. Her eyes measured me up and down, locking onto mine.

"Hey, Sam. We were just dancing. No reason for you to get jealous.

There's plenty of me to go around." Rory winked and smiled broadly at her. His eyes roamed over her body. His body language said he was into her, but his eyes held something close to fear in them. One hand pushed me slightly behind him.

I sidestepped him and held my hand toward her.

"Hi, I don't think we've had the chance to meet. I'm Sloane." I smiled my sweetest smile.

She glanced at my hand and folded her arms, the best she could, over her sizable chest. I dropped my hand but kept my smile.

"I'm Samantha Harris. The Protector." She slid the black glove off her right hand, and this time she held her hand out to me with a small smile on her dark red lips.

"Sloane, wait." Rory lurched toward me to grab my hand, but my hand landed in hers first.

An electric shock shot through my arm and buzzed through my ears, as our hands met. Stars burst from my eyes. I dimly remembered falling to my knees.

————

I FOUND myself standing in a ruined old house, one that had been burned and left to the elements. A painful wind whipped around me, lashing at my clothes and body. A dark mist clung to the floor and what was left of the ceiling. The mist clung to my clothes and grabbed hold of them. I tried to move, but it was like I was in wet cement. My legs were sluggish and could barely keep my weight supported.

Now, where was I?

I pulled my weight across the room inch by inch to the leftovers of the door. The world outside burned. Falling down, with dark mist clinging to every surface. The wind whipped dirt, and whatever else through the air, flinging it in every direction. The world was deserted.

I blinked.

I then stood on the front porch of the once dilapidated house but what was now whole and new. The smell of wet paint had freshly been applied onto the siding. Shutters hung on the windows were painted a bright blue. The world was now filled with bright sunshine and a blue sky. Flowers were scattered across the fields. I blinked a few more times and stared in wonder at the world around me.

The dark mist had evaporated.

I stepped off the porch and onto the grass. As the sun hit my skin, the light bounced off and shimmered like tiny stars embedded into my arms and hands. I lifted my hands up to the sky and twirled. My heartfelt light and self-assured. I had never felt such weightlessness. I felt like I could fly and never touch the ground again.

A bright light, brighter than the sun, appeared in the sky. It seemed to be the sun, but the light moved closer and closer. The brightness of the light blinded me. The light hit me. It drove through me, searing my soul.

I burned from the inside out.

Unexplainable pain tore through me. The smell of dirt enveloped my senses as I tried to catch my breath. I turned my head to the side as the house wavered. I tried to block the pain. Tears leaked out of the corners of my eyes, my hands grappled at the ground grasping at the grass and twigs while the house crumbled away.

———

People yelling made me aware that I was in a different place. I opened my eyes to find I was on the floor again. A few feet from me, curled into a fetal position, was Samantha. Her eye make-up was smeared all over her face, along with her red lipstick.

The whole bar huddled around us. Ashlen knelt beside me with a damp towel and wiped at my face and neck.

"Sloane? Are you okay? Sloane?" her face creased with fear and concern. "Sloane? Talk to me," her voice shook as she spoke.

I felt my head. "Yeah, I'm okay, I think."

"I'm so sorry. I was trying to get you away from stress. Instead, you got deeper in it."

I limply flicked my hand at her, "It's alright. Don't worry about it. I blacked out again."

People watched and whispered. I quickly shielded my face and turned away from them.

Ashlen stood, "Okay, people, the show is over. Move it."

Slowly, they filtered out. A small group stayed around Samantha. She wasn't responding.

Ashlen knelt back down, "After you and Samantha touched, we couldn't separate you. Rory screamed about Samantha's powers. Apparently, part of her powers is inflicting pain when she touches someone, but," Ashlen turned to Samantha, "it seems her power backfired." She gave me a sly smile, implying the bitch deserved it. I tended to agree.

"Yeah, when our hands met, I was teleported, metaphysically, to some world I have never seen before." I rubbed my temples, "It was weird. The place was destroyed one moment, and when I blinked, it changed. I guess, at the same time you separated us, that's when I saw this huge light high up in the sky. It careened down and struck me, tearing through me like it was setting my insides on fire, then I woke up here." I rubbed my arms like I could feel the light burning. Ashlen studied me.

"Move. Get out of my way." Callum pushed through the crowd around me. He stopped, looking me over.

"You okay?" His voice wasn't kind. His eyes were blank and void of emotion.

I nodded, "Yes, I'm fine, thank you," my voice was level, and I made sure to keep as much emotion out of it as I could.

"Come on, let's get you back." He moved forward like he was going to help get me up, but I got up before he could touch me.

"It's okay. I got it." I grabbed Ashlen's arm and pulled her through the crowd to the outside, not even glancing at Samantha.

We trudged up the hill to the main building. The buildings along the way were mostly dark, with only a couple of windows bright with candlelight. It had to be close to midnight by now. The streets were deserted. Most people were either asleep, out at the bar, or up at the main building.

Ashlen squeezed my arm, "I'm sorry."

"Ash, it's okay, I promise. Don't worry about it." I patted her hand. "It was great to get out."

She laughed.

I could feel Callum's presence behind us, but I refused to acknowledge him. Ashlen and I walked into the main building. A lot of the people were in the dining hall dancing, discussing, or eating; it was definitely time for me to go to bed. Ashlen and I threaded through the people in the direction of our room.

"Sloane," he spoke without trying to raise his voice over all the noise.

I stopped in the middle of the floor with people bumping into me and yelling all around. Ashlen apparently didn't hear him because she kept winding through the crowd to the hallway. I saw her stop and search for me. She finally spotted me and started to make her way back, but I waved her to stop. She frowned for a moment. I saw her gaze shift behind me. Her eyes moved back to me, and she nodded once, spinning on her heel, and continuing on down the hall.

I took a deep breath and slowly faced Callum.

His hair fell in his eyes, so I could barely see them, and he towered over me. His mouth was set into a straight line. The lines of his face were hard. I squared my shoulders and lifted my chin up. I passed by him and back to the outside. I walked steadily toward the barn but stopped at a fallen tree to sit down. I guessed it was around nine or ten at night. Callum was a few yards behind and stopped in front of me. He crossed his arms across his chest, but his eyes didn't meet mine.

"Alright, say what you want to say. Let's just get this over with." I crossed my arms across my chest and glared up at him. What in the world does he have to say to me?

Callum stood very still, this time he looked straight at me, "I need you to understand..."

I lifted an eyebrow and waited.

His arms fell to his sides, and he took a deep breath. He ran his hands through his hair.

He was nervous. My anger subsided, and confusion took its place.

"Why is it so hard to talk to you?" His eyes were filled with anger and frustration. "You have got to be the most infuriating..." he clenched his teeth, "person."

I stood to give myself more height, "Hey, you do not get to be mad at me, because I have done absolutely nothing to deserve it." I almost jabbed my finger in his chest but refrained. "Don't you remember? You're the one who keeps yo-yoing."

He made an exasperated noise then ran both hands through his hair.

"I've lost my whole family," he almost whispered.

Rushing through my mind had been choices of words that I thought of yelling at him, those words suddenly crashed. Replaced with a prominent question mark.

He slowly faced me. His eyes landed on mine for a split second then darted away.

"I didn't tell you that to get you to pity me. I told you, so maybe you can better understand my reasoning behind my actions toward you." His hands were balled into fists at his sides, but his voice was steady.

"I like you ..." he seemed startled by his own confession. "I consider you to be my friend. I don't know why I like you, but whenever I'm around you, some of the weight on my shoulders seems to lift." His mouth slowly curled at the edges, and his eyes met mine more steadily, "I've liked you ever since I saw you walking through the forest in your pajamas. I don't know, something told me I needed to take care of you." His eyes studied me for a reaction, which I tried my best not to give him.

"As I'm sure you've noticed, I'm not a very social person. Honestly, I think you are the only person who consistently stays around. At the risk of sounding like an emotional twat. You mean a lot to me..."

I stopped breathing.

He paused, "I don't have many I can rely on. But you make me feel like I belong."

The air that had been thick with hostility was now lighter.

I studied him for a moment, and my heartbeat again, "So, that's why you've been acting weird?"

He nodded slowly, "I wanted to make sure you weren't leaving. You make it hard for me to watch out for you." His hands were loose at his sides now.

I wasn't sure what to say or how to react. *Why was everything so complicated?*

"So, friends?" I extended my hand out to him with a slight smile on my face.

He watched me, a small chuckle escaped his lips, and he shook his head like he was laughing at me. He took my hand in his.

"Friends."

Was it weird my stomach did some somersaults at that moment? Maybe tinged with sadness at being called a friend by a hot man? *I can't ever win in my head.*

"And Sloane, you shouldn't be afraid because you're different. Embrace it. Besides, the white eyes look good on you." One corner of his mouth lifted, and his eyes laughed at me.

I scoffed and rolled my eyes, "Thanks, I guess."

Callum tilted his head like he heard something, then someone shouted off in the distance. My hand released his, dropping to my side. I turned in the direction of the noise.

We silently moved toward the noise. The yelling came from the front gate, so we hurried down the path as fast as we could. About forty or more people were gathered near the gate.

Callum made a path to see about the commotion. I followed on his heels. The people gave way a bit, and we stumbled into the middle of the gathering. Graham and a few of the warriors he had left with were gathered together in the center of the group. My eyes immediately sought him. A small group of what appeared to be Watchers were covered in mud and grime.

The small group was being hugged and given pats on the backs by all the others gathered around us. People were laughing and crying. Graham and the other warriors were being greeted by their family and friends. Graham's eyes locked onto mine, but when I smiled at him, he did not return it. My smile faltered, and I turned my attention back to the Watchers.

There was something different about Graham. Something in his eyes. They were hollow.

The Watchers looked spent, but relieved. They had tired smiles on their dirty faces.

We eventually moved toward the main building. I vaguely remembered Callum walking around the perimeter of the group like he was keeping watch. I could almost feel Callum watching my reaction to Graham. As we moved toward the main door, I saw Graham and his friends separate from the main group and disappear around a corner. He never looked back at me.

My group went on into the main building where Chuck had arranged for the seven Watchers to get washed up for a party. The group consisted of five girls and two boys. I did recognize the faces, but I didn't know them personally. They disappeared to the second floor to get cleaned up.

Chuck had food brought out for all. A welcome home party for them that I'm sure they would never forget ensued. Dancing, singing, and eating were the main goals for the night. The seven survivors were seated at a table in the middle of the room. My table was to the right of where they sat, so I had a clear view of them. Ashlen, Raleigh, and Harris were seated at the table with me.

Callum stood at the survivors' table talking to the two guys, getting information from them about their journey.

Graham led the seven back to Kingston, so twelve of his warriors traveled on to the camp to see what they could find. Graham would travel back to the camp later to meet up with the rest of the group.

I kept scanning the crowd for Graham, but he never showed. Maybe they were setting up their plans for the return journey to the camp.

Callum was laughing with the two guys, Caleb and Evan. He

made no sense whatsoever. This whole time I've never seen him laugh like that except when I was hitting him. What was his deal? I couldn't help but watch him interact with the two guys.

"You okay?" Ashlen leaned over, her arms on the table and a concerned expression on her face.

I flicked my eyes over to Callum again, "I'm fine, just thinking." I smiled.

Ashlen had followed my glance. She nodded knowingly, "He seems to make you think a lot. You know I think I'm going to have to change what I had first said about him," she ran a finger along the stained wood table and started tapping her fingers, "I think he's a good guy, slightly misunderstood sometimes, but overall a good guy. He cares a lot about what he does, and he seems to always be watching out for you too."

She leaned back in her chair, "Graham though," her smile widened, "he's a *great* guy. I mean, his biceps surely make up for any faults."

I rolled my eyes and gently pushed the leg of her chair to make her have to catch herself from falling backwards. "Be quiet. They are both just friends. That is all. Even Callum told me that he pretty much thinks of me as a sister or a best friend. As for Graham, he's ignoring me."

Ashlen spoke eagerly, "Really? Callum told you *all* that? Why would Graham ignore you?" A line formed between her eyebrows and her head tilted.

I shrugged and glanced at Callum, "I don't know. Callum and I had a conversation," she raised her eyebrows to that and bit back a smile. "And I haven't been able to talk to Graham, so I don't know what's with him."

Her eyes grew larger, and her voice was anxious, "Well, what *exactly* did Callum say?"

I smiled and shook my head. "Just that he felt like he needed to protect me, and he's always liked me from the moment we met, even in my silly pjs, and I am his only friend." The more I thought about Callum, warmth spread across my face.

Ashlen laughed. Her eyes sparkled with laughter, and her head went back as she laughed.

"Why is that funny?"

She laughed some more, then covered her mouth with her hand, trying to stifle her laughter, which didn't really work. She answered, "I'm sorry, girl, what are you doing?"

My eyebrows in surprise. "What?"

"Sloane, he *likes* you. He didn't say anything about you being his sister." She studied me some more. "Obviously, you don't know much about guys."

I shifted uncomfortably. "Yeah, not really. I'm not used to the attention."

She nodded.

I looked back over to see what Callum was doing now. Our eyes met. I know my face immediately showed surprise, but I smiled, trying to cover up my embarrassment. He studied me for a moment then smiled back. He continued speaking to the guys.

Raleigh, who had been sitting at the end of the table, stood, and disappeared through the crowd of people dancing on the floor. Harris leaned over and whispered to Ashlen. She glanced at me with a smile.

"Hey, did you hear if that Samantha girl was okay?"

Ashlen frowned for a moment in thought, "Oh yeah, the pain girl. She's okay though she will have to stay in the infirmary for a few nights."

"Oh, wow, okay."

"She's fine. Don't worry about it." Harris whispered in her ear again, making her giggle, "We will discuss this topic later." She patted my back as she and Harris both got up, holding hands leaving the table.

My eyes grew heavy, so I got up and headed in the direction of my room for some sleep. It had been such a long day. Ashlen and Harris were on the dance floor having a great time, so I didn't bother them. I scanned over the crowd one more time, hoping to see Graham, but of course, he wasn't there. I couldn't find Raleigh at all, so I went to the room by myself. My feet were lead as I forced myself up the stairs, not passing a soul. I tumbled straight into bed, falling on top of the sheets without changing my clothes, and fell right to sleep.

The Dark

THE DARKENED creature that was once a man stalked across the room to stare out the window. His fingers, now razor-sharp claws, dug into the wooden window sill. The light was about to make its brief appearance. As the hazy light crept in, he pulled the shutters and thick draperies across the window to extinguish the light. He turned back to what was his bed, torn parts of cloth, dirt, and shavings, and sat down.

The mission was a failure.

They had been close and, yet, *he* fell through their grasp. The creature hadn't expected the realmer to be that fast, but maybe he got the message. Maybe the realmer will try to find them.

The creature needed *him*.

The Nightlins needed *him* to be a part of their family. *He* has to become one of the Nights. There must be a way to capture *him*, the dark ones say *he* is one of the best, but the realmer had to have seen the sign, to recognize it.

The realmer will come. *He* won't be able to stay away. If *he* saw the sign, the creature knew the realmer couldn't have missed it, then *he* would find them.

14

I AWOKE WITH A JOLT.

"Training!" I gritted my teeth, throwing the covers off of me in the process. I jumped out of bed and ran around the room, throwing on clothes and armor, stuffing food in my mouth. The room was empty, so the girls were already down at practice. *Why didn't they wake me?*

My armor rubbed and bumped as I ran down the hallway. I kept running all the way to the main gate and out to the field. They fought in their circles, each hitting and blocking, the metal clanging as they moved.

Callum and Irene were on the sidelines of the fighting rings, giving advice and encouragement.

Callum was the first to see me. He stopped when he caught sight of me and wasn't very happy. He said something to Irene, who noticed me. She nodded and continued speaking to the others. Callum moved around the circle and toward my direction.

His dark hair hung across his forehead and into his eyes. He had on lighter armor, which fit close to his toned body. He moved with grace and confidence of a jungle cat. His eyes stayed on mine the entire time it took for him to reach me.

For some reason, I felt cognizant, like maybe I should have taken more time to look in a mirror.

"I should have known you wouldn't stay away." He crossed his arms across his chest and pinned me with his eyes, they were accusing.

My defenses went up, "Why would I stay away?"

"Sloane, you've had a draining past few days both physically and mentally, which literally knocked you out and, on your ass, twice. I told the girls to let you rest for a little while, so maybe you can get fully charged." His eyes were measuring me again.

I rolled my eyes, "I'm fine, I need to be training anyways, and you know it, so let's go." I moved to pass him, except he grabbed my arm, stopping me. I glared.

"Hold on. I want to make sure you're okay, so we're going to start out slow. Alright?" He was stern as he waited for my response.

I let out a slow breath, "Okay, fine, I'll take it slow." Why does he annoy me so much?

He nodded and let go of my arm. I continued my stroll toward the group of fighters.

He's always telling me what to do or not to do.

Irene stopped her interjection to Raleigh and Jordan, who were sparring, and started in my direction, with a wooden sword in each hand. Her dark red wavy hair bounced as she walked. The ends touched the base of her back. She smiled and held out a sword for me to take.

I took the wooden sword wrapping my hand around the hilt, "Thanks."

"Glad you could make it," she moved about ten feet away, so she was at an angle from me and took a fighting stance.

I smiled, "Me too." I glanced back at Callum, who stood about twenty feet away with arms crossed watching us.

I squared my shoulders and centered my body over my feet, tightening my thighs so I could prepare myself for the blows.

"We're going slow. If you move too fast then, I'll stop, and we'll start over again."

She moved toward me, arching her sword upwards and bringing it down, aiming at my head, but it was in slow-motion, so I was able to block her movements. The slow-motion fighting continued for a couple of hours, like a dance. I would move forward, and she would move back then she would advance. I thought it would be easy, but my arms felt ready to fall off by the time we took a break. Ashlen, Harris, and Raleigh were fighting at full speed. The wood made loud smacks as it hit their armor. Every now and then, Ashlen would make grunting noises, or Raleigh would yell. Harris was in full concentration when he was fighting, barely making any noise.

Callum sat at the edge of the fighting ring the entire time. His legs crossed with his hands folded in his lap.

"Okay, everyone, let's take a ten-minute break," Jess yelled, his Russian accent thick from exertion.

I made my way over to sit by Ashlen, Raleigh, and Harris.

"Hey! You look better!"

"Thanks, Harris." I laughed, "So I looked terrible before, hmm?"

"What? Oh, no, you know that's not what I meant. I'm glad you're here."

"Thanks, me too," I patted his arm.

"I'm sorry I didn't wake you; I knew you would be upset that we left you," Ashlen said quietly.

"It's okay, Callum said that he told you to let me sleep."

We ended up lying back on the grass and letting the minutes tick by until we had to get up again. The Protectors and Hunters were either lounging next to us or talking to each other in twos or threes. Jess jumped up and started stretching, I guessed that was our sign to get up and stretch too. The four of us looked at each other, groaning as we stood. We spread out on the field and touched our toes or swung our arms. We went to our own little corners of the field with our trainers and started to fight.

This time Callum stood in front of me. He held his wooden sword loosely in his right hand, but I could see the muscles in his arms, contracting and loosening. He rolled his head around his neck then straightened with a smirk planted on his face.

"Okay, I'm going a little faster this time."

Oh, great.

I set my shoulders, narrowed my eyes at him, and tightened my grip on the hilt of the sword.

When he lunged at me, he was definitely faster. I almost missed the block. Our swords hit with a loud slap that jarred my arms. He moved gracefully through the air as he leapt up and started coming back down to earth again. His sword swung downward, slicing through the air aiming for my middle. Somehow, I twisted around and pushed his sword away from me. He landed lightly on his feet, but he was already raising his sword for another attack.

I was going to have to go on the offense if I wanted to beat him, so that's exactly what I did.

He raised his arms to bring his sword up, but I didn't give him the time. I immediately lunged at him. He had to react fast to block my aim, which he did at the last second. But his eyes grew wider when he looked at me, filling with surprise and amusement etched onto his face.

I kept on pushing at him, moving faster and faster. I wasn't supposed to be traveling that fast, but I kept moving. I shifted my weight from leg to leg, dancing on the balls of my feet. My arms were strong and moved quickly with the sword, acting as an extension. This time when the world around me started to slow so that I could see every movement, I pushed harder. Every detail of Callum stood out right down to the hairs on his arms. It was like my eyes had optimized into a microscope. His movements became slow motion.

One moment I was positioned in front of him parrying his small blows, and the next, I was behind him. I pushed him straight to the ground by hitting him squarely in the back with my shoulder. As he fell to the ground, I moved my knee so that I would hit the middle of his back, pinning him. My sword fell to the ground beside us. My hands hit the dirt on either side of his head.

Silence fell.

15

Sloane

MY HEAVY BREATHING punctuated the stillness. I peered around the field to see that everyone had come to a standstill. Harris actually had his mouth hanging open. Raleigh's eyes were the size of saucers, and Ashlen's face was filled with astonishment and pride.

"Ugh, get off me," Callum twisted to the side so he could breathe more easily.

"Oops, sorry," I rolled off him and kneeled beside him. "You okay?"

Callum coughed a couple of times and wiped the dirt off his face. "Yeah, I'll be fine." He grimaced in pain, but when he opened his eyes to look at me, they brimmed with happiness. That same little boy happiness that had filled his face the first time I had fought him.

"So, Sloane, can you explain how you were able to do that?" Jess had come to stand beside me. His arms again crossed over his chest.

The corners of my mouth lifted, "Well, no, I don't think I can."

"Ohmygosh, Sloane, that. Was. So. Cool!" Ashlen bounded up to me and threw her arms around me, tugging me off the ground. Her words ran together. She talked so fast, "That was so unbelievable. You were going super-fast all your movements were a blur! And then that moment you were in front of him and then BAM! You were behind him, knocking him to the ground. That was amazing." Her eyes were wide, and she was breathing hard from the excitement.

Raleigh shook her head in disbelief, "That was amazing."

Harris guffawed.

Callum, at this point, was trying to sit up, but he wasn't succeeding, "Can I get some help here?"

We had forgotten about him. We immediately made a fuss over him, helping him get up.

"Callum, I'm so sorry. You sure you're okay?" I was still kneeling on the ground with my hands resting on my thighs.

He nodded, "Yeah, that was the most fun I've had in a long time." He pushed his hair out of his face. "We'll have to have more one-on-one sessions," he grinned.

I smiled and looked down at the ground, feeling kind of bashful. *I'm so weird.* I jumped to my feet and brushed the dirt from my knees. I held out a hand to help Callum. He grabbed my hand and pulled up, swaying when he stood. I put my hands on his arms to help him steady his balance.

"I'm alright, I didn't think you had hit me that hard, but I guess I was wrong. Hey, don't worry about it, though. I need that kind of practice all the time." His hand was at the base of his back like he was trying to rub the pain out of it.

"Hey, honey, if he can't take the pain, I sure can," Rory replied with a satisfied tone and devilish smile.

Callum turned slowly to face him and straightened, demonstrating the full magnitude of his height and muscular build. He lowered his hands and erased the pain from his face. He might as well have killed Rory with his eyes. I hoped my face hadn't turned red.

"I never said I couldn't take the pain." Ohh, things were getting interesting.

Rory smiled broadly at him, but then winked at me, "You just let me know, I'm here anytime you want me."

Out of the corner of my eye, I saw Callum's hands tighten into fists, and his teeth clench, making the line of his jaw sharp. I subconsciously took a step-in front of Callum.

Rory is full of it, whatever it is. I rolled my eyes and turned back to Jess and the others but kept a cautious eye on Callum.

Jess and Irene were scrutinizing me. The others were watching us as if we were entertainment.

Jess took a step toward me, his eyes boring into mine. I self-consciously thought that my eyes had probably changed white. He twirled his sword at his side, "Let's see if you can do it again." He smiled, rolling his shoulders, and taking a fighter's stance.

Everyone that was gathered around us cleared a circle. Callum got up and limped to the edge of the circle and sat down. The circle was about a twenty-foot radius giving us plenty of room.

I shook my arms out and took my stance as well, facing him squarely. We began to circle each other. He went to the right, and I followed, then he lunged straight for my core. I met his sword with mine and twisted it away. He immediately aimed closer for my legs, but I leapt to the side, swinging my sword at the same time, slicing through the air, trying to aim for his neck. He ducked and spun elbowing me in the side. I landed on one foot, almost tilting off balance, but I let my knee hit the ground. When my knee landed on the dirt, I swung upward, bringing my sword to run straight up the middle of Jess. He had to take a step back to avoid getting sliced and diced.

Blinding white light erupted from his palm, forming a circular shield. My heart raced. My wooden sword meekly bounced off the shield. His feet left the ground as he hovered a few inches from the ground. *Shit.* I scrambled to keep up. He seemed to be everywhere at once, barely touching the ground. His white shield deflected my blows easily. Tendrils of light fell, disappearing into the dirt. I had to do something. My adrenaline kicked into overdrive, and the blood in my veins thundered.

He was going to beat me.

No.

Every muscle in my body tensed, blood cells surged through my veins, and oxygen sang into my lungs. I swung my sword around, and everything slowed to a near standstill.

Jess's face scrunched in concentration, his arms swinging around to aim a blow. Beads of sweat ran down his forehead and dotted his shirt. His left foot stayed flat, moving slightly forward as he arced the sword. His right leg came up on the ball of his foot, the heel moving up, pushing his body forward. The sword swung closer; it was going to hit my thigh and slice up to my chest. I instantly braced myself for the hit, blocking the blow by mere seconds, while at the same time, I suddenly appeared on his left side. I hit his ribs full force with my shoulder, making him bend inward and causing him to lose balance and fall.

"Holy shhhhiii..." Harris exclaimed. He glanced at us, "sorry, ladies."

"Dang," Ashlen replied with a huge smile plastered on her lovely face.

I looked at everyone and down at Jess. Jess propped up on his elbows and tilted his head up at me. He smiled and shook his head. I think that was the first smile I had seen from him.

"Alright, let's figure this out," Jess hopped up, and everyone gathered around us. "We are going to change the training. You," he pointed to me, "will fight against each person, making them better too." He studied me for a moment and then turned to the other three.

"We are still going to meet each morning with our regular training sessions, but right now, we're going to shake things up. We've got a couple more hours before dinner. I want you and you," he pointed to Harris and Raleigh, "to both attack Sloane, then we will see what else we can throw at you."

I stayed standing in the middle of the field. Raleigh and Harris both spread out on either side of me.

This was going to be an exciting matchup. Why do I feel like everyone is ganging up on me? How I miss the days of being able to go swimming or watch television. Oh, to be able to just sit on a sofa, letting my mind drift off in bliss. The only downtime I got was when I'm unconscious, which seemed to be happening a lot lately.

Raleigh moved out on my right, Harris circling around on my left. Raleigh let out a battle cry and charged for me, as she ran toward me Harris came in silently at the opposite side. I met Raleigh first. Our wooden swords were hitting and sliding along the blades as they met. I shoved with my arms pushing Raleigh back. I spun around to meet Harris's onslaught.

I barely had time to deflect his advance. His sword came in high, aiming a mark to my neck, which would have left an awful bruise. Our swords met, his sword came down, and my sword swung upward. I could feel Raleigh coming in from my left. I twisted around so I could meet her advances, barely having the time to miss Harris.

Time slowed again.

The pounding in my head escalated. Raleigh's and Harris's movements seemed long and slow, then Jordan and Stephen were suddenly on top of us. The world shifted into fast action again. They didn't only go after me, but after Raleigh and Harris too. Harris had one second to switch his offensive tactic to defense. Stephen went straight for Harris while he was occupied with me. Stephen's sword clipped Harris's shoulder, making him stumble and fall to the ground. He rolled into Raleigh, forcing her to leap over him to counter-attack Jordan's strike.

Power rippled through the circle and light erupted from the ground running along Stephen's legs and arms. He moved faster, and if we got too close, the hair on my arms stood at attention. The electricity pulsing from him was almost too much.

An oval shield formed in front of Jordan. The light forming his shield had a yellow tint. Jordan's eyes were solid black as he danced around the circle.

Water smacked my face. Stephen again threw more water at me as if he was holding a baseball. Balls of water sailed through the air. What the hell was happening?? I jumped, ran, and tried whatever I could to miss the water balls. If one hit me, electricity would zing behind it, causing tiny shocks. I was quickly becoming soaked and tired. With only my wooden sword, I wasn't much of a match against

Realmers with superpowers. I had to tap into that energy inside of me, somehow.

A buzzing thundered in my ears and traveled through my body. So much was going on around me. I felt a thin thread of energy in my core, and I pulled at it. The movement around me slowed even more than it ever had before. I moved around the four of them in a blur, blocking blows before they even made them, ducking around them so fast they couldn't see me. I was behind them one second and in front of them in another. *Was I turning into the freaking Flash or Quicksilver?*

I ended with a three-hundred-sixty-degree turn. Everyone was laid out on the ground.

Raleigh was on her back, Harris was on his stomach with one arm tucked under him, Jordan was on his side, his left arm stretched out above his head, but Stephen was the only one moving. Jess, Callum, Irene, Miranda, Molly, Rory, and Ashlen all had varying degrees of surprise on their faces.

I was beginning to get scared.

"I believe you are getting better," Jess replied.

16

After our training session, we traveled back up the hill to eat dinner. The dining hall boomed with activity. People passed food back and forth and talked uproariously. I spotted Chuck, the seven survivors, and Patrice at a large round table situated close to the fire. We pushed through the crowd of people to find a seat. I glanced to my right and caught sight of long golden hair disappearing through an archway that led to a patio. I stopped, trying to figure out if I wanted to follow him. He was different, and I wanted to help him, or at least know what happened. My dumb curiosity.

I grabbed Ashlen's arm, "Hey, I'm going to be back in a few, so don't worry."

Ashlen studied me for a moment, wrinkles creasing her forehead. "Okay, I'll save you a spot at the table." She carried on with Harris to find a seat.

I turned my feet toward the archway that Graham had disappeared through and started down the hallway. The hallway took a right, leading to a large wooden door with brass studs forming designs in the wood. I pushed the door open and out onto the stone patio. My feet clicked on the stones echoing around me. Only the crescent moon gave a little light to the grounds. A darkened form sat at the corner of the building. He was partly shadowed by the masonry.

I took a deep breath and tredded quietly to him. His body stiffened when he heard me approach. His head tilted slightly toward my direction.

"Mind if I sit down?" I spoke quietly, afraid my voice would scare him away.

His response to my question was a shrug. I knelt down on my knees and scooted to the edge of the patio, swinging my legs over the edge, there was a ten-foot drop below. We sat in silence for a few minutes. I was trying to collect my thoughts and hoping he would speak first. I guess I would have to do the speaking.

"Graham? What's going on?"

He glanced at me, "Listen, I don't know why you're here, but I came out here to be alone. If I had wanted company, I would have asked for it." He swung his legs up and pushed himself up. He strode to the door.

I was in shock. Where had that come from?

"Wait. I said wait," I jumped up and stalked toward him. "Why the hostility?"

He paused at the doorway and turned slightly toward me, "I don't have to answer your questions." He turned on his heel and stalked down the hall.

I went after him.

I caught up with him in the middle of the hall. I wrapped my fingers tightly around his forearm, stopping him from moving forward. He spun around so fast I barely saw him move. He pushed me up against the wall, his face right in front of mine. His chest moved quickly up and down. This wasn't a seductive move, this was predatorial and angry.

"Sloane, what don't you understand about me saying, leave me alone?" his voice came out hollow and hard.

My heart thumped loudly in my ears, and I was having trouble swallowing. I was able to squeak out, "What happened? What happened those two weeks you were gone?"

He never released his stare. I could see anger, fear, and hate coming through his eyes, but what I could see the most was sadness. He blinked and glanced away. The grief from his eyes flowed onto his features. The hard lines of his face cracked. His mask of certainty tainted by his emotions.

He shook his head, "I'm sorry. I can't tell you, but don't worry about it." He took a step closer to me, and this time he brought his hand up slowly, brushing my hair away from my face. As if the tender touch could erase the harsh, angry words. "It's something I'm going to have to figure out on my own."

"Let me help you. You know I can. My powers have grown since you've left," I pleaded with him.

"Sloane, I know you probably could help, but you have all these powers for a reason, and I won't have you waste them on my problems," he shook his head again and turned me in the direction of the dining hall, "time for you to go back." He pushed me toward the archway.

I stopped and looked back at him, "Just ask me for help if you get too deep, okay?"

The corners of his mouth lifted slightly, and he nodded. The darkness in the hall covered him, so I couldn't see his eyes. "Go on," he waited for me to continue down the hall before going back to the patio.

I traveled back inside the loud dining hall, picking out Ashlen and Harris at a far table in a corner with food piled high. I pushed through the crowds of people and finally made it to the table. Ashlen pulled a seat out for me. I sat beside her, and she pushed a plate in front of me. I felt like I was sitting in the background with the world passing by.

I couldn't get the way Graham's eyes had been so haunted out of my mind. He was planning something, and I knew he would act fast. I hoped he didn't do anything stupid.

17

Graham

GRAHAM STEPPED out onto the stone patio. The moon casting deep shadows along the brick buildings. The small amount of light glinted off his bare arms. The night breeze blew strands of his hair across his shoulders and face. The air caressed his skin.

He took a deep breath of the night air, maybe one of the last he would take.

Worry and sorrow creased his usually smooth features. He was going to need to plan. He paced across the stones, trying to come up with something that he could maybe do, something that would save her and keep her safe.

He was going to have to move fast so no one would know what he was up to because he was sure someone would try to stop him. He had no doubt about that.

He never thought he would be contacted by *them*, that they would have something to say. Who knew they could even say something?

His shoulders and back tightened with the stress coursing through his body. His mind spun with questions.

"If I'm going to act, it should be now." He tilted his head back to look at the moon, the tiny sliver barely giving off any light.

He made his decision, turning from the door that leads to the dining hall, and going to another door that would take him to his room. He moved quickly through the door and up the stairs, taking the steps two at a time. Walking quickly down the hall to his room, he did not pass a soul. He entered his room quietly and grabbed his bag to pack. He stuffed it with some food, more knives, some matches, and a small blanket, also putting some weapons into the bag. He strapped the bag onto his back, tightening it across his chest. He picked up his bow and arrows as he left. He went down the same way he had gone up to the room. He stepped out onto the stone patio and in the direction that would take him away from people. Quietly walking away from the main building, he made his way to a small clearing.

He took another deep breath, pulling the air in deep to fill his whole chest. His chest and shoulders moved up and down as the air filled his lungs. He turned his face up to the night sky. The space around him became charged, bits of electricity flickering around his body. The air crackled and sizzled. His ears filled with a humming noise that changed into a loud droning sound. He spread his arms out wide.

Electricity erupted from the ground, traveled up his legs, along his body, and out his fingertips. A bright light erupted from his heart and burned through his veins down his arms transforming the light into fire. The light and energy cascaded from his fingers, forming a large orb suspended in the air directly in front of him; it glistened and glowed. The energy powering it hummed. The orb hovered for a moment then began to bend and lengthen, forming into wings. A body could be distinguished. The skin along the body moved and shifted into scales and gold feathers. The wings spread out wide, flexing, and stretching. The large head rose and spread its mouth wide, exposing rows of gleaming white sharp teeth. Smoke curled out its nostrils. The enormous black eyes turned and blinked at its creator.

He patted the creature's scaly neck. He made sure his pack was tight then climbed on top of the giant dragon's back, making sure to sit above the wings, so he had a good hold around its neck.

"Alright, little man, let's do some hunting."

The Czar looked around him then, spread his wings, and pushed off with his feet, soaring into the night sky. He turned in a wide circle and aligned himself toward the shadowed mountain that sat in the North like a dark beacon.

———

New York City, N.Y
6:00 p.m.
W.A.F.F. Broadcast Station

A WOMAN with short dark brown hair, wearing a dark blue tailored suit, sat at a stained cherry desk with a stack of neatly placed papers on the right-hand side. The news anchor kept her eyes on the camera, waiting for her performance to begin. The cameraman started counting down the seconds before air time. The red light flicked on, and the woman quickly set a compliant smile on her doctor-enriched face.

"Good evening everyone, we have a special report tonight that is a cautionary warning to all of us, and will be disturbing to younger viewers. We have been in contact with local Police and residents about their neighborhood disappearances, the death of pets, vandalism, thefts, and other forms of violence. The findings are disturbing, to say the least, but our problems are a part of a national crisis. Violence of all kinds are rising all across the nation," she paused dramatically.

"Police have confirmed that muggings, as well as senseless beatings on streets, have risen twenty percent from last year. Homicide has had a ten percent increase. Car accidents have even increased fifteen percent, with motorists claiming complete loss of control of their vehicles. Those involved have vehicles of varying makes, models, and production years. The Police Chief says they are adding more men on the streets for prevention. The added manpower should help deviate criminals, and hopefully, save on time if there is an emergency." The broadcaster brought her hands together and pursed her lips.

"The police have stated to take the usual precautions during your daily tasks. Make sure to park and walk in well-lit areas. Keep all doors and windows locked and secured. Bring your pets indoors. Most importantly, do not travel anywhere by yourself and possibly avoid being out after dark. It seems these monsters are using the darkness as a shield." She shook her head in anger.

"We will be keeping a close eye on the increase in violence and keep you posted on any more occurrences. Please feel free to call our hotline if you have any information on this story..."

18

THAT NIGHT AFTER EATING, I made my way to the library. It had been almost a week since I had last been there.

I found my man, Clifford, where I had first met him at the big table in the center of the library hiding behind a stack of books. His large glasses seemed to have made his eyes appear larger. His bushy eyebrows were bushier, and he seemed to hunch over slightly more. When he spotted me, he hopped off his chair and came around the table to take my hand.

"Sloane, where have you been off to?" His eyes twinkled with happiness when he noticed me.

"I know I'm sorry that it has been so long since I've been here. I have no excuse except for my memory."

He grinned, "Oh dear, I have heard about your adventures, so I forgive you, but I've wanted to tell you that I took it upon myself to keep your research going during your absence." He immediately turned from me and headed down an aisle.

I knew he was heading for my table, so I didn't try to keep up. I wound through the aisles of books, running my fingers over their spines, feeling the rough leather and paper that made the covers; dust and sand covered each shelf and the floor. I came out at the end of the aisle where my table was placed near the windows. The papers, books, and journals were still where I had left them. Clifford was rifling through the papers like some kind of fiend. He pulled out one very crinkled paper; the paper's edge had been torn away and was now a light tea color.

Clifford brandished the paper in my face, "Come, come look at what I found. I think you will enjoy this very much."

I smiled softly and walked around the table to stand beside him. He handed the paper to me. It was a journal page dated 1990 the year my father had disappeared, but it wasn't signed by anyone.

17 November 1990

Today was a slow one. I miss home. I miss movies and air conditioning. Cars. Regular shower times. I even miss school. I wish I was at home with Anna. I hope she's okay. She must think I'm the worst...

Training was as usual today. My Protector abilities have begun as the training has gotten more strenuous. I have been using Artemis a lot more lately. She helps me get out of trouble. I try not to use her when I don't need her, but it's hard not to use her for the little things too. These aides are supposed to help me, but I think some of them can cause more problems because I rely on them so much. Masada has yet to be used. He is patiently waiting, though.

My father passed the aides on to me to help me with my training and for when I become a Hunter and then maybe the Leader. He always keeps Willow by his side. He says he will never part with her, which I guess I'll have to live with. He says that even in death, he will not part with her. I don't understand his reluctance or stubbornness about her, oh well. Jacob was given Yumi, which I really didn't think was fair. I'm the best at archery. Yumi is beautiful, and it always hits its intended mark, much like Willow.

THE REST of the paper had been burned or torn. Wrinkles creased my forehead with confusion and concentration.

"Can you tell me what this means exactly?",

Clifford smiled and nodded excitedly, "Yes, of course, the author is giving you the names of their aides."

"Okay, I know it's a stupid question, but what is an aide?"

"Well, that's what your necklace is, Artemis is her name?"

"Uh, yeah, how'd you know that?"

"Well, I figured that out from reading one of the other pages, but I assumed you had learned her name already?"

"Yes, I did learn its name. Um, why do you call the necklace *her*?"

"They have always called the aides a female or male. It is a way to hide the true identity of the aide to keep the name safe from those who don't own it. As I'm sure you have learned, the name is an immensely powerful tool in using the aide," his eyes watched my face to see if I understood. "Of course, if someone learns the name, but is not a part of the family, the aide cannot be used to the greatest of its ability, only because their blood is not an ingredient."

I nodded to show I was listening, "So according to this, my dagger's name is Masada?"

Clifford took the page from my hand and scanned the page again. He began nodding, "Yes, I believe that is what this document is telling us." He handed the page back to me.

"Would you know where..." I looked back at the page, "Willow and Yumi are then?"

"Hmm, well, no. Jacob disappeared, and I think along with him, Yumi went too. Now, as for your grandfather," Clifford scratched his head, "I think Willow was indeed buried with him just like he wanted. Charles was buried underneath this building in the hall of legends."

My eyebrows rose, and my mouth forming a small O, "There's a cemetery underneath this building?" My voice kind of squeaked when it came out.

Clifford nodded his wrinkled head, "Yes, it has been there since this Realm began. The tomb was built first, and when they decided to build the city, they put the main building on top as a way to secure the restfulness of the bodies below."

Just hearing him talk of bodies underneath us, made my skin want to crawl off my body and hide under a rock. I'm sorry, but I get squeamish with talk of blood and dead things. I can't help it. I shivered, and goosebumps appeared along my arms.

"So, is there a way I might be able to retrieve Willow?"

This time it was Clifford's eyes that grew larger, "Retrieve Willow? Why would you want to get her?"

I shrugged, "Wouldn't she be helpful if we're going to have to do some serious damage to the Nightlins?"

Clifford turned his back to me to look out the window. He stayed quiet for several minutes before he turned back to me. "I think you might be right, but I know that it won't be easy to retrieve Willow. If I remember correctly, Charles was a sneaky fellow, and like your father says in that note, Charles would never give Willow up to anyone even in death. He might be stingy."

"Alright, I will need a plan."

Footsteps echoed in the library; they were moving fast between the aisles. Stephen appeared at the end of an aisle, searching for someone, he spotted us and quickly made his way toward us.

"Have you seen Graham?"

My heart instantly pumped harder.

"No, what's wrong?"

"No one can find him. We've been looking all over the grounds for him."

"The last time I saw him was at dinner. He was out on the patio, but I haven't seen him since. That was hours ago."

Stephen ran his fingers through his dark hair and then balled his fists. "This is when I hate it when we don't have fucking technology like in the Norm, we could be using fucking cell phones! Instead, we have to live like dumb ass cavemen." His sea-colored eyes were pinpoints of anger. I knew exactly how he felt.

"So, what can we do?"

Stephen growled, "Absolutely nothing. We have no way of finding him or contacting him. Damn Realm." A long line of expletives flowed out of his mouth.

"Wait!" I pulled my necklace up and over the collar of my shirt, "I can use this."

I took off through the hallways until I found the patio. The crescent moon was beginning to disappear. The cool night air was refreshing after being in the moldy library. I stood on the edge of the stone and held Artemis out in front of me. Stephen arrived a few seconds later and stood behind me. Clifford announced his arrival by way of breathing heavily.

I whispered to her, "Artemis, find Graham." The needle started spinning rapidly around then, slowed. It swung to the North and stilled. A mountain broke the line of the horizon. I looked at Stephen and Clifford.

"She points to the North at that mountain."

Stephen's eyes flickered to the mountain and then away. He grumbled some more. Pretty sure I heard a few more curses. He came over to stand by me.

"Why would he go near the mountain?" he spoke low, it was a rhetorical question. Stephen's eyes locked onto the black mountain; strands of his black hair blew across his forehead, making his hair more disheveled.

"What's the significance of the mountain?"

Stephen turned his attention to me, "It is the beginning of the Nightlin territory. We've never been able to penetrate the area, but we know they are there. We believe they live under the mountain in some sort of underground system." He shook his head, "I need to go tell the others. Why would he go near that place?" He headed for the door, "thanks, Sloane." He disappeared through the doorway.

I stared at the mountain. The massive dark peaks were barely visible in the night sky. Could someone even climb it? Clifford came to stand beside me.

"Only trouble will he find if he goes to that place," Clifford stared fixedly at the mountain. *Sheesh, Yoda much?*

"Is there something we can do? We have to go after him." My heartbeat faster, and thoughts rushed through my mind, thoughts of

actions to take, what might be happening to Graham, and the conse-
quences if we didn't act.

"No, you cannot. You will surely die; then how would you find
your answers?" Clifford asked. His bushy eyebrows were pushed
together, making a straight line above his eyes.

A headache pounded behind my eyes again, though this time, I
was sure it was because of Graham and the Nightlins. I massaged my
temples in clockwise motions, trying to ease the tension.

"So, what can we do?"

"We can only wait. You can't be going off to fight thousands of
Nightlins by yourself. You still need training, and if need be, we will
find Willow too." Clifford patted my arm, "Graham left without a
word because he knew some journeys must be taken alone." He
paused and looked me in the eyes, "One day, I'm sure you will have to
take the same kind of journey. Come, let's go back inside, they will
tell you what they plan to do." He took my hand and tugged me in the
direction of the hall.

I followed him on auto-pilot. My mind was in a haze. There must
be something I could do to help Graham. Surely, there's something.
Why else would I be here, but to help in any way I can? Clifford led
me to the stairway.

"Can you make it to your room?"

I nodded slowly.

"Okay, I will see you tomorrow. We have work to do."

This time I met his eyes and nodded again. I smiled slightly, "I'll
see you tomorrow."

19

Sloane

I WOKE UP EARLY. Raleigh and Ashlen were still asleep. Ashlen was tangled up in her sheets, while Raleigh had her mouth open, her arms hung off the bed, and the sheets were on the floor. The moonlight shone in through the windows. The once-hot fire was now mere embers.

Rolling out of bed as quietly as I could, I tiptoed to the kitchen area to get a fire going. I placed a bucket on the fire to boil some water, then eventually to make coffee. I sat at the counter with my head resting in my hands. I closed my eyes for a few seconds, trying to straighten out my thoughts.

The water boiled, and I got up. I poured the coffee into a mug along with milk and sugar. My spoon clinked methodically against the clay mug as I stirred in the sugar.

Things had been happening so fast. I didn't really know if I had absorbed it all. Okay, let me lay out the problems: first, I had no clue what happened to my father except he was possibly taken by the Nightlins and killed. Second, the crime and death rates had risen in the Norm, because the Nightlins may be creating their own portals. Third, Nightlins are being more aggressive in the Realm causing more deaths. Fourth, Graham disappeared probably off to try and conquer the Nightlin Mountain alone. *Are those all the problems? Oh, right, I can't forget my physical problems, which consist of getting new abilities that aren't normal for others. I have no idea what it means or how in the world I am going to develop these new abilities. Hopefully, those problems will sort themselves out. Oh, and then there's this whole thing about retrieving my grandfather's sword? In a tomb. Great. Just wonderful. Everything keeps getting better. Why does it all seem to come down to a tomb filled with dead people, spiders, spider webs, and who knows what else? And then, of course, there is Callum...not even going to touch that one right now. Uggggg. Can't I catch a break?*

The second and third problems I couldn't solve myself. The first problem I had been working on consistently. At least, I'm here. I can't solve my father's disappearance in one week, so I'm learning the history behind him. With Graham, I have no idea what to do, except maybe find Willow, which I don't even know if I can do that. I think I'm going to put my physical abnormalities on the back burner for now.

There's never a simple answer.

I used to be a somewhat 'normal' human being. Now I might not even be called human. Oh, wow, I might not be a human anymore. I guess I'm not really. I'm a Realmer now, no complaints there since I am more comfortable here than I've ever been on the Norm side.

So, the only thing left to do was to visit my dead grandfather.

———

THE GIRLS STIRRED about an hour later, while I strapped on my armor. They got up and fixed breakfast.

"So, what are your plans for today?" Ashlen was busy putting a mixture of vegetables in her soup and chopping up fruit.

"Funny you should ask that particular question on this particular day," I looked at her with I knew what was amusement on my face.

Ashlen looked up from what she was doing. Surprise overtook her features, and then she asked skeptically, "What makes you say that?"

"Well, I've been going over everything that I'm going to have to do and this particular activity I am going to have to perform, especially since Graham disappeared."

Raleigh's head snapped up, "He what?"

"Oh, yeah, he's gone. My necklace said that he went to Nightlin Mountain."

This time Raleigh was the skeptical one, "Your necklace said?"

"Yes, while you've been out with all your men, I've been hunting down clues. My necklace can tell me where to find people or how to find them."

Raleigh raised her eyebrows.

"Yeah, so my grandfather is buried underneath us by the way, and has a sword buried with him that might be able to help fight against the Nightlins. I'm not sure why yet, but I need it."

"So, you're saying we are standing above a cemetery?" Raleigh looked incredulous.

I nodded with a slight smile on my lips, "Yep, full of skeletons."

Raleigh and Ashlen made faces at each other. They silently exchanged words. Finally, Raleigh shrugged.

"Alright, let's go," Ashlen smiled.

"I should warn you about one thing."

They looked at me, waiting.

"Okay, so, apparently, there might be some sort of enchantment on the sword, which will make it difficult to retrieve..."

Raleigh narrowed her eyes, "Difficult?"

I shuffled in my spot, "Umm, yeah. I won't know how much until I get down there."

Raleigh glanced at Ashlen, "Well, if we can't fight an enchantment, then we have no business to fight Nightlins."

"That is exactly right," Ashlen nodded. "When do we go?"

"How about when the light appears?"

They both nodded.

"What about practice?" Ashlen asked.

Oh, right, forgot about practice, "Uh, we can still go and then take a small break," I smiled sweetly.

Ashlen chuckled, shaking her head, and Raleigh laughed. We gathered our weapons and made our way down to the training field.

As usual, the Protectors and Hunters were already waiting for us. Harris was starting to make us look bad. He usually arrived a few minutes before us. This time Harris was stretching already.

Callum watched us approach. He stood in the group with Irene, Jess, Jordan, and Miranda. Rory and Stephen were sparring together to the side of the group. Molly sat with her legs stretched out on the ground and her arms out behind her, propping herself up, watching the two guys.

Jess met us, "Now that everyone is here, let's do some warm-ups."

We split up and moved to our spots on the field. We began stretching. Then we started doing flips, twists, and somersaults, racing each other to see who was the best.

Callum was paying me more attention than usual. Every time I turned around; he was watching me.

"Callum, what is it?" I asked as we finished warming-up.

He stretched down to touch his toes, "What do you mean?"

"You've had that funny smile on your face all morning."

He rose and glanced at Jess, "You have a plan, and I'm going."

My face filled with surprise no matter how hard I tried to hide it. I looked at Jess and the others.

I whispered as low as I dared, "How did you know?"

He moved to stand directly in front of me and spoke low, "I know you. I knew you would want to do something about Graham, so I assumed you were planning something for tonight. And, I have amazing hearing."

My eyes grew slightly wider, "Amazing hearing? How amazing?"

He smiled slightly, "Very."

I crossed my arms across my chest, "You know it just occurred to me that I never asked you about your abilities."

His smile widened, and he messed his hair, "Yeah, you don't ask, I don't tell."

I threw my hands up in the air, "Shit! There's no telling what you've heard."

He smiled again, this time the corners of his eyes crinkling, and shrugged.

I narrowed my eyes at him, "Oh well, it doesn't matter what you might have heard. There certainly isn't anything I can do about it now."

He continued to smile.

I leaned in close to him, "But just so you know, we aren't planning on going after Graham yet. I have something else we need to do first."

That wiped the smile off his face. His face filled with confusion.

"Well, whatever you're planning, I'm still going with you. Remember our deal?"

I let out an exasperated sigh, "Yes, I remember."

"When?"

"When the light appears."

He nodded once then turned away.

I started sparring with Irene. We were still using our wooden swords, so the blows didn't cut, but they still left nasty bruises. As we were fighting, the sun began to break the horizon. I broke off from fighting to bend over and take a breath. I looked over at the girls. Raleigh was fighting with Molly. Molly was actually fast enough to keep up with her. Ashlen was sparring with Rory. Rory had to work hard to keep up. He had sweat running down his face and dripping off his chin. Not very attractive.

I waved off Irene and went over to a patch of non-trampled grass to sit down.

Irene came over to me, "Hey, you okay?"

"Oh, yeah, I'm fine. I just needed a breather."

She studied me for a moment then nodded. She walked over to talk to Callum. Callum was watching me again. I focused my attention back to the girls. Both of them had stopped sparring and were sitting on the ground. They watched me, both asking me a question with their expressions. I nodded to each of them.

Ashlen got up and made some remark to Rory, who just nodded and shrugged, he gestured with his hands toward the city. Ashlen nodded and started walking toward the main gate. She passed by and winked.

Raleigh went over to talk to Jess, who was coaching Harris. Jess nodded, and Raleigh spun on her heel toward the main gate too.

Now it was up to me. Callum, like usual, had his eyes on me, so when I nodded at him, he knew I was ready. He said something to Irene to make her look at me. She said something, then Callum sauntered over to me. He held out his hand to help me up. I grasped his right hand, and he pulled me swiftly up, bringing me lightly up to my feet.

"Okay, we got the green light. They won't know anything for at least an hour, so we better get moving with whatever crazy idea that you thought up."

I glared at him, "It wasn't just my idea. Clifford helped too."

His eyebrows raised, "Then I really should be worried."

I rolled my eyes and kept walking. We were almost to the gate when Callum started drilling me again.

"What are we doing?"

I glanced at him and waited a few moments before I answered him, "We are going to go retrieve a family heirloom."

He was quiet for a second, "Where is this, heirloom?"

I smiled, "Always know what questions to ask. It's in the cemetery."

Callum stopped abruptly, "The cemetery? Are you crazy?" He grabbed my arm, "We can't go traipsing through the cemetery. You do know what's down there, right?"

"Yes, skeletons, bugs, spiders, a little dirt. I'm surprised you'd be so worried about some little bugs."

He shook his head, "That wasn't the only thing that I was talking about. There are things down there, including your grandfather, that won't want to be disturbed. Things that won't be friendly if we disturb them."

"You can't be serious, so you're telling me that in this world, things that die don't always stay dead?"

He nodded his head slowly, "It won't exactly be the person, but the essence of them. I know Charles will probably be one of the worst he was as stubborn and selfish as they come."

"Well, we better get going. We don't have all day," I smiled audaciously, "literally."

We continued up to the main building to find Ashlen and Raleigh. I felt terrible about leaving Harris behind. He wasn't going to be very happy with us later, but he loved to train with the Protectors and Hunters. Hopefully, he wouldn't hold it against us for too long. We found the girls in the dining hall. They each had a bulging backpack hanging over their shoulders—no telling what they had decided to pack. Ashlen held out a pack to me; mine looked slightly lighter than theirs.

"Okay, let's go find Clifford. He has to tell us where we can locate the door."

"I can lead us there," replied Callum.

I shifted my attention to Callum, "Why didn't you say that in the first place?"

"Well, I kind of was hoping that I could talk you out of it, but seeing how you're set on it... well, I'm going with you, so let's go." Callum moved toward the door, his weapons strapped across shoulders and back, swung back and forth as he walked.

20

CALLUM TOOK THE LEAD, and I gestured to Ashlen and Raleigh, "After you."

They followed Callum.

Callum walked swiftly around to the back of the main building. He stopped in the middle of the grounds. He seemed to scan the wall like he was looking for something. He walked to the edge of the cliff-side and jumped. I nearly screamed. I raced to the edge and leaned over to see Callum about ten feet below, with a smile on his face.

"Didn't know you cared so much," he laughed and went down a set of rough stone stairs.

I was going to strangle him one of these days, "Idiot."

"I heard that!" he joyfully replied.

I clenched my fists in frustration. Raleigh and Ashlen craned over my shoulder, their eyes watching Callum go down the stairs.

"After you," Ashlen gestured with her hand to the stone stairs below us.

"Hardy harr harr," I jumped down, landing on my feet, one hand hit the soil beneath me. I didn't check to see if the girls were follow-ing, I hurried after Callum. He had already disappeared around a bend in the staircase. The rough stone stairs were wide and had a shallow step, so running was slightly awkward. The stairs had been cut into the side of the hill, so the right side of the staircase had a dirt wall, the stairway slowly curved around the hillside. The thick masonry wall that ran along the whole city was on the left side of the stairs, about twenty feet away. I ran steadily down the stairs. Ashlen and Raleigh tromped down behind me, along with Ashlen's heavy breathing. The stairs widened, and as I came around the bend, it opened up to reveal a vast cut out on the side of the hill.

We arrived at the large opening at the base of the hill. The opening was about ten feet across and fifteen feet tall. They had cut out the tunnel from the side of the hill; the tunnel shrank as we trekked farther in. At the entry of the tunnel, we were stopped by an incredibly thick and ornate wrought iron gate. The iron gate was about six feet wide and ten feet tall.

The gate swung inward when I pushed it, letting out a loud screeching noise as it swung on its hinges. We came to a bend in the tunnel, which brought us to another door. This door was made out of walnut. A mass of carvings made up the door. At first, I couldn't tell what the picture was, but as we grew closer, I could pick out the details. Skeletons that belonged to people and animals were at the bottom of the door, their hands reaching out and their mouths gaping in a silent scream. Floating above the skeletons were a host of angels, their wings and robes flowing out behind them. Large trees framed the picture, the roots entangled with skeletons, and the branches and leaves brushed the faces of the angels.

A keyhole was set into the middle of the two doors.

"Alright, now what?" Callum turned his dark eyes to me questioningly.

I stepped toward the door to investigate and bent down to inspect the keyhole. It wasn't a regular keyhole. This one had a simple small round hole.

"I don't think it takes a regular key," I turned back to my friends.

Ashlen came closer to look for herself. She traced the keyhole with her fingers, "It obviously doesn't take a Norm key," she turned to me, "but a Realm one."

My eyebrows rose, "Realm key?"

Callum was the one to answer, "Yes, a Realm key. They can be any shape or size. We need a key that is small and round and comes to a point."

We all looked at each other. Great, where am I going to get a key?

"We could go back to the library to see what Clifford might be able to tell us?"

"Well, why didn't we do that before we made our way down here?" Callum didn't sound amused.

"Well, if I remember correctly, someone said we didn't need to go see Clifford." I looked at him accusingly. He answered me by rolling his eyes.

Light reflected off the gold of my necklace. The needles moved slightly. I picked it up, holding it in the palm of my hand. The necklace had two points, one at the top and the bottom. Both points were two inches long. I studied the necklace then at the keyhole. Could it be that simple?

I lifted the necklace off my neck and over my head. I fit the point into the keyhole, pushing it as far it would go. There was a soft click and a hum started thrumming. Everyone gathered around me watching. I twisted the necklace to the right. Several clicks sounded inside the door and ended with a loud snap. Dust sprayed out from the cracks in the doors. We immediately took several steps back. Of course, Callum jumped in front of me, blocking the door in case something emerged so he would be attacked first.

As the dust settled, the doors made a popping noise and came apart, pushing outward by an inch. Callum stepped forward and heaved the doors back to reveal a dark hallway. Callum walked into the dark. He struck a match, and a torch that had been hanging on the wall ignited. The torch was simply made. It had a metal cone shape bottom that supported the wood. The cone sat in a small wooden ring that had been set into the rock wall. He turned to the opposite wall and lit another torch. He took one of the torches. We entered the tunnel, and at every ten feet, Callum would light the torches that adorned the walls.

The tunnel beneath the main building was like the kind you see in every horror film. Dark, wet, moldy, humid, spiders, insects, rats, mice, webs, and the atmosphere had that ominous feeling like around the next corner, some creature or murderer would jump out. We were all jumpy, and our eyes wide, trying to keep on the lookout for anything. The tunnel was made out of block masonry, something like sandstone because it was crumbling away, and they had gone back with wood to try and stabilize the tunnel. The floor was made up of leveled dirt. Torches lined the immensely long hallway. The fire waved back and forth as we passed by them or by some slight breeze that blew through the tunnel. The breeze blew strands of hair from my face.

Callum was in the lead. I peered around him to see the tunnel was opening up into a large cavern. Callum stepped to the end of the tunnel, swinging his torch to the right of the large room. Fire leapt up from along the edge of the wall and traveled around the whole room. The fire lit the entire space. A kind of shallow trough lined the room, filled with kindling, so the fire was able to travel quickly. The fire crackled, and the warmth of the flames began to heat the room, almost making it hard to breathe.

The large room was maybe fifty feet wide, other tunnels were arranged along the walls, there were ten tunnels in all. In the middle of the space was a round dais, and on top of it was a stone statue of a man with a sword. The fire threw strange shadows across him. The man had all his armor on, including his helmet, so his face was partly covered. A cloak was tied around his neck and hit the ground at his feet, pooling on the ground. The statue looked almost personified.

"This is Jonathon Smith, the first Leader," Callum replied.

Something like a whisper traveled through the room. The statue seemed to light within, the stone changing to a stark white. Light burst forth from the statue; it engulfed us and traveled through each of us. The white light blinded my sight, except the light came out my eyes. All of us screamed, whether from the pain or the surprise of the unknown. The light disintegrated as quickly as it had engulfed us.

We were left standing, though we were bent over trying to catch our breaths and waiting for our eyesight to readjust.

"What was that?" gasped Raleigh.

Callum stood up straight, "A test, to see if we were part of the Realm."

I turned wide eyes to look at Callum, "What would have happened if we hadn't been?"

"I'm not sure, but my imagination is supplying my mind with plenty of things that could have happened. Okay, so each of these tunnels is dated. See," Callum walked over to one of the openings, he pointed to a set of numbers that had been carved into the stone, "these give the years, so we need to find the one that has the 1990s."

Raleigh grabbed my arm. Her fingers dug into my skin, "Do you see that?"

I looked around the room then back at her to see where she was focused, "See what?"

She glanced at me then back to one of the tunnels, "I, uh, a woman is standing there watching us."

My eyes grew larger, and my body and mind instantly said to run. Callum stopped, and Ashlen turned slowly to survey the room, her eyes about to pop out of her head. I clenched my teeth to keep them from chattering.

"Are you being serious?"

Raleigh nodded and continued to stare at the tunnel. Her eyes swung to her left, and her grip on my arm tightened. Her nostrils flared. I looked over at the tunnel next to us and saw nothing.

"Let's just get a move on. I want to get out of here right now."

I nodded, "Okay." I lowered my voice, "Do you see anything else?"

"A little boy," she whispered. She swallowed hard, then tightened her shoulders and lifted her chin. I could see resolve and determination settling into her features. Her fingers released my arm. "Let's go."

Callum continued around the room, looking over each set of numbers. "Here it is," he stopped at the side of one of the openings to the left of the tunnel that we had traveled through; it had the numbers 1950-2000 carved into the stone.

Of course, this tunnel was dark as well. Callum stepped forward and lit another trough of kindling that was along the side. The fire leapt up and traveled down the tunnel and disappeared into another room. Callum took the lead and headed down the tunnel. This tunnel was a little smaller than the first, so we had to walk single file. As we traveled down the hall, we passed extended rectangular cut-outs in the brick. Raleigh stayed as far away from them as she could.

I stopped suddenly and pointed to one of the rectangular boxes, "Are these, what I think they are?"

Callum stopped and looked back over his shoulder, "Yep, tombs." He kept walking.

I stared wearily at the tombs set into the walls and shuddered. I'm sorry, but it's creepy. I can't help it. We were surrounded by dead bodies. I turned to the girls; they had the same look on their faces as I did, and Ashlen was trying to get as far away from them as she could without catching on fire. We walked cautiously down the hall. The tombs had each person's name and the dates of their reign carved into the stonework. We passed about twenty of the tombs. These people had died in the nineteen-fifties. The farther we traveled through the tunnel, the more the dates began to increase.

The tunnel opened up into a long oval room. Another tunnel was at the opposite end of the room. A large three-foot-wide wall was centered in the room; more tombs were inside the wall. Callum walked to the other tunnel, and lit a torch within then, came back into the room.

"Okay, look through the tombs for Charles Tomas Sullivan," he immediately started scrutinizing each tomb.

The stone wall next to me was rough and crumbling away at the edges. I hesitantly ran my fingers over the edge of the rectangle that had been carved into the masonry. I looked around the room. Ashlen and Raleigh were spread out, inspecting the tombs.

My eyes landed on the wall, situated in the middle of the room. I walked unhurriedly to stand in front of the wall; it felt as if it loomed over me. I scanned the stones, and the names ran together. I knelt down, resting my knees on the dirt floor. I reached out with my right hand and brushed the dirt off the carvings. My fingers scraped over a name and dates, revealing Charles Tomas Sullivan, 1934-1994. I let my breath escape from my mouth.

"I found him," I spoke softly, but Callum appeared at my side at once.

Callum ran his hands over the tomb, rubbing the excess dirt off. The dirt piled on the floor underneath the tomb. He looked at me.

"We are going to have to tear the brick apart," his mouth set into a line. He wasn't very happy with the idea.

"I'll break it."

"No. No way am I letting you," his eyes were adamant and his face stern.

I studied him for a moment, "I'm sorry, but I'm going to have to do this, whether it's by myself or with you helping me."

"I'm opting for me helping you."

"Okay, let's get started," I scooted away from the tomb, about a foot, and put my feet against the rock.

Callum smiled and copied me. The girls stood behind us, waiting. We braced our hands behind us on the dirt floor.

"One, two, three," simultaneously, we pulled our knees up to our chest then kicked out. The whole wall shook. Nothing happened to the tomb.

"Umm, I don't think kicking it is going to do anything," Callum said softly.

Dammit, why can't things be simple?

"Okay, any ideas?" I raised one eyebrow.

Callum ran his fingers along the edge of the rectangle. He unsheathed a small knife and started digging his knife into the crevice. Dirt fell out onto the ground. He was at one end, so I pulled out my small knife, Masada, and started scraping the crevice too.

"Okay, Masada, help us out."

My knife glowed a soft blue. I dropped it.

"What is it?" Callum stopped what he was doing.

"Her knife turned blue," Ashlen said from behind me.

He craned his neck over to look at her then over to me, "It

changed colors?" he focused on the knife, which had changed back to its normal silver color.

I nodded.

He picked it up, turning it over in his hands. He put the blade up to the crevice and pushed the knife into the stone. Blue light ran from the tip to the handle. Callum turned his wide eyes to me. He let go of the knife, leaving it pushed into the stone. The knife still glowed pale blue.

I tentatively pulled the knife out again. It turned back to the steel color. I plunged the knife into the stone again and held it there, where the blue point of the knife had been embedded. The blue light began to travel out across the stone like veins of electricity. Slowly the stone crumbled away.

A dusty skeleton laid inside.

"So, I wasn't expecting him to look like... that," I said. I'm not quite sure what I was expecting, maybe pristine bones? Or maybe a body untouched by the elements. Not the pile of bones before me seemed kind of disappointing. Callum had a disgusted look on his face.

Ashlen pressed herself up against the wall, and Raleigh's face had an 'ugh' expression written across it. I turned back to the tomb and carefully bent forward so I could see inside.

"Ugh, be careful," Ashlen replied from against the wall. "Don't touch it."

I paused then peered closer at the skeleton. I was not about to call it a body. His clothes had rotted away and his hands were clasped over where his stomach had been. Dirt had fallen around and on top of the skeleton. I scooted forward on my knees and reached inside the darkened tomb to see if I could feel something that resembled a sword. I grasped something and pulled it out. A femur was held in my palm. I gasped and immediately dropped it, wiping my hand on my pants.

"Shit," I shook my head, took a breath careful not to breathe in the dead smell, and reached back in with my eyes closed.

"I think I could have given up on opening this tomb a long time ago," Ashlen replied, this time she was leaning over my shoulder.

"I have to agree with her," Raleigh said from her spot against the wall, her eyes roamed across the expansive room.

"You know what would help is if someone would shine a light in here," I glared at Callum, who was kneeling on the ground beside me just watching.

Callum fished in his pocket and pulled out something that resembled a small stick. It was maybe a foot long, but only a couple centimeters in diameter. It was smooth and had a sheen that made it appear as if it glowed from the inside. He placed the stick, so it was inside the tomb.

I stared at him like he was crazy, "How is a stick going to…"

The stick became a pulsing white light. It blinded me for an instant then dimmed slightly, so my eyes could adjust. The entire stick glowed steadily, illuminating the whole tomb. The light glowed through Callum's hand, making his hand red. It was so bright you could see the bones in his hand. I looked at Callum with a shocked expression on my face.

"Remind me to ask you about that later."

He smiled slightly and nodded; his eyes were locked onto the skeleton.

I tried to see through the dirt and skeletal remains for the sword. I moved slightly closer to the edge of the tomb to feel on the opposite side. I swept my hand over the dirt, trying not to let my arm touch the bones. I dug my fingers into the dirt and felt a hard-cool metal. My heart leapt for joy, and I smiled. I wrapped my fingers around the metal and started pulling it up and over the skeleton.

"I got it."

21

As the sword cleared the remains, it hummed. The sound filled my ears, blocking out any other. I watched as the sword started to emit a red glow. The red light filled my vision. I barely registered seeing movement. I squeezed my eyes shut. The floor dropped out from beneath me. I screamed. I tried to open my eyes, but they wouldn't open, making me scream even more.

"Would you shut up?"

My eyes snapped open to a world where the sun was shining bright, and a breeze blew across my face. I turned slowly around from where I was sitting on a soft bed of grass and saw the same white house with the front porch and blue shutters—the one that I saw when that girl in the bar had grabbed my hand, and I passed out. A man sat on the porch step, watching me. He motioned for me to sit by him. I looked around incredulously, trying to see a way out. I peered up into the pale blue sky to see if I spotted the bright white light again, nothing appeared. I shifted my eyes back to the man.

He sat with his broad shoulders slightly rolled inward, his elbows resting on his thighs. His dark blue jeans, slate gray shirt, and brown leather shoes were clean and unruffled. He had thick salt and pepper hair and gray-blue eyes. His eyes were demanding and restless. He tapped the boards beside him.

I looked around again then walked hesitantly toward him. I watched him as I sat on the porch. I made sure there was a good two feet between us.

"You weren't who I was expecting. Who are you?" His voice was hard and authoritative.

"I'm Sloane."

"I'm guessing you broke into my tomb?" he asked me accusingly.

"Well, I was trying to retrieve Willow."

"Willow? Of course, you want to try and use her power, but you can't unless you're blood, and there's no way you are. I only had two sons, and they disappeared before I died."

"Well, remember that girl James told you about? She's my mother. My father never knew about me."

His eyes became unfocused like he remembered something. The man studied me for a few minutes, "Give me your hand." He held out his hand, waiting for me to respond.

I weighed my decision. I laid my right hand gently in his. His hand was large and rough. His fingers wrapped tightly around my hand, squeezing uncomfortably hard.

Before I knew what he was doing, he had swiftly cut my palm. A sharp sting ran up my arm from my palm. I stared, with my mouth open, at the red welling up from a long gash that ran from my pinky finger to my thumb. I looked up at him. He was watching the blood run down my arm. He quickly sliced his hand, which I noticed wasn't as deep as my cut. He wrapped his hand around mine, and it burned. My mouth stayed open in a silent scream. Our hands started to change colors. I watched in horror as our linked hands became blinding white. Light exuded from our hands. I searched his face, which intently watched our hands.

The light suddenly extinguished, and he released my hand. I stared at my palm, which was now unscarred and slightly pink.

"What the hell?"

"It was a test to see if you were indeed family," he crossed his arms over his chest, "it appears that you are." He didn't look overly excited about the idea. He turned his gaze out over the bright green grass and flowers.

"So, what does that mean?"

He didn't answer right away. He clasped his hands in front of him and looked down at his interlocked fingers.

He met my eyes, "The sword you found is not Willow, but it will help you release her." He nodded toward me, "I notice you have James' necklace, Artemis, she will help you find the sword. It won't be easy, though. When you find her, you will have to fight for her. She is a great prize, and I made sure that when I concealed her that the only person who could retrieve her would be someone worthy." He looked at me carefully before he continued. "The sword you currently have can still be used, but you will have to activate it. Once you activate the energy within your blood, it will answer you and become yours fully."

"How am I going to activate it?" I was quite sure I wasn't going to like the answer.

"You're of my blood. I have no doubt you will discover that answer quickly."

"So you're not going to answer me?" my mouth was slightly open because it was hard for me to believe that he wasn't giving me real answers.

"You have the same strong will and stubbornness of James..."

He looked down at the boards of the porch. I didn't know what to say, although my heart kind of swelled when he said that, so I watched him, waiting for him to do something.

"Have you found James?"

I took my time answering him, "No, I'm sorry I haven't. That's part of the reason why I'm trying to find Willow."

He nodded and continued to stare at the boards.

"If you do see him, will you tell him I'm sorry for not listening to him?" he watched my expression.

I smiled slightly, "Sure."

He nodded and looked back out across the pastures.

"Wait a second, how are you here?" I blurted out.

He looked at me with a half-smile that somehow transformed his hard, stern features into a handsome, gentle face, "I'm a collection of memories that were stored within the sword so that when someone tried to engage the sword, I would act as a sort of security system. I am a way to prevent the sword and our family secrets from falling into the wrong hands..." He shrugged his massive shoulders.

"Can you tell me what kind of powers Willow holds?"

He locked his eyes on me, making me want to squirm. He turned his gaze back to the green pastures, "Willow is an old artifact from the beginning. She was forged here in this world using the magic and resources from the very ground you walk on. Anything she cuts through will fall, no matter what." He looked at me, "She will be the key to the destruction of the Nightlins if only you can strike the heart of them."

"The heart? Do you know where it is?"

He shook his head, "We never were able to locate that information. I only know that somehow they are able to move it when it senses danger."

I ran my fingers across the boards of the porch, "Therefore, it has to be small, easily carried."

He nodded again, "Of course, but don't think of it being an actual heart. Things in this world are never really as they seem. I may speak more metaphorically than literally."

This was definitely not going to be easy. Why would I even dream to think that it would be? I sighed out of habit and rubbed my hands together, dirt and dust falling away.

"Okay, next question," I looked around at the unfamiliar sloping hills and bright blue sky, "how am I going to get back?"

"Oh, that's easy," he grasped my arm. I instantly tried to pull away, but he held my arm firmly. His eyes swept across my face and finally locked onto my eyes like he was taking a picture of my face. "You look like him." A sharp pain sliced up my arm and through my mind. A white light pounded through my senses, shutting out everything around me. I gasped to catch my breath.

Someone was shaking me. Things in my head were being rattled.

My eyes fluttered open, and a bright light was shining in my eyes. I tried to focus on what was going on around me, but everything was very fuzzy. Sound slowly began to filter into my ears. Three dark shapes hovered around me. I tried to tell them to move away, but I'm pretty sure what came out was a jumbled mess.

I could feel them lifting me up, but my body wasn't fully cooperating. I felt like Jell-O.

"Sloane?" said a female voice

Oh, someone was saying something. What were they saying? I was bouncing around as someone carried me. Fire light blinked in and out as we rushed by. Fresh air hit my face as we came out of the tunnels.

"Sloane, are you there?" a different female voice.

"What's wrong with her?" the first female.

"I don't know. You saw her. When she touched that sword, her mind went to a different place," a male voice this time, "Sloane?"

"Her arm, it looks like she's bleeding!" said a second female voice.

Someone's fingers rubbed lightly over my arm.

"It's blood, but she just has a red line on her skin," the male voice responded.

I tried extra hard to focus. The dark hovering shapes became people. Those people turned into Ashlen, Callum, and Raleigh. I smiled slightly. Their faces grew more concerned.

Callum had me in his strong warm arms, "Sloane, you okay?" His eyes were anxious for my answer.

I patted his cheek, "Callum."

"That is going to be a no," he started to lift me up more, but I pushed him off.

"I'm fine, okay? Just let me be for a minute." My head was beginning to clear. I pressed my hand to my forehead. Callum backed up a little, but not much. His hands still rested on my arms.

"Cal, I need some more room."

Callum's eyebrows rose slightly, and the corners of his mouth tugged, but he scooted back some more.

I was sitting outside the opening of the tombs on the grass. The sun was about to peek out for its morning tease, so we hadn't been down there for long, maybe three hours. The world felt tilted. I leaned my head back with my eyes shut, letting my face soak up the sun's meager rays. It was gone before I knew it.

"Okay, Sloane, what happened for the umpteenth time?" Callum kneeled on the ground in front of me.

"Long story short, I met my grandfather in a metaphysical kind of way, and he told me how I can get Willow."

"Well, that's great. How do we get her?" Ashlen asked.

I looked around and spotted the sword lying a few feet away. I pointed to it, "With that and my necklace." I noticed my arm where the red line ran down from my shoulder and curved slightly to the inside of my arm near my elbow. It was a smooth, clean red line that was slowly turning to pink like my hand had.

Raleigh picked the sword up. She examined across the sword, inspecting it, "How will this sword help us to find the real one?" She walked back toward us.

"He said that this sword would release Willow, and Artemis will help us find the real sword."

"Release from what I wonder." Callum looked over at me.

I lifted one shoulder in a shrug, "He said it would be challenging and that the task would only be for someone that is worthy, so let's hope that I am."

I held out my hand toward Raleigh, "Here, let me see."

She handed me the sword hilt first. The metal gleamed in the sunlight; it was clean and untarnished. I ran my hand over the cool smooth blade. It vibrated slightly in my hands.

"Oh, wow, it just shook in my hands." I looked up at them.

"Here, let me look at it," Callum moved closer to take the sword. "It didn't do anything with me."

"Maybe it's like Artemis, and it only answers to me."

He looked back at the sword, pulling it closer to his face, apparently to get a better look at it. His eyes roamed over the surface of the blade, trying to find some sort of sign or scribble. "I wonder if there might be any clues hidden in this blade. Maybe heat or cold would bring out some pattern that we could decipher."

"You think something needs to be added?" I leaned over and studied the sword, thinking.

"Well, he told you that it would tell us how to release her, so I think that there would be some sign or inscription on the sword somewhere that we could see. Of course, you might need to be near the real Willow for some kind of sign to become more apparent."

I looked at Ashlen and Raleigh's faces, trying to come up with something. My eyes landed on my right hand. The pink line across my palm began to fade.

"What exactly did he say?" Callum asked.

Could it be that easy? Or really that painful? I smiled. My grandfather would be that nasty to come up with something like this. Without further thought, I took the sword from Callum and swiftly ran the blade across my palm. My brain registered the pain efficiently. The others around me yelled, asking me what I was doing, and if I was crazy. Someone, I think Callum, tried to pull the sword from me, but I moved away from him.

My blood ran slowly down the edge of the blade, falling toward the hilt. As the blood swam along the hilt, the sword exuded a white light, and the blade burst into a blue-white flame that licked up to the tip of the sword. I held the sword out in front of me. Designs suddenly illuminated. The fire died slowly and cooled instantly, but it still hummed slightly in my hands. The designs that I could now see etched into the sword were a sterling blue hue, which started at the hilt and traveled down the length of the sword, curving across the blade.

22

Sloane

WE TRAVELED to the front of the main building and stood near the front door. Callum and I waited on the girls, who had run upstairs to grab some supplies. Callum held the fake Willow, inspecting the designs etched into the metal.

"Well, what do you think that means?" I watched him as he looked over the blade.

Callum looked over at me, "I'm not sure. There are no definite patterns or any kind of language hiding in the designs, so your guess is as good as mine." I saw him try not to smile, which he covered up by studying the sword very carefully. He kept turning it every which way so he could get a better angle. The mystery excited him.

He held the sword out to me, being careful not to let the edge of the blade get too close to me, "Here you go."

The moment my flesh touched the cold metal, it shivered in my palm and a faint humming noise emanated from it. This sword spooked me a little, but no way was I admitting that to Callum.

"I know you're anxious, but there's not much else we can do to prepare for something like this." Callum was studying my face, trying to gauge my emotions.

The corners of my mouth lifted faintly, "You're right. I just like to have my plans in order, even though the whole time I've been here, I haven't been able to rely on my planning." I shook my head out of wonder; it was hard to get out of a routine even if your whole world had been knocked off its axis.

I looked back at the main building.

"Where are those girls?" I muttered to myself.

Callum coughed, "Uh, Sloane?"

I turned back to look at him, "Yeah?"

He reached up and ran his hand through his dark hair. It almost appeared as if his neck was turning red, "I've been meaning to ask you something."

An eyebrow arched, "Yeah?"

A loud racket erupted from the main building. The girls had pushed through the doors with bags hanging from their backs and off their shoulders. They were arguing, and I saw what I assumed was the reason for their disagreement, walking behind them was Harris. He had a huge shit-eating grin on his face. He also had a large bulging bag strapped across his back.

"Alright, people, let's get going. We got us some relics to go get." Harris came up to me and slapped my back a little too hard, making me have to take a couple of steps to steady myself.

"Sorry, we were trying to get out without anyone seeing us, but Harris was camped outside our door," Ashlen replied in an apologetic tone. She stepped closer to me, "You know I can't tell him no."

I laughed, "Ashlen, it's okay, I love Harris. He can come. It wouldn't be the same without him."

Raleigh stood off to the side with her arms crossed over her chest, "Harris, you better keep your stories and little country remarks to yourself."

"Who me?" He winked at her and wrapped an arm around her shoulders. Raleigh slipped out from under his arm and rolled her eyes.

"And don't touch me," she sauntered over to me. Raleigh held out a long piece of cloth for my hand. I took it and wrapped it carefully around the new gash. Raleigh tied the material ends securely. I closed my fist, trying not to let the pain show on my face. Great, why did I cut my dominant hand?

People passed us as we walked along the road—the guards stationed heavily at the front gate. One of the men called out to us. Callum greeted him and spoke with him for a minute. We waited right outside the gate. Not that many people were leaving the city, most were entering. Callum slapped the guy on the back with a big smile on his face and turned back toward us. He really kept surprising me.

"What's that look for?" he asked.

I blinked and shook my head, "You just keep me thinking is all." I gestured to the guard, "What did he say?"

Callum glanced behind him, "He was asking where we were going."

"What did you say?"

He smiled, "I said we were going on an adventure to find a magical sword and to destroy the Nightlins." His eyes were gauging my reaction.

I shoved him, not too hard but enough to make him back up a couple of steps. He laughed. I continued along the stone wall toward the stream that ran through the city. Raleigh and Ashlen walked on either side of me. Harris was directly behind the three of us. Callum was still chuckling behind us as his boots crunched on the rocks. The fake Willow was slung across my back and tied safely with a strip of leather.

Along the wall, were numbers, marking each portal.

"We need number three to take us to the river." Callum walked up to the wall and pounded on number three, three times. The portal shimmered as it activated. "Alright, who's first?"

Raleigh said, "Me." And without hesitation, she stepped through the portal.

Callum watched as I took my spot in front of the shimmering wall. One big deep breath in, and I stepped through.

Cold air rushed through me, and my stomach flipped. I barely had time to think to brace myself before my feet hit the ground.

Raleigh grabbed me from the spot before Ashlen smacked into me. Next, Harris sailed through the opening above us, then Callum, cool as a cucumber.

I gingerly picked up Artemis; the needles were lazily swinging back and forth. I whispered to her, "Artemis," the necklace hummed in answer, "find Willow."

The needles frantically spun around and around. Everyone gathered around me watching the necklace, awaiting its decision. The large needle stopped abruptly, and the smaller one began to slow until it rested, pointing toward the North. The humming quieted a little, but I could still hear it faintly, tickling my ears.

"It's pointing in the same direction as the stream," Callum offered.

"Okay, come on, let's go,"

We walked along the river bank. Harris dropped back and chatted with Callum. I hopped down to stand on the narrow shore. The others jumped down to stand beside me, or in Ashlen's case, slid down. I looked over my shoulder to find Callum's eyes. He pushed between Raleigh and Harris to stand beside me. I watched Artemis as the needles moved to the left, pointing west following the path of the river.

"Onward we go, we are sticking with the river for now." I hitched the bag on my shoulders, trying to shift some of the weight, then followed along the bank. I glanced behind me to check that everyone was following.

Raleigh was right beside me, "Raleigh, have you seen ghosts before?"

Her mouth became a firm line, and she shook her head, "No, not ever." She kept her attention focused ahead.

I grabbed her arm, easing her to a stop and studied her eyes. I took a step toward her, "I wonder."

"What are you doing?" She asked carefully.

Her dark brown eyes were their normal shape and color.

"I thought maybe your eyes had begun to change. But of course, we are out of there, so even if your eyes had changed to black, we wouldn't know." I studied her and smiled, "Next time, I'll stop you and check."

She laughed, "Okay, deal."

———

WE KEPT A STEADY PACE. Eventually, we had to travel above the river because the bank became too narrow for all of us. The moonlight reflected off the water. Callum acted as a guard, following behind. Raleigh was behind me, followed by Ashlen then Harris.

Harris whistled some tune I couldn't place until Raleigh yelled at him, "Harris, would you shut the fuck up! We do not want to hear that godforsaken song. Celine Dion's, *My Heart Will Go On,* has been overplayed without having you whistle it too."

I couldn't help but giggle, which earned me a punch in the arm.

We found a large tree that was probably six feet in diameter and had stood close to fifty feet tall; it had fallen over alongside the river, like some sleeping giant. We decided to make camp beside it, thinking it would act as some kind of protector. We made a small fire so we could cook some food and get warm, but then we doused it for fear of any kind of creature lurking.

I rolled out my sleeping pad, making sure my back was to the tree. Everyone followed suit, except for Callum and Harris, who both decided they would take turns watching over us. Forever our personal guardians.

For some reason, I fell asleep pretty quickly and dreamed. My dreams began with me running through the forest, hunting for something. Although I couldn't remember what it was, I had lost. I stepped into a stream and instantly fell through landing into another dream. In this one, I was with Callum, Ashlen, Harris, and Raleigh. We were out camping, and somehow, we are back in the Norm, just camping in your run of the mill forests. We seemed happy and carefree. Harris had us all laughing hysterically. Callum stretched out on the ground, his face smooth with no lines of worry or stress. He barely resembled the Callum I knew. Ashlen propped against Harris's legs. Her head tilted back so she could watch him. Raleigh laughed and threw peanuts into the air then caught them in her awaiting mouth as they came back down.

It was pitch black, but I felt safe, then the screaming started, and we stopped to look around. Everyone transitioned back to their protective and watchful stances as if we had never left the Night Realm. We stood with our backs to the fire in a tight circle and waited.

Without warning, they dropped from the trees within a matter of seconds.

We tried to fight back, but they were too fast. The monsters' long, sharp claws tore through our skin like it was made of tissue paper. Callum was throwing fireballs at them, while Harris tried to shoot them with arrows. Raleigh used her sword to hack through their limbs. Black blood coated her face and arms. Her white teeth gleamed when she smiled. I tried to use my sword, but the animals kept tearing at me. The bones of my arms peeked through the shredded skin.

I woke up with a hand over my mouth and whispering in my ear.

"Sloane, Sloane, wake up. It's a dream, Sloane. Wake up." His voice tickled my ear and made the hairs on my neck stand up.

"Are you awake?"

I nodded.

"Stay quiet. I heard something." Callum took his hand from my mouth and sat back on his heels. He watched the sky like he was listening to something I couldn't hear. I strained my hearing as much as I could, but the woods had fallen deathly quiet, which made me feel uneasy.

Callum and I were the only ones awake. The fire was completely out I could barely see the embers twinkling in the ash, which meant we had been sleeping for several hours at least. The moon was shining brightly, but it was nearing its descent. The night was a tad chilly, enough to make me pull my blanket up to my chin and make my breath appear faintly in the air before me.

Callum slowly stood and pulled his sword from the sheath. I

reached behind me to grab mine. I positioned myself beside him and unsheathed my sword. The metal glowed a faint blue. I immediately turned to Callum for guidance, but he only nodded and motioned for me to stay quiet. He pointed to the other sleeping bodies and gestured for me to wake them. I very slowly and carefully tiptoed over to Ashlen and knelt beside her. I pushed her gently and put my hand over her lips before she could speak. She noticed my sword's blue glow. She understood instantly. She woke Harris, and then I roused Raleigh. Our placement around the fire reminded me of my dream from a few minutes before. We stood in a circle with our backs to each other, all straining to listen.

Callum was the only one who had *super* hearing, so I mostly kept my eyes on him. My sword slowly grew darker, and my heart resumed its natural pace.

"What did you hear?" Ashlen turned to us.

Callum replied, "They got pretty close. I was certain they had heard us or at least smelled us, but I guess not." He smiled softly.

A loud shrieking erupted through the night, and I could hear what sounded like thousands of wings beating the air. My sword lit up like a beacon, and before anyone could react. A large Nightlin dropped down from one of the treetops. His vast wings berated the ground, and his sharp talons latched onto Ashlen's shoulder. They were gone in the blink of an eye. Ashlen's screams echoed as it carried her through the trees. I stood motionless. I couldn't believe it. Harris took off at a charge through the forest. I could hear him yelling all the way. Callum was throwing things into a bag in a frenzied panic. I looked around me in slow motion.

To my left, Raleigh scrambled around our campsite, trying to pick things up. She dashed up to me and slapped me across the face. Her eyes were solid black. She looked furious and scared.

"SNAP OUT OF IT!!" she whipped around and darted toward her bag, grabbing it and slinging it across her shoulders; she disappeared through the dark forest.

"Sloane? You okay?" Callum had his hand on my shoulder and was shaking me slightly.

The sting from her hand hitting my face reverberated through my head like my brain was knocking back and forth against my skull. I gently rubbed my cheek to make sure it was still there.

I nodded solemnly.

"Come on." He spun on his heel and sprinted through the trees.

My bag rested by my feet. I scooped it up and ran after them. Twigs snapped, and heavy footfalls crashed through the underbrush, every now and then Harris yelled Ashlen's name. My eyes, I assumed, were solid black as well, because their night sensitivity was heightened. I could see every leaf on all the trees and on the ground. I leapt over every obstacle and dodged every low lying limb.

Callum yelled for Harris to stop.

Two figures stood in the middle of an open field. Callum was running a slight distance in front of me. I slowed as we neared the other two. Harris paced back and forth with his fists clenched at his sides. Raleigh stood near him. She kept scanning the area.

"Guys, we need to use Sloane's necklace to find her. We won't have any luck finding her just running through the woods yelling her name." Callum grabbed Harris's arm, making him stop. "Are you listening to me?"

Harris glanced at Callum, his jaw tightened. He nodded once. Callum dropped his grip on Harris. His eyes had changed back to their normal green color.

"Sloane."

I nodded, trying to collect my thoughts and feelings and trying not to panic.

"Okay."

I picked up my necklace and held it in my hand, "Artemis, we need your help to find Ashlen."

The needles swung back and forth, then, around and around in a blur. They stopped. The needles pointed to the North West. The Nightlin Mountain sat in the North blocking out part of the sky.

"Let's head that way." Callum tightened his bag's straps around his shoulders and torso then led us through the trees.

Harris fell behind us but kept within a safe distance. Raleigh marched in front of him, only a short distance away. I trudged behind Callum.

"Callum, why would they take Ashlen?"

He glanced back at me, his tone was angry, and he seemed to bite each word off when he spoke, "I'm not sure. We never are sure what their motives are for anything they do. I'm not even sure they can think constructive thoughts."

We continued moving in silence for a few moments.

When he spoke again, it was so softly I had to strain to hear him, "We will get her back. And if it's up to me, we will destroy every last one of them." He turned back to me, "We will get her back. I promise Sloane."

His eyes bored into mine, daring me to say no.

"I know we will." I squeezed his arm.

He nodded and kept on.

I HAD to stop several times and ask Artemis for directions. The Nightlins seemed to be trying to lose us; little did they know that wasn't going to happen. The top of the moon was sliding past the horizon, and the sun was on its way up when we were finally closing in on them. They had to find shelter fast, so we were gaining.

Harris was out in front this time. He charged ahead, slashing through limbs and tall stalks of grass. Raleigh jogged behind him. Somehow, I had fallen to the rear of the group.

"Harris, slow it down. We don't want them to hear us coming at them." Callum stated.

Harris looked at Callum briefly. I had never seen him so serious or angry before. He definitely was not the Harris I had come to love as my friend. Raleigh had her sword out, ready to go.

We were in a large open field. Tips of the tall yellow grass brushed the tops of my shoulders. The sky was a light gray, where the sun was coming up, a tinge of orange was painting the sky with tiny brushstrokes. The sun was just about to break over the top of the trees. I knew the Nightlins didn't have much longer.

We made it to the edge of the woods with no more hints of noises or broken twigs. The large trees loomed over us. What made me the most nervous was how quiet everything had settled. No insects sang in the morning, and birds didn't flutter from limb to limb, in the midst of catching their morning breakfast. The four of us stood like statues at the edge, waiting and listening. Callum was the first to hear something.

He motioned with his hand to follow him.

Walking at a slow pace, we entered the woods. We were light on our feet, so as not to crunch any leaves or disturb any animals.

Callum picked up his pace. Even his feet barely seemed to touch the ground. We wove in and out of the trees, only using Callum as our guide. He came to an abrupt stop and motioned for us to stay still. He disappeared behind a tree without a sound. We stood for a few minutes, not risking a sound. I could barely breathe. Harris stood rigidly; every muscle in his body was tense and ready to spring into action. Raleigh was bouncing on her toes, getting ready to move. I seemed to be the only one who didn't want to go into a fight against the Nightlins. I tightened my grip around the hilt of my sword.

Callum reappeared, and air whooshed into my lungs again. He knelt down before us. We gathered around him.

"Here's the deal. They're underground. There are two entrances, although one is very small." He looked at me.

"Small enough for girls to fit through?" I sarcastically asked, knowing the answer.

He nodded grimly.

Raleigh unsheathed her sword and smiled fiercely; her white teeth a stark contrast.

"Tell me where."

Callum knelt on the ground and drew a rough map of where the hole would be.

"From what I could tell, you'll have to crawl with your weapons sheathed, then when you get out of the tunnel, you will have enough room to attack. I'm not sure how far in the tunnel goes, so you may very well be at risk of dumping out into their main cavern. I suggest you wait at the end of your tunnel until you hear us come through on the other side, then you can join us."

I nodded, "Sounds reasonable." I waited on Raleigh for her acceptance.

She smiled, "Let's get on with it."

"We can take 'em," Harris replied matter-of-factly.

Callum nodded, "I didn't see her, but I saw her bag in a pile of things. We can't just go in there with guns blazing. We need a thought-out plan. I'm not about to risk losing any more of you."

Harris was tense and ready for action. Raleigh had her war face on ready to go. My eyes met Callum's, who was watching me. He raised an eyebrow. So?

I took a deep breath, "Give us a few minutes to get around to our position."

Callum nodded, "Be careful. I'll make sure to get Ashlen out."

I nodded, sure of him and his words.

Callum motioned for us to follow. We traveled in line with one another, making sure to be as silent as we possibly could be. He led us through some tightly grown trees; their branches were woven together, making a kind of canopy above us, which blocked out most of the light. I peered around Harris to see a large fallen tree. The roots were spread out in every direction like they were searching for something. Where the roots had previously resided, there was a large gaping black hole in the ground, tall and wide enough for the boys to go through somewhat comfortably.

It was very shaded around the tree. I could see why the Nightlins had chosen it for refuge. I had my sword grasped in both hands, ready to swing just in case the creatures came out.

Callum pointed to the left of the gaping hole, telling us which way Raleigh and I were to take.

I gestured to Raleigh, "Come on, girl."

She smiled her megawatt smile, and we moved off in the direction Callum had indicated.

We weaved through the trees, traveling maybe a hundred yards or so. We came to two trees that were large at their base, but as the trees grew upwards, the boughs and branches intertwined, making an arch. The ground rose slightly from the roots of the trees, and I could just make out a small darkened hole.

Callum had been right. There was no way we could have our weapons out or even be able to pull them out if the beasts came after us. I looked over at Raleigh, gauging her expression. Her eyes were narrowed, examining the surroundings. She frowned then shrugged at me as if to say, oh well, let's go.

I whispered, "I'll go first."

"Move fast. I want some action."

I rolled my eyes and moved toward the black hole.

Peering inside, I could see absolutely nothing. I pushed the branches and leaves out of the way. I tightened the straps that kept my weapons in place then placed my arms inside. I carefully inched myself into the blackness, trying to calm my nerves and the part of me that was afraid of the unknown and tight spaces. I took a shallow breath and pulled myself in deeper. Raleigh felt the need to push my feet a little, which didn't sit that well with me, so I kicked back at her. She didn't try that again.

The hole was so narrow it was hard to get my knees up under me to help with my progression, so I was mostly using my arms, which might harm me later when I was going to have to wield my sword, but I pushed on, vowing to do more arm and shoulder exercises when this was over.

The darkness swallowed me whole, making it hard for any of my senses to function. My nose only smelled musty dirt and old water. My hearing wasn't as good as Callum's, so I had to strain to hear anything at all, besides mine and Raleigh's huffing.

The change in the air is what first made me aware that we were at our destination. The second was the stench of the Nightlin bodies. I couldn't see them at all, because it was completely dark, but for the moment their smell hit my nose. My Watcher senses took over. My hands wrapped around the edge of the hole, ready to push myself out with as much force as I could muster. I felt Raleigh tense behind me. She had moved up as close as she could beside me.

A few minutes passed of intense, uninterrupted silence.

The first thing to break the blackness was Callum's wand of light, and then total chaos ensued. I didn't have to think twice to leap down into the cavern. All hell had broken loose.

Pulling my sword from its scabbard, the white light erupted, nearly blinding me, but it did stun some of the Nightlins that were about to attack us. They reared back, and it gave us the opportunity to slash across their abdomens and lop their heads off. Black liquid sprayed us. A Nightlin ran toward me. His claws were outstretched, ready to slice. I swiftly swung my sword. The creature's claws fell to the ground. It screamed a piercing wail, and I finished him off, ending his misery. Raleigh and I swung around and met the next onslaught of demons. We hacked and chopped with every bit of energy we had until nothing was left.

My sword hung loosely at my side. We were both breathing heavily, which was hard to do with the stench of the creatures' death surrounding us.

Black guts and blood anointed the dirt walls and floor. My two men were in the middle of the melee, all but painted black with blood and dirt. They looked haggard and ready to pass out. My sword blazed white casting eerie shadows on the cave walls. As the last Nightlin fell, my sword's light dimmed, becoming an eerie glow within the depth of the black hole.

Black bodies and limbs covered the cavern floor.

"Spread out. She's got to be in here somewhere."

I started lifting some of the dead bodies trying to see if Ashlen might be under them. Callum's light bobbed through the darkness and swept the cavern. My sword was getting darker and darker by the second. I grew frantic. Harris called out to her. He was in a frenzy, pushing the creatures out of the way or nearly tossing them to the side.

Callum jerked up, saying, "Wait, I hear something. Be quiet."

Instantly, we stilled. I strained my hearing, trying to hear anything at all except the beat of my own heart.

"Over there!" Callum leapt over the creatures and ran to the farthest corner from me. When I made it to where they were, I could see a body wrapped up in dirty rags.

It was Ashlen. She was lifeless.

What was left of a Nightlin laid beside her, his torso was all that remained of him. It stretched toward her with its claws scraping the dirt floor. Callum raised his sword and finished the beast off. The creature's head rolled along the cave wall.

Harris pushed Callum out of the way and scooped Ashlen up in his arms. He made his way to the tunnel and walked out. We followed quickly. He gently laid her down on the damp ground outside. I knelt beside her and brushed the dirt and leaves away from her face. Harris tore the rags from her body and wadded them up. He threw the rags back into the cave.

When he turned back to Ashlen, I had never seen someone with so much anguish and heartache on their face. He gently took her hand in both of his, enclosing it between his own. He bowed his head over her and kissed her knuckles.

"Ashlen, wake up. Baby, please wake up for me. Please, I beg you." Harris whispered over and over.

I looked back at her face. She was so pale. Her pretty skin had scratches along her jaw and cheeks. Her bottom lip had been sliced open. Blood had dried along her chin. I gently rubbed the blood and dirt off. Raleigh sank to the ground beside me. She took Ashlen's other hand between hers. A sob broke from Harris, and he lifted Ashlen back into his lap and laid her head against his chest. He squeezed her tightly.

"Ughh, you're hurting me."

Harris froze, and his eyes roamed over Ashlen's face. Her eyes fluttered open lazily, and she peered up at him. A huge smile broke across his face, and he hugged her again.

"Hurts." She feebly pushed him away.

Harris laughed and released her gently to the ground, "I'm sorry. I'm so happy you're okay." He laughed again from relief. He took her hand in his and kissed her palm.

She smiled tenderly and patted his head, combing her fingers through his hair. "I'm glad I am too. Thank you for rescuing me."

She looked at all of us, "You all look horrible like something chewed you up and shat you out." She shuddered, "Stop staring at me; it's eerie having those black eyes stare at you, especially your white eyes, Sloane."

24

Sloane

"I STILL CAN'T BELIEVE they took me." Ashlen kept repeating.

"Do you remember anything at all?" Raleigh asked.

She frowned for a moment, trying to recall, "I honestly don't. I remember lots of pain and that horrible smell of theirs. They kind of hit me a few times, so I passed out several times." She glanced at Harris, whose jaw was getting so tight I thought he might crack some teeth.

I lightly squeezed her arm, "I'm so thankful we found you. Without everyone, I'm not sure we would have."

She gestured to the boys, "Thank you, guys."

Harris smiled, and Callum grunted in reply.

Raleigh hit my arm, "We would have found her."

I rubbed my arm, where she had hit me, "I'm sure, but it would have taken us longer."

Raleigh narrowed her eyes at me but dropped the subject.

We started out at a slow pace, to give Ashlen plenty of time. We would need to find a spot to make camp within the next hour. Birds chirped, and little animals scurried through the treetops or underbrush, as we disturbed their habitats. The girls were quiet while we walked. Harris was the only one that I could really hear, but that wasn't a surprise. He kept a short distance from Ashlen, making sure he was only a few steps away from her.

Callum and Harris seemed to be in some kind of interesting conversation.

There was no telling what he and Harris were discussing. He looked up quickly when he realized I was speaking to him.

"We probably won't find it today, will we?" I was watching the ground as I spoke, trying to make sure I didn't trip over any roots or rocks. I glanced over my shoulder at him.

He shrugged and looked up at the moon, "You're probably right."

The moonlight filtered through the trees, lighting up patches of grass and sparkling off the water. A lazy breeze blew, moving the limbs back and forth like the trees were dancing to an unheard tune. The river was quiet as it moved over the sands and rocks. The only sounds I could hear were made from our shoes crunching on twigs, leaves, and pebbles. Harris also seemed to not want to disrupt the quiet. Ashlen had dropped back at some point to be beside him. Callum allowed them a little room and was now a few steps behind them. He seemed lost in thought.

It was at moments like this when all you can do is think, that my thoughts turned to my mother, wondering what she was doing or saying, wondering if she's okay. Will I see her again? I have to erase that question from my mind.

"What are you thinking about?"

I glanced over at Raleigh. She stared at me with curiosity.

"My mom," I smiled slightly at her.

She nodded, "Yeah, I was thinking about my family too. It's kind of crazy to think that here we are in this world, while their lives are still going on in another."

I nodded and stopped so I could climb over a fallen tree. The top had fallen into the water. The roots disappeared through the foliage. It was massive. The circumference was bigger than me by maybe a couple of feet. I used the limbs to help hoist myself up. I threw my legs over the rough bark and pulled and pushed till I was sitting straight. The trees surrounding us seemed to lean toward the fallen mass as if trying to help it up again.

I looked down at the group.

"We probably could have just walked around," Callum said with way too much pizzazz.

I decided not to give him satisfaction by answering.

I sat on top of the tree trunk, preparing myself to slide off the other side.

"Yeah, I think we should be able to go home at some point. I mean, I don't see why not." I pushed off and slid to the ground about seven feet below. I landed on my feet, but my knees and hands hit the ground too. I stood up and brushed the dirt from my hands. A snake slid out from underneath the fallen tree toward me. I did what any other girl would have done, I screamed.

I jumped up and down and ran to the edge of the bank. The snake followed me. I might have screamed again.

Raleigh leapt from the top of the trunk, rolling on the ground and springing up with her sword drawn. Callum somehow leapt right over the whole tree. He landed a few feet from me and grabbed me before I could fall into the river. The snake slipped over the edge of the bank and plopped into the water.

I did a little dance trying to shake off the snake jitters, "Ugh, gross, gross, gross." Callum laughed at me, while Raleigh stood to the side with her sword still in her hand and a huge smile. Harris had a surprised and confused look on his face. Ashlen was still trying to climb over the tree. Callum couldn't seem to stop laughing. He was bent over with both hands on his knees.

"You should have seen the look on your face." It felt weird to see Callum showing so much emotion, even stranger to see him laugh so hard that he could barely breathe.

I straightened my back and shoulders, righteously, "It's not that funny." My hands clenched at my sides. I narrowed my eyes and folded my arms across my chest. "Callum."

He still laughed at me. I slowly smiled. Soon, all of us were laughing. Tears ran down my cheeks, and my face began to hurt.

Something moved across my foot. I looked down, wiping tears from my eyes. Another snake slid across my foot. I immediately stopped breathing, laughing, and moving. Everyone registered that I had stopped all movement. Callum became quiet and watched the snake that had slid off my foot and was making his way toward the river. The fallen tree had more snakes slithering out from underneath the bark.

"Look over there, that might be something." Callum pointed to the base of the tree, where a small hill rose from behind it.

"A hole?" I glared at the snakes. There seemed to be more of them appearing out of nowhere.

Callum nodded. He studied the fallen tree. "They seem to be traveling from the roots." As he spoke, I noticed a bright green snake, about a foot long, moving along the tree trunk.

We moved toward the roots, which were withered and splayed outward like they were stretching to touch the sky. The base of the tree had been planted up against a small hill. As I studied the area, I could see where large rocks had been placed against the hillside forming an archway. Since the tree had fallen, the archway had crumbled, making the hole larger. Snakes were streaming out of the tunnel.

My insides instantly recoiled and screamed. We immediately backed away from the edge. The snakes were clamoring over each other to get out.

I tried to peer past the snakes to see inside the deep black nothingness. There seemed to be no way through.

Callum made a faint noise and scratched his head, "I think we're supposed to go in there." He looked at each of us.

"Ha, no way, Jose," Ashlen replied. She took several more steps away from the snake-filled hole.

Raleigh shook her head, making her hair hit her face.

Harris took a step forward and bent to get a better look. "Well, if those snakes don't bite, then I'm up for adventurin' down there." He winked.

My insides were literally squirming. What am I going to do? I stared at the snakes. I watched Callum gauge his reaction, "I don't know if I can go down there."

His mouth lifted slightly at the side. He took a step toward me and patted my arm, "Sure you can. I believe in you."

I ran a hand through my hair. Choices, choices. I narrowed my eyes at Callum. He raised his hands like he was surrendering.

"Hey, I'm just trying to help."

"I know," I ground the words out of my clenched teeth. "I hate snakes."

Callum walked over to the roots and pulled a long rope out of his backpack. He tied one end around a knotted root. He uncoiled the rope and threw the other end down the black hole. Snakes moved around the rope, making it hard to distinguish the rope from the snakes. My head argued with me again.

"I'll go down first, and I'll yell when I make it to the bottom to let you know if it's okay," Callum studied me for a moment. When I didn't argue, he nodded and faced the tree.

Callum wrapped part of the rope around his arm once, pushed some snakes out of the way so he could place his feet, and slowly eased his way into the hole. Amazingly, the snakes moved around his feet like he was part of the earth. He dug in his back pocket and pulled out the mysterious stick. I saw him whisper to it, and then the stick lit up with the same bright light. He disappeared. I could barely see the light shining because of all the snakes. We were silent the entire time he descended. My ears were straining to hear him, and I bit my nails to calm my nerves. The rope grew taut and then slacked.

"Hey! It's okay, climb down!" Callum's voice echoed as it passed through the hole.

I looked around at everyone, who, in turn, looked at me.

"Harris?"

Harris's eyebrows rose. "Umm, sure, okay," he took a step toward the hole.

"Sloane! Get down here!" Callum bellowed.

"Why do I have to go next?" I yelled back.

"Just come on!"

I took a deep breath, pulling the air in through my nose and blowing out through my mouth. I very slowly turned toward the hole. I tentatively wrapped my right hand around the rope and then my left hand. The fibers of the rope jabbed into my skin. Snakes slid over my boots. I internally screamed, and I may have whimpered out loud. I clenched my teeth to keep from screaming audibly. I peered into the dark hole.

"Callum?" I asked unsurely.

"Sloane, just get down here already!"

I squeezed my eyes shut and excruciatingly lowered myself one step at a time. Surprisingly, I didn't step on any snakes. They seemed to know where my feet were going to fall and would move right before my boot hit the ground. My friends' faces peered over the rim of the hole, watching my descent. The snakes continuously glided up the dirt to escape. I was no longer touched by the moonlight, the darkness settled around me, and the smell of earth filled my senses. I tried to see what was around me, but it was completely dark. The tunnel began to level out so that I was walking upright.

I peeked behind me. I could see a pinprick of white light. I hoped it belonged to Callum. The tunnel turned sharply and opened up into a massive cavern. My mouth fell open. Light poured into the middle of the cave. Water was streaming in through the opening, falling into a bright blue-green pool of water. The moonlight reflected from the underground pool, making the light dance on the dirt walls. Large stalagmites and stalactites were littered around the cavern. Callum was standing next to the pool. The light moved across his skin. He smiled at me.

"I told you it wasn't bad."

"I know... where are the snakes?"

He gestured for me to come closer, "Over here."

I walked to him. As I drew closer, I noticed the water was moving. Snakes were swimming, hundreds of them. I looked up at the opening and noticed that water wasn't the only thing falling into the pool. Snakes were falling too. I took a few steps back. Callum grabbed my hand and pulled me up to the edge of the water.

"That's disgusting."

"It's not that bad," his eyes laughed at me.

I glared at him.

"You know Indiana Jones was terrified of snakes." I raised an eyebrow.

"Surely, you aren't comparing yourself to Indiana Jones?" he raised one of his eyebrows.

My eyes narrowed even more.

"Hey, don't start this whole being mad at me thing again. I haven't done anything yet."

I laughed, "The keyword is yet." He smiled.

Callum's fingers slid through mine, but he carefully slid his arm around my waist, pulling me in closer to him and pinning my arm against my back. He squeezed me against his side. I looked up at him. He had his eyes locked onto the pool, but I saw his jaw clench. The light reflecting from the pool highlighted his features and made the angles of his face harder, more striking.

His gaze shifted to mine, and he studied my face. Strands of his hair covered his eyes, making me want to brush them away. The way he looked at me like he was really seeing me for the first time made my stomach flutter. I swallowed hard. I couldn't look away, and I didn't want to.

His other hand moved up toward my face, and he glided his fingers along my jaw. His eyes followed the movement of his hand, and then I knew he was studying my mouth. My heart was in my throat, and my breaths came out shallow and quick, and at the same time, I don't think I was breathing at all.

"Sloane?" he barely whispered. His eyes bore into mine, asking me the same question. His thumb brushed across my bottom lip. He leaned in closer to me.

"Whoa! This wasn't what I was expecting." Harris stumbled toward us, "this place is real purdy." He was in complete awe, his mouth hanging open.

Callum dropped his arm from around me and took a step back. I caught myself before I stepped toward him. His attention again locked onto the snake-filled pool. I tried not to burn Harris with my eyes, turning my attention back to the snakes. I placed my hands on my hips because my hands had started to shake, and tried not to think of snakes running over my toes or the way Callum had looked at me. I glanced at him, but his expression was bland and almost bored. His mask once again locked back into place.

"Whoa," Ashlen stepped out from the tunnel. The water reflected in her eyes. "This is amazing."

Raleigh tripped out of the tunnel. She caught herself against a stalagmite.

"Awesome," Raleigh stared wide-eyed around the cavern. "Where are we?"

Callum replied, "I think we are directly underneath the riverbed."

The moonlight shining off the water rippled across the cave walls, making the walls look as if they undulated.

"So, have you asked your necklace where to next?" Ashlen came to stand beside me, but her eyes were on our beautiful surroundings.

I picked up Artemis, "No, not yet."

"Well, hop to it. We haven't got all day."

I smiled and shook my head at her, but I lifted the necklace to my mouth and breathed, "Artemis, take us to Willow."

The large needle began to vibrate and started spinning frantically, then it stopped just as quickly, pointing to the corner of the cave.

I pointed to the dark corner, "She says over there."

Everyone moved toward the corner and tried pushing on the walls.

"Nothin' is workin'," Harris heaved with all of his strength. Sweat accumulated on his upper lip. His hair stuck to the sides of his face.

Raleigh was kneeling on the ground, running her hands along the base of the wall. Callum was on the other side of Harris pushing and testing the walls, much like Harris, with the same effect.

"This isn't working..." Ashlen stopped and folded her arms across her chest. "We aren't getting anywhere."

"I don't think you're looking in the right spot," said a throaty voice.

Ashlen squealed and jumped five feet away from the dark space where she had stopped. We spun to the sound of the voice. I stared hard at the dark corner, trying to see a form. A very tall, robust man stepped out of the shadows. He was dressed in a dark blue button-down shirt, brown pants, and heavy-duty hiking boots laced halfway up his calves. His dark brown hair fell past his shoulders, falling in large waves; gray streaked his hair around his face. A large bushy beard fell nearly to the middle of his chest. But it was his eyes that captured my attention first. They were black as the night sky with no stars. He seemed to look through us.

"What can I do for you?" he spoke again.

No one said a word just stared. I looked at Callum, who had his mouth open. That was a first for him, and he turned to me. All I could do was shrug. I scrutinized the stranger.

"I'm guessing you don't know how to get out of here since you just appeared out of nowhere?"

The man looked slightly amused by what I could tell by his mouth, twitching, "Follow me." He moved into the darkness and disappeared. "Watch your step."

We collectively looked at each other, measuring the decision to follow.

"I'm not waiting."

I glanced at everyone first then followed the mysterious man. I stepped into the dark corner, having to squeeze past a large stalagmite in the process, and came out on the other side into another larger tunnel. The man stood a few feet away, waiting. He watched me for a moment. Callum appeared right behind me with Ashlen, Harris, and Raleigh bringing up the rear. The man continued on at a slow and deliberate gait, his left foot dragging slightly. We walked for maybe twenty to thirty minutes. The tunnel began to slope upward, which signaled that we were heading to the surface.

"So, sir, how is it that you came to be here?" I asked, somewhat tentatively.

"First of all, my name is Morgan, in no way am I a sir. And I will tell you my story when I'm good and ready." His deep rough voice replied smartly.

Well, he was certainly snippy.

The only light we had to see by was Callum's mysterious little stick. Callum had his fingers wrapped around my upper arm. He constantly bumped into me. I was slightly annoyed and amused about him being so close. I couldn't help but think about that moment in the cavern. I glanced at him, but we were mostly in the dark, so all I could see was the light reflecting off of his eyes.

I heard rather than saw the end of the tunnel. A roaring sound echoed through the darkness. I knew the end was close. We finally saw the light at the end of the tunnel. It opened up into a small cave that sat behind a large waterfall. The water thundered and splashed over the rocks. A cool breeze blew through, bringing with it the smell of clean, freshwater, and mud. I took a deep breath letting the scent coat my lungs; it smelled wonderful.

Morgan sat down at the edge of the cave, staring off into the open; his scraggly hair stood to attention around his head like a halo. Everyone had caution and wonder creased onto their faces. Ashlen gestured me toward him. I walked over to the man and sat with my knees tucked under me. Callum came and sat beside me. Ashlen, Harris, and Raleigh cautiously settled beside us. They still looked pretty wary of our new friend.

The man faced us, "I'm guessing you're part of Charles' family because there's no one else who would be carrying that damn sword across their back."

25

Graham

HE WOKE up lying on his stomach. He kept breathing in the moist smell of dirt. The dripping of water annoyed him. His body felt sore and exhausted like he had run a fifty-mile marathon.

Slowly he rolled over to lie on his back, every muscle and bone protesting as he maneuvered his body. A groan escaped his lips. Rocks jabbed into his back. He hated the feeling of uselessness.

His eyes slowly opened to reveal a cave. He needed to get up and move. He needed to move quickly. It hurt so much. Slowly, he sat up. His arms were laid by his sides, and his head drooped forward. He carefully tucked his legs under him and pushed to a standing position. He braced himself against the cave wall. Mud seeped under his fingernails as he dug his fingers into the wall, trying to keep his balance. His breathing labored, and it wasn't getting easier.

His bag was near the opening of the cave. He staggered toward it and slid down the wall to the floor so he could easily pick it up. He pulled out his shirt and tugged it over his head. He carefully strapped his weapons onto his back, legs, and chest. Slowly, he gained strength as he went through the motions. Strapping the bag back onto his back was the finishing touch.

He leaned against the opening of the cave, trying to ensnare some remnants of energy that might be lying around inside of him. The dark mountain loomed over the cave. The tallest peak stood like a beacon to the right of the opening.

With the pulse of light giving way back to darkness, he pushed away from his crutch by the wall and headed for the tallest peak.

The Dark

THE QUICK BURST of sunlight receded.

He would be free to fly in minutes, free to let the beast go. Tonight, was the night for the Nightlins to take back what rightfully belonged to them.

He stretched his limbs out to the maximum point, the slick black skin pulling tight, feeling the strength pulse through his veins. His wings flexed, and his claws extended. The power was intoxicating, and he wanted more. They had said he would have more power, but now he wanted his power crammed to capacity. He wanted the power to fill him up so much that he thought he might burst.

The night was almost there again. He could taste it on his tongue and breathe it into his lungs. He reveled in the thought of soaring through the air. They will be so surprised. Oh, how he couldn't wait to see their faces.

He walked to the window and yanked the sheets away. Remnants of light seeped through the cracked shutters the light hit part of his arm, he hissed and instinctively moved away from the sun streaming in. He studied his arm to see that some of the black skin now had blisters. He made a low animalistic noise. Leaning against the wall, he waited patiently for those pesky sun rays to disappear completely. The past twenty years had taught him well at being patient.

26

OUTSIDE, the cave entrance was a small pond. Where the water was so clear that, even in the dark, I could see the bottom. Around the pond were thin, delicate trees. Large boulders were littered across the grass and next to the water. Moss and algae grew along the entrance of the cave. Green ferns and vines dangled off the edge of the waterfall and grew from cracks in the rocks.

The mountainside began where the pond ended. The side of the mountain traveled straight up about a hundred feet; there was no way to climb up it without some rigging and ropes. The rock face was completely smooth. The smoothness continued on either side, traveling off into the distance for five hundred yards or more. At the top, trees were leaning over, and the mountain kept sloping upward, blocking out part of the sky.

"So, are you a Realmer like us?" I asked.

We were seated around a small crackling fire mostly made up of small, wiry twigs that were burning up pretty quickly.

The man nodded, one long leg propped up with his elbow sitting on his knee, "Yes, when things began to go to pot, I decided to leave Kingston. Things changed so much that it was time to go. There was so much conflict between everyone. I wasn't going to be part of it." He tilted his head, as if thinking, "I was one of Charles's generals and a trusted friend. Well, as good of a friend as he could have. He wasn't the nicest man."

I nodded, "Yeah, I know. I read about him."

Morgan leaned back with his legs stretched out in front of him, resting his elbows behind him. "Charles told me that he was going to entrust me with the secret of Willow, but I never really believed him. I've tried to find it. Maybe you will have better luck than me." He gazed outside the cave, "We will have to wait till daylight though. The light will show you the way."

We sat in silence for a few minutes. Callum's body radiated heat next to mine. His tension was almost palpable. He didn't trust Morgan. I looked around at everyone, "So you've been out here all this time?"

He lifted a shoulder, "Yes after I left, your grandfather came to see me a short time later and told me the secret of the sword. He asked me to stay and guard it until his son came for it," He gestured to me with a flick of his hand. "Of course, your father wasn't the one to come."

Callum measured him closely, "I assume you are a Hunter, then?"

Morgan nodded, "Yes, I am. Although my Czar and I have not seen much in over twenty years." He seemed almost sad when he admitted that. "I miss the battles and the killings."

I shivered.

"So, what have you been doing?" Ashlen asked.

"We have been here guarding the sword and its secrets."

I studied him for a moment. His deep black eyes were focused away from everyone as if he might be ashamed.

"Do you know the secrets?"

His head jerked up, and his eyes locked onto me. He seemed to be studying me as well.

"Only time will tell what secrets I have been given, and that time will only present itself when or if you are the chosen one to pluck the sword from the shallow grasps of which it is held."

We all sat in uncomfortable silence for several minutes. Our little group managed to move closer together silently. Morgan's eyes leveled at me, and I tried not to look at him, afraid he might take it as a challenge.

Callum cleared his throat, "So your Czar doesn't try and come out on its own? Or try to speak to you?"

Morgan's eyes locked onto me, "My Czar is always with me."

His eyes filled with despair, pain, and maybe anger. Pretty sure he had gone a little crazy. I don't know if I could let myself be so consumed by something like he had been. Callum studied the floor pretty hard and leaned in closer to me. Our shoulders were touching at this point, while Ashlen and Harris whispered to each other. Raleigh made designs in the dirt with her finger.

"It takes a lot of energy to form a Czar, though it makes traveling a lot easier. The moment the Czar dissipates, your energy levels sink to zero, so the majority of the time, people choose to use their Czar for dire emergencies."

"Hey, I have a question. Why were snakes having a party in that river?" Raleigh had stopped doodling and looked expectantly at Morgan.

Morgan chuckled. From what I could tell, it sounded like a chuckle and replied, "We've never really been able to figure out why they are in the river, but from what some scientists guessed is there's something in the water. They don't stay at the river all year long. It's mostly during the summer months, but as I'm sure you noticed, they don't bite. Their main goal is to jump in the river and then slide back; they're on a continuous cycle. I mean, look at the world we live in."

Our little group fell into silence again. Morgan studied the fire and poked it with a long stick.

"How about telling me something about my family? Something about my father, James?" Somehow, I couldn't resist asking.

He watched me for a moment, "Well, what would you like to know?"

I shrugged, "Anything would be great."

He nodded, "Okay, your father drove me crazy."

I laughed, "Yeah, I've heard that from some other people."

"Before I became a Hunter, your father, uncle, and I were good friends. I will tell you something though, Jacob was pretty jealous of your father."

My eyebrows shot up. "Really? No one ever said anything about jealousy."

"They were only candid around their friends, and they didn't get close to people, because, according to them, they were here to fight, not to make friends. Your father was... great at everything when he applied himself. Jacob always tried to please Charles, but it seemed like whatever he did never satisfied your grandfather or James would do it better. Charles blamed a lot of what happened on himself, so I'm glad that in his final days, he was sorry for the way he had treated Jacob."

"When I met him, he said to tell James that he was sorry."

"When you met him?"

I gestured to Willow, "When I first touched the sword, it transported me into some other dimension of time where Charles was waiting."

He tilted his head. I couldn't help but think of how odd the motion looked on him.

"That's interesting. Well, those three years after your father came back, he was a very different person from when I knew him as a kid. He was very upset about your mother. He practically stopped talking to Charles. I know he never forgave Charles for not letting him go back to your mother."

I nodded. It was weird, but it felt like some weight had lifted from me. At the same time, more mysteries and confusions wove together. I never imagined that jealousy might be a part of my father's history.

"Wait, you were part of the dirty dozen. Weren't you?" My heart felt like it skipped a few beats.

Morgan looked at me sideways, "Haven't heard that name in a long time." He dug through his beard to scratch his cheek.

I scooted forward, "What can you tell me? Who were the others?"

He blinked at me for a few seconds before speaking, "I don't remember much of those days."

I thought my heart was going to either implode or I was about to shake the man to make him talk.

"Please, anything you can tell me."

Morgan seemed to wrestle with his thoughts, his mouth worked back and forth as if he was turning the thoughts around in his mouth.

"We had Georgie, Bails, beautiful Ava, snarky Samantha," he paused thinking some more. "Chris and Alvaro." He shook his head, "that's about all I can think of."

I looked excitedly at Callum. He nodded his head and smiled.

"Samantha and Alvaro are new. Thank you for telling me."

He nodded, "Georgie, Bails, Ava, and Dorian all died."

Crap. I felt like time wasn't on my side.

I pressed my lips together out of determination, "You gave me some new names so that helps." I smiled reassuringly at him.

We sat around the small fire that Callum had made, trying to keep warm. The waterfall didn't sound as loud. The moonlight reflected off the water and into the cave. Something crossed in front of the moon, making the cave fall into darkness for an instant. All of our heads whipped to the outside. Morgan got up and shuffled to the edge of the cave staring out through the breaks in the waterfall. Callum jumped up and moved to stand behind Morgan; his hand was bracing against the rock, his face tilted up toward the sky.

Callum talked over his shoulder, "You all need to see this."

I hurried to stand beside Callum. He moved to the side so I could stand in front of him. At first, all I could see was the moon and a dark sky, but then something moved across the moon. The shape was immense and black. My eyes followed the movement. The form became a bird, a very large bird. My eyes seemed to adjust to the night, allowing me to see that the whole sky was filled with birds. On closer look, we realized they were not birds, but Nightlins. My mouth fell open, and my neck started hurting from leaning my head back.

Callum turned quickly away, walking toward our bags. He began throwing things in the bags with no consideration of what went where or how they fitted into the packs.

"We need to leave now," he pointed toward the outside, "those things are going to Kingston," he jabbed his finger at his chest, "and I have to be there. I'm not going to let those people die without me there trying to defend them."

I stood at the mouth of the cave watching Callum pack. Harris had his hands on Ashlen's shoulders, both of them watching Callum too. Raleigh was peering outside, watching every movement that the Nightlins were making. Morgan sat, staring absentmindedly at the waterfall.

At some point, my body and mind started moving again. I found myself automatically moving and ended up standing beside Callum. I knelt beside him, "What about Willow?"

He glanced at me. His face held fury, "Don't you get it? People are going to die, and they are going to need every single kind of defense."

I nodded, "We'll come back for her." I turned to the others, "You heard the man we've got to go."

I stood up, placing my hands on my hips. They seemed to come out of their daydreams and moved frantically around the cave. Dirt and dust flew up as we maneuvered around the cave. Morgan stayed seated at the cave entrance. All of the packs were filled and ready to go. I slid the pack onto my back, securing it around my chest and middle. I made sure the fake Willow was secured and moved to stand beside Morgan. He looked at me for a second, then focused his attention back to the waterfall.

"You've got a long road ahead of you." The words came slow and filled with sadness.

I looked down at him, "Yes, I know. We'll see you soon, I'm sure."

Morgan kept his eyes on the pool, "The Willow you seek is buried. Buried deep inside of the Willow. This Willow you will find deep in the pool, deep in the caverns. You will have to use all of your power and the things given to you to pry her out of the cold fingers of death." He turned to me as he spoke the last words. "You won't find me here the next time you come."

"We won't?"

He shook his head, "No, something is coming." He stared fixedly on nothing of importance; he was thinking very hard. I could almost see thoughts running through his mind. "I can feel it." He looked up at me, "You take care of yourselves."

I reached out and grabbed his arm, "Why not go with us? Fight with us?"

He studied me for a moment, and his black eyes stared straight through me, "I can't. I can't be part of that world anymore." He lifted his bag up to his shoulder. Stopping at the edge of the cave entrance, he looked back at all of us, like he was trying to memorize our faces or the moment, but sympathy etched into the lines of his face. He turned his back on us and jumped through the streaming water. Hopping around the rocks and sprinting through the dense trees, he moved quickly and with determination like he was on a mission.

27

I STOOD behind the falling water, watching him run through the forest. I waited until I could no longer see him darting between the trees. I looked over my shoulder at Harris, Raleigh, Ashlen, and Callum. All of their eyes were on me, waiting.

I spoke softly, "Let's go."

I grabbed one of the rocks, pulling myself up one inch at a time. Someone took hold of one of my feet and lifted. Callum pushed my feet upward. I lurched upward and grabbed onto whatever I could find. A short laugh came out of my mouth as I was propelled up. It felt like I was flying. I cleared the top. I grabbed hold of a tree root and pulled myself up with all the strength I had in me. I collapsed on the ground with my arms spread out and one foot dangling over the edge. Callum jumped up beside me. My heart almost leapt out of my chest.

"You scared me." I pulled the hair off my face and was shocked by how breathy my voice was.

He was kneeling beside me. He pulled some strands of hair from my cheek, "You're a mess," his eyes glittered with a smile. Adrenaline pumped through both of us. If one of us leaned forward a little, something could happen.

"Thanks." I sat up on one elbow. We both heard a noise.

He smiled and went back to the edge of the cliff to help Raleigh scale the rocks. He wrapped his hand around her forearm. She clambered up and practically fell onto the ground. She lifted up with a huge toothy grin on her face.

"That was graceful."

I smiled back at her, "That is your middle name."

Ashlen appeared at the edge of the rock. She had her arms under her pushing up. Callum and I reached out to help her. We each grasped one arm and pulled her up, her stomach sliding along the ground.

"Geez! Be careful. I'm delicate." She rolled over onto her back, placing her hand on her stomach. She pulled her shirt up to show that her skin was turning red.

"Sorry, Ash, we didn't mean to."

"Yeah, yeah, okay," she grimaced then, slowly sat up.

Harris hopped over the rim of the overhang, "That was fun. Used to go climbing all the time back home."

Ashlen glared at him.

"Hey, you okay?" Harris stooped down and took her hand, pulling her up.

"Yeah, I'm fine. I decided I needed to exfoliate." Ashlen narrowed her eyes at Callum and me.

I rolled my eyes at her, "Stop being such a baby. We need to get going." I looked toward the sky. The Nightlins were still flying overhead. "And be quiet," I gestured toward the sky, "we can't afford for them to hear us."

They became quiet. Callum stepped in front of me and started leading the way back to the city. We started out at a brisk jog. Leaping over rocks and sticking close to the river. The moonlight painted the path so we could see. We were moving pretty fast. It had taken us maybe five hours to find the waterfall. We were going to make it back to Kingston in less than two hours.

My hair became untied, so it was whipping around my neck and flying out behind me. My legs stretched to cover the most ground. I pumped my arms hard to help propel me faster. Every now and then, a small branch would whip across my face, stinging my skin. A humming whispered through my mind. Every leaf, rock, and detail down to the creases in Callum's clothes were thrown into high definition. A headache throbbed behind my eyes. I started moving faster. Grass and trees became a blur. I overtook Callum, passing him breathlessly. We were almost to the city perimeter.

I stopped.

Dirt and grass flew around me as I braked. The sight of the Kingston mountain was astonishing. I had stopped where the thickness of the trees dissipated. We stood on the edge of the line of trees, watching the massacre unfold. Black portals dotted the sky above the ridge. The Nightlins were savagely attacking the city, swooping down and snatching people up before they dropped them again. It was a scene from a nightmare or a horror movie. It was surreal. Screams erupted. We could hear shouting and some roars and bellows. Nightlins swarmed around the highest point of the city, like giant black vultures circling the dead.

I heard the others stop behind me. We were stunned from disbelief. Callum was the first to move again.

"Come on. We can enter at the river portal." He took my hand and pulled me forward.

We ran along the bank of the river, keeping low and in the shadows. Nightlins flew overhead. They circled over the mountain then dove straight down. A black hole formed, and the Nightlins disappeared through it. Screams echoed as the Nightlins vanished.

What the literal fuck? How did they do that?

"How the fuck did they do that?" Harris yelled.

Callum shook his head, "No time."

We made it to the small raft. Callum didn't hesitate; he jumped into the river. We followed him, eagerly jumping off the edge. The portal swallowed us whole. We broke the surface and ran to the wall.

People yelled, trying to escape. Arrows shot into the air intermittently at the Nightlins, some hitting their targets and some being an annoyance. Nightlins constantly attacked, catching people in their large teeth.

Something exploded within the city, causing my heart to beat faster. Harris and Ashlen moved so they would have some safety against the wall.

Callum peered around the edge of the building. His dark hair plastered to his head and dripped with sweat. I crawled over to him and looked over his shoulder—several bodies laid in the street. Fire consumed the houses, as it leapt from one house to the next. Callum glanced back at me.

"We need to get to the main building. That's where everyone will be holding up. I think our best chance is to go through the cemetery."

I know my face showed surprise because he smiled slightly and shook his head.

"Listen, it'll be okay. It's the safest way to go without having Nightlins dive bomb us."

I nodded, "You have a point. Show us the way."

He smiled and looked around me at the other three, who leaned heavily against the wall. "Hey, everyone get ready. We're about to go to the tombs and get inside the main building from there."

They nodded and sat up either resting on their knees or by squatting. The air was so dry because of the heat from the fire that our clothes were nearly dried out.

Callum stood up, "Stay close."

He took off around the perimeter of the buildings. He skidded to a stop by one large building. He held a finger up to his lips and pointed around the corner. I was right behind him, so I leaned around him to see why he was gesturing.

A large black creature came out of the building. It was taller than an average man and yet looked like a man except it had immensely large wings folded against its back. The bend of the wings extended a foot or more over its head, and the tips barely brushed the dirt as it walked. Walking didn't accurately describe its gait; it was more staggering. The creature's two legs, which were thick with muscle, were bent at the knee, making the rest of its body lean slightly forward. Its back was rounded and broad. Large painful-looking nodules covered its whole body. Its arms were large and corded with muscle, so they looked too big for its body. Long shiny talons and fingers were at the end of the arms.

What disturbed me the most was the creature's face.

A shadow of humanity was etched into its features. You could tell that at one time, whatever this creature was now, had at one point been human. But now its face was hollow and stretched. It had nothing where its nose should have been and no ears. The face was a combination of bone and taut skin. Like dried leather. Its skull and the parts where it was supposed to have eyes were made of bone, but the rest of its face moved with no structure to hold it together.

Goosebumps rose along my arms. I was fixated. I hadn't realized I had started walking toward the creature until Callum grabbed me and pushed me against the side of the building.

"What do you think you're doing?" he ground the words out as quietly as he could.

I blinked and shook my head. Sweat appeared on my forehead and slid down my temple. My breath was shaky as I blew the air out.

"I, I, don't know... I don't know what came over me," My hand shook as I wiped the sweat from my eyes.

Callum peered around the building again. The creature pierced the night with a guttural scream. Its wings beat the air as it soared into the sky. My breathing leveled out, and my heart began to beat normally. Callum's hand was still pressed against my shoulder. He had placed one foot between mine so that the right side of his body was pressed against me. I pushed him. He jerked around to look at me.

"I'm fine."

"Settle down," but he moved away from me, "as long as you don't go out walking toward death again, we should be fine."

I glared at him. He had a point, though. Why had I moved toward that creature? What was the pull that it had on me? Just thinking about it made my heart hammer in my chest again.

Ashlen stood right behind us, her eyes were big and round, "What was that?"

Callum had his focus on the sky, "I have no idea." Callum looked back at us, "Come on, we need to get to the tombs as fast as we can, so stay close to one another and keep your eyes open to the sky."

He ran to the neighboring building, keeping to the shadows. We stayed right on top of him. At one point, we had to run up a slight hill, and we no longer had cover from the buildings. We ran along the wall, trying to stay in the shadows. Nightlins continually flew and circled over the buildings. The main building was ravaged with fire, but the structure was still holding up.

Callum didn't wait to see if we were behind him when he reached the cliff, he dropped straight from sight. We followed him. He was crouched on the floor when I landed beside him. He registered my arrival, with a quick glance, and started running down the steps. My weapons slapped against my legs and back as I bounded down the steps after him. We were silent as we ran down. Only the noise of our feet hitting the stones, our heavy breathing, and the movement of our weapons resounded. We made it to the iron gate. Callum threw the gate open, and we continued running into the tunnel. I was already pulling my necklace out when we came to the large walnut door. I knelt swiftly and inserted the key into the door, turning it quickly and pushing the door inward once I heard the click.

We ran inside until we came to the chamber where Jonathon Smith stood memorialized. This time when we barged in, it was like we had breached an invisible layer. It slowed me down like I was suddenly wading through a gel. Something brushed against my skin and pulled on my body then, I broke through the layer and stumbled. I leaned against the dais. The others were panting beside me.

"Okay, now where do we go from here?" The room had several tunnels that led to only God knows where. I glanced over my shoulder. Raleigh was wide-eyed and staring at one of the tunnels. "Raleigh?"

She flicked her gaze at me, then back to the tunnel. She pointed, "I think we need to go that way."

We turned in the direction she had pointed. The tunnel had spider webs covering the entrance. Callum walked up to it and lit the torch inside. The light spread across the wall and ground in a warm glow. He pushed the webs out of the way and looked inside the tunnel. Webs covered the tunnel as far as we could see.

Raleigh was standing very still, breathing shallow, and her eyes had changed completely black. I slowly touched her arm. She jumped but settled when she realized it was me.

"Why do you say we need to go that way?"

Her voice shook as she spoke, "There's a woman standing there beckoning with her hands to follow her. She keeps coming back to the entrance. She looks... anxious." As her voice trailed off, it held a thoughtful and calm undertone. She took several steps toward the tunnel and stopped at the entrance. "Come on. I think it will be okay."

"You think?" Harris asked uncertainly. He looked kind of spooked.

Raleigh walked into the tunnel, grabbing a torch as she passed by it. We filed in after her. She hesitated when we came to three more tunnels, but then quickly walked down the left tunnel.

"Hurry."

Our steps quickened as we followed her through the tunnel. We slowly moved upward. We took another turn and reached... a dead end.

28

Graham

HE TRUDGED along the base of the mountain, trying to find a secure place to climb, a spot where the slope was slight, and trees dotted the area, making it easier to hold on to as he ascended the Nightlin mountain. He tied his hair back with a string and climbed. The mountainside was steep, and his thighs burned halfway up. Grabbing hold of the tree trunks, helped propel himself forward.

He scrutinized the landscape, trying to find something that didn't quite fit.

He came to the ridge and stopped. He gazed into a valley. A large onyx lake nestled between the mountain ranges. A river fed the lake; it wound its way between the mountains and disappeared. Scores of trees dotted the land like a thick blanket. The moon hung high, and the stars showed in full force.

He spotted several creatures flying over the mountain like they were flying toward the city. Maybe more will fly out of their hiding place so that he could find them.

He stayed in that same spot for an hour, maybe more, his eyes locked onto the mountain ranges. He scanned every inch of the rocky terrain. A black creature sprung into the air, but he couldn't tell where it had come from. He was getting annoyed and desperate.

Then he heard a splash, and his eyes instantly fixed onto the lake. Ripples moved across the still surface of the black water. He leaned forward, trying to pick out a shape. His fingers dug into the soil, rigid with anticipation.

Again, a black creature leapt into the air. Flecks of water flew as its wings beat the air. He needed to get closer to the lake. He hurdled from the ridge and landed at a run. He dodged and bounded over fallen trees and roots.

His heart hit his rib cage with excitement. This would be the day he found her. He would rescue her. They would leave, go far from these creatures that had brought him so much grief, where the two of them could be together without interruption, and forget about these past years.

His feet hit the ground assuredly. He barely touched the ground.

He glided to a stop a few feet from the water. He didn't want to chance being seen now, so he knelt behind a tree and waited.

The ripples announced something was coming first, as it broke the surface. The inky black water made it hard to see, but he spotted a pair of eyes turn in his direction. The creature's nostrils flared. His breath stopped. The eyes moved to the other side of the lake. It swam to the opposite bank. He let out the breath he had been holding. The creature slid out. Its body shook, slinging the water off. Its wings spread as it soared into the air. It flew around the lake once and then headed in the direction of the city, the same as the others.

He hated to admit that anytime he saw a Nightlin, his muscles quivered with fear.

His heart faltered at the black water. He had never been a great swimmer, but that's because he had been made for the sky. The black depths frightened him, but he would do anything for her, anything to see her again, to hold her.

No matter what, he would dive into the water.

Funny, how he had told her he would travel to the center of the earth and back because that's precisely what he was going to do.

———

The Dark

THE FEEL of the cool air that ran along his body felt like heaven, like fingers caressing his face.

His wings were outstretched and moved up and down, propelling his body forward. The feathers laid flat against his body from the air pushing against him. It felt so good to beat the air, to breathe in the cold. The moon was exceptionally bright tonight. It was a good omen. The moon gave them the light they needed so they could vanquish their enemies.

The land below him flew by fast. The forest stretched out beneath him. He focused on the city that he was about to destroy. The portals were opened right where they needed to be. The lights from the city flickered with the gusts of the wind created by his beating wings. People walked along the deserted roads. The tallest building on the hill stood out like a beacon, calling to him.

He was going to enjoy this moment very much.

The servants beside and behind him stayed quiet. They knew what would happen if they disturbed the moment. Their eyes were locked onto the city, and he could feel their anticipation. The ones who could not fly were being carried on the servant's backs or in their claws. They would be released once they reached the city walls.

He had been waiting for this for a long, long time. He could barely contain his joy. His brother had said their day would come, and they would finally be able to get what they had always wanted.

29

Sloane

"Umm... Raleigh?"

"Hold on. She's saying something..." Raleigh lifted her torch upwards toward the dirt ceiling. "I think she's saying to go up."

Callum moved toward her and started hitting the ceiling with the hilt of his sword. Ashlen and I moved away from the falling dirt. Harris moved forward to help. Dirt rained down on top of them, their damp hair catching the soil easily. The guys struck something. We looked up to see cracks of light shining through slats of wood.

"Harris, give me a boost up," Callum said.

Harris locked his hands and Callum set one foot in Harris's hands. Harris lifted while Callum pushed on the boards. The boards creaked and whined as he pushed, but finally, a little trap door opened. Harris pushed Callum through the opening. Callum pulled himself up, sitting on the edge of the gap, and turned around to help us up through the hole. Harris stayed in the tunnel with us, giving us a leg up.

Before we closed the door back, Raleigh ran to the edge and leaned over, yelling, "Thank you," into the dark tunnel. She stood, brushing her hands off on her pants, beaming.

We were in the kitchen of the main building. Shelves lined the walls with food piled on them. Callum opened the door and peeked around the corner. The halls deserted. We walked out to the dining hall, but no one was there either. I moved over to the staircase that led to our rooms, but it had crumbled and caved in.

"This way!" Callum directed us through a hallway and down a set of stairs.

We entered a room that was missing part of the exterior wall and ceiling. The Realmers had pushed tables, chairs, and whatever else they could find in the middle of the room, providing a barrier from the flying Nightlins. Watchers and Protectors gathered under the barrier, each holding several weapons. Several of the Hunters and their Czars perched along the wall, their massive bodies were having a hard time fitting into the cramped quarters. The colors of the Czars' scales and feathers ranged from black, purple, gold, white, and any variance in-between. They easily dwarfed us.

Chuck came through the far door. The only way to describe the way he looked was to say that he glowed. His skin appeared to have a hint of brownness to it, but some sort of light pushed through, making him seem almost like one of the Greek gods from one of my school books. His eyes caught my attention because they also glowed, except that they looked like dragon's eyes like he was about to shift into his Hunter form. His eyes were yellow and gold. The pupil was large and black, looking more and more like the eyes of a bird. Yellow electrical currents lazily whipped around his hands and feet. He headed in our direction, those yellow eyes staring right at me.

I couldn't control my heart from speeding up.

"I'm glad you decided to show. We are organizing a counter-attack." Chuck's voice had become gravelly and deeper; the effects of him about to change. "We have our air support waiting in the room through that door. I am sending the rest of you to the ground to attack the ground anchored Nightlins. The children have been relocated to a part of the tombs. If everyone will get to their positions, we will then give a signal for our counter-attack to begin." Chuck walked over to the next room. The muscles in his body were tense and rigid.

His eyes darted back and forth, watching every movement. He was immensely scary.

I caught myself staring, and Callum was watching me.

Movement began in haste all around me, while everyone rushed to get to their posts. Watchers and Protectors were getting in position as we traveled down to the ground level with some of the Protectors. We congregated in the entry of the main building, and people were passing out weapons and armor. The fires that were usually lit in the dining hall had been left unattended, so the embers glowed faintly, making the room feel less inviting.

Callum came to stand in front of me. His eyes roamed over every inch of me. I squirmed. He moved to stand behind me and started tightening the straps of my armor. Some he tightened so much that my limbs tingled.

I cleared my throat, "You know you're kind of scaring me?"

He kept his focus on tightening each strap, but I saw the corners of his mouth tug slightly, "Remember what I said?"

I let out a sigh and mumbled, "Yes." I flicked my eyes behind me to see his reaction.

This time the smile spread across his whole face, "I'm making sure you will be safe, so no more arguing or whining."

I rolled my eyes as an answer.

Raleigh and Ashlen were standing next to me. Each ran their fingers across each piece of armor. Ashlen's fingers trembled slightly. She jerked her head up to look at me. Her eyes were wide, but there was determination shining through; her hands stilled. Harris was standing off to the side; he looked lost in thought, but he didn't seem scared. I scanned the crowd of beings. Everyone was pacing either because they were nervous or anxious, maybe both. You could see the fear on their faces or in the way they huddled together.

I spotted Molly and Rory standing in a far corner. They had numerous amounts of weapons strapped across their bodies. Stephen was closest to the door; his black hair hid his eyes, and his head was bowed like in prayer. A long wooden staff was held between his hands. The staff was a foot taller than him and looked smooth except for the carvings that decorated the top.

A large white Czar nearly knocked me over; it looked over its shoulder at me. Its eyes were boring into me, the sharp teeth gleaming from its mouth, its talons clicking on the stone floor as it pushed through the crowd of people. I laid my hand out along its long tail, the feathers and scales sliding through my hand effortlessly, and it whacked me in the face with it. Miranda followed after it. She lumbered on through the crowd, pushing people out of her way.

You know how in books or in movies when they describe the calm before the storm or right before the big battle there's a heavy silence? Well, they don't describe it well enough. The silence wasn't calm but ratcheted with nervousness. The air smelled of fear, failure, and death. To me, silence didn't exist at that moment. The air buzzed with noise.

Something roared. Everyone stood straighter, and the group tightened. The people closest to the door pulled the massive double doors back. The moon shone brightly over the whole city. The shadows of the building were like gaping holes, waiting to swallow us whole. Sounds like birds could be heard flapping and screeching through the night. We filed out the doors in two long lines. The Hunters marched along the lines acting as a barrier. Electricity moved in currents up and down their arms. Their Czars were about to be called forth. We stood with our backs to the building, facing our death.

30

AT FIRST, I couldn't see anything moving, but then my eyes seemed to adjust to the darkness. The shadows moved restlessly. Now and then, a dark figure ran from one shadow to the next. They were coming for us. I looked down the lines to see everyone pulling out their weapons, preparing for the onslaught.

The long claws of the Nightlins clung to the edges and roofs of the buildings. Sometimes, pinpricks of light reflected from the shadows; their eyes watched us.

One figure stepped out from the shadows. It almost looked like the creature that we had run upon earlier when we entered the city, but this one didn't have wings. Instead, it had what looked like razors growing out of its back and along the backs of its arms. Dark strips of cloth hung from its body. Again, I couldn't see its eyes just the spaces where they should have been. It didn't have lips. Its long sharp teeth pierced through the holes in its mouth.

Something inside of me perked up.

This thing in front of me was calling to me, or I was calling it. I felt a connection. The creature studied me. It raised its arm and made an inarticulate noise. The shadows unfolded to reveal more Nightlins waiting. They crept from behind the buildings. Some looked like a bunch of bones held together with ligaments. They had the same dark, stretched skin with gaping holes for eyes and noses.

The hairs on my arms stood to attention, and goosebumps ran up my arms and down my legs. I turned to Callum standing beside me. His lips were in a thin line, and his teeth clenched.

He spoke to me without taking his eyes from the creatures, "Remember what you've trained to do, and I'll be right beside you the whole time."

The Nightlins stood in a line maybe a hundred yards away. When they breathed, steam issued out of the holes in their bodies. The breeze blew the strips of black cloth that hung from their limbs. A few of them had drool hanging from their mouths.

I heard Jess yell, "Fit your bows!"

At once, everyone lifted an arrow to the bows and sighted on the Nightlins. Some of the Hunters took off into the sky, their Czars swiftly soaring straight for the Nightlins circling above our heads. The massive creature raised his arm again, and the Nightlins shifted their weight and kneeled, preparing to run or jump at us. I had my arrow pointed directly at the supposed leader of the Nightlins. I aimed right at his chest.

Jess yelled, "Now!"

Hundreds of arrows whistled through the air toward the horde of Nightlins. At the same time, the Nightlins sprinted toward us. As the first set of arrows left the bows, we immediately fitted another arrow and let them fly. Some of the arrows struck their intended targets while others seemed to disintegrate before they hit their mark as my arrow did. The Nightlins were on top of us before I could string another arrow. They crashed into us.

I remember hearing Jess yell then, there was a loud pop, and his Czar appeared, his energy melting into black feathers and scales like liquid poured from a glass. Jess swung up onto the back of the ferocious animal. The muscles bulged and moved effortlessly through his body. He looked like a black eagle on steroids, which began tearing into any black creature he could touch.

White streaks of light, as if it were electricity, erupted from the ground from all around me. Protectors formed their shields. The Hunters and their Czars took to the air. Watchers, Protectors, Hunters, and Czars yelled their battle cries and lunged at the creatures. Everything blurred. Some of the Protectors moved at super-speed, hacking and chopping at the Nightlins. Black fluid sprayed out in every direction.

I picked out Miranda, on her bright white Czar, leaping through the air toward a nasty looking Nightlin. Assuming it was Jess's black Czar, took down another Nightlin. In a matter of seconds a Nightlin appeared before me. I arched an arrow, and it hit the creature between its eyes. It crumpled to the ground, and I pulled out my knife and stabbed it in the chest for good measure. My knife, Masada, glowed blue, the black blood running down the carved blade. The creature disintegrated. I looked to see if anyone else had witnessed its demise, but another Nightlin was on top of me.

This creature was bonier with long needle-like claws, which it tried to use on my face. I twisted away from it and dropped my bow to the ground. I grabbed for my sword, yanking it from the scabbard. The buzzing noise started in the front of my head right behind my eyes. I ran toward the creature. It reared as I got closer. Its claws sliced through the air coming toward my head. I ducked, sliding on my knees with my arms raised, bracing the sword. The sword cut through its middle. Black blood sprayed across my face. I hopped up and spun around for another attack, but the creature collapsed to the ground in two pieces. Its life fluids quickly spilled out of it onto the dirt path.

Realmers were scattered everywhere. Nightlins laid in heaps. I was standing closest to the main building. People and creatures fought below me. I took off at a sprint around the carnage of bodies toward the last survivors. I tried to search for my friends, but there was too much going on. I think I spotted Ashlen's dark hair swirling around her, but she disappeared behind the others.

I jumped into the action, swinging my sword around at every black creature. I ran my sword through the things tearing off limbs and depositing their heads onto the dirt. I was soon covered in black oily blood. It stained my clothes and made my hair look brown.

A sound like a fog horn erupted from the top of the main building. I jerked my head up to the sound only to see hundreds of Nightlins flying through the air, circling the building. Czars of all shapes flew into the sky toward the Nightlins. They rammed against the dark creatures, but several of the birds plummeted to the ground. Screeching noises and caws could be heard at every moment.

Something sliced through my arm, bringing my attention back to the fight before me. I rolled without seeing where I was going. I rolled into a body. I stopped. The body had raven black hair. He looked like Stephen. My heart instantly seized, and I let out a sob. I reached out to touch him to see if it was really him, but I recoiled. I gripped my sword to my chest and turned toward the Nightlin that was climbing over bodies to get to me.

The buzzing started again in my head. I stood with the sword gripped so tightly in my hand that my fingers began to hurt and burn. My anger coursed through me, and I used it against the Nightlin. It cleared one of the bodies, jumping toward me. Its razor-sharp teeth gleamed in the moonlight, and spittle flew from its gaping mouth. Its long claws reached me first. They sliced my arm, but I dropped to the ground and swung my arm away from it. I leaned into the right, raising the sword up toward its chest. The sword hit its chest and embedded in the black flesh. The creature screamed a high-pitched wail. My body shook from the noise. It landed on top of me with either hand to each side of me. Its face was mere inches from mine. I could smell its distinct odor like raw sewage. The creature brought its face closer to mine, opening its jaws wide like it was about to take a huge bite out of me, then it stopped. It reared back, and a sword point appeared in its middle. Someone yanked the sword out, and the creature fell to the side, revealing Callum as my savior.

He had black goo all over him. It was caked on his clothes and dripped down his face. His hair was plastered to his head. Exhaustion was clearly written across his face and body. His sword hung loosely in his hand by his side. He held out his left hand to help me up. I grabbed his hand with my right, and he pulled with every muscle in his body straining. I bent down to pick my sword back up and turned to Callum.

He wiped some of the black blood from his eyes with his forearm, "Some of us are holed up in a building over here, follow me."

He started jogging and leaping over the fallen. His sword was still held in his hand. He took a sharp right down a small alley between the buildings and stopped at a small door. He pushed the door open, and briskly pulled me inside. People talked, and some yelled. The room we had entered into was dark; I couldn't make out any shape, but Callum seemed to know where to go. He took my hand and led me through the room and to another door. We walked through the doorway onto a scene of a huddled group of every kind of Realmer. Part of the far wall had been either pushed out or blown away. The Realmers had pushed tables and other things they could use as protection against the hole in the building. Now and then, a Nightlin's claw or hand would try to grapple inside of the hole only to be burned or hacked. People would stand and fire arrows through the opening, striking whatever they sighted.

I moved to a corner where I could see out a small window. Nightlins were packed around the small building. I spotted the larger Nightlin leader in the middle of the group who towered above all the rest. Its broad boney chest glistened with blood; I hoped it was its own. Its attention seemed to swing around to where I was at the window. I stepped back, putting my face in the shadows. Its focus stayed transfixed on the window for several minutes before one of the creatures interrupted. It swung around to the beast hitting it. The smaller creature fell against the dirt and slithered away. It slowly turned back to the building. I retreated to stand next to Callum.

"What's going on? Where are the girls and Harris?"

Callum looked down at his arm, which I had subconsciously wrapped my hand around. I released his arm quickly, rubbing the palm of my hand on my pants. I saw a smirk appear on his lips, but he instantly diminished it.

"We're about to storm the gates." He focused his gaze back to the action.

"Callum, where is everyone else?" I asked hesitantly.

He glanced at me, his mouth growing thin.

"Sloane, have some patience. We will find them."

A noise broke through the fighting sounds, something that screeched like a horned owl. We collectively moved to the small opening in the wall so we could see out. The leader seemed to be yelling at the other Nightlins; they shrunk away from him. He yelled again, and they slowly gathered around him. He turned toward our small building, his shoulders rolling, and his teeth gleaming. His mouth opened like it was on a hinge, opening farther than any normal mouth. He screamed then sprinted toward us. He leapt through the air and hit the face of the building.

The building shook.

Dust and dirt fell from the ceiling. The opening began to crumble even more. The creature's black arms and claws appeared through the opening. Everyone swiftly moved to block his entry. We rammed the tables and pieces of wood against the gap. The Nightlins kept trying to tear through. The smaller Nightlins attacked whatever they could. Screeching and screams filled the night.

Callum pushed his way to the front. I scrambled behind him. He pushed against the boards, trying to lift the board to bar the way of the creatures. I was blocked from advancing toward Callum. A warm light interrupted the darkness. I tried to peer around everyone to see where the light was coming from, but all I could see were arms and heads.

The light grew brighter then, something burst into flames. Nightlins screeched. Fireballs were being thrown at the retreating Nightlins, eating them up. People started pushing me back. I stumbled and fell against the floor. Everyone moved around me so I could see what had caused the commotion.

A man stood by the opening of the structure we had used to block the hole. His back faced me. His head bent forward, looking at the ground. He lifted his hands like he was inspecting them. Flames moved across his fingers and hands as he moved each appendage.

The realmers around me stepped back. They appeared to be as surprised as I was. The man looked directly at me.

His eyes were pure white.

Fire engulfed his arms. It flickered and moved as it traveled across his skin and clothes. His clothes still looked intact. He glowed in warm colors of red and orange. He started to walk toward me. As he moved closer, the fire seemed to extinguish; his clothes and skin were becoming their natural color again. He knelt in front of me. The flames were last to leave from the tips of his fingers, but I had known who it was. Callum smiled. The only remnants of the fire shined through his eyes. The white dimmed to a soft yellow, but when he blinked, the fire left them, changing back to the deep, forest green color I had become accustomed to always find watching. He held his hand out to me. I looked at his hand then back at his face. Steam rose from his olive skin.

I slipped my hand into his, electricity ran up my arm, and he pulled me to my feet. His hand was slightly warmer than usual. I stood there watching him for several seconds.

"We need to figure out how we are going to get back to the main building," a voice replied.

Callum turned his attention to the guy that had spoken. A guy I had seen a few times, but never learned his name. He was slightly taller than Callum but wiry.

"We can move from one building to the next until we reach the main one. We should separate into groups that way if the Nightlins do attack, then they won't be able to get all of us."

The guy nodded. I noticed some of the others putting their weapons back into their holders and tightening their armor.

Callum turned back to me. His voice lowered as he spoke, "You okay?"

My eyebrows rose, "Yeah, I'm fine."

He studied the hole in the building, "I'm not sure what happened to the others."

My heart dropped. "But that doesn't mean that they aren't okay?"

He shook his head, "No, it doesn't. They are fighters like us," his mouth lifted slightly.

People around us moved toward the small door. Jordan came over to speak to Callum, and they moved away from me. Watchers and Protectors brushed by me. Callum moved back to stand beside me; his fingers wrapped around my elbow. He gently pushed me toward the door. A group of three or four disappeared into the night. We waited in the dark for what felt like an hour. The small amount of light that I could see would appear whenever someone would enter or leave. The only sound was the steady opening and closing of the door.

I stood close to Callum. I was very aware of how close he was next to me. The top of my head came to his chin, so he watched everything going on over my head. We were mere inches away from each other. The light reflected in his eyes.

His arm tightened around me, and before I knew what had happened, his soft lips kissed mine. A tender second passed. It was over before I could react. I gasped. He turned to the door listening again to the noises outside. He squeezed me tighter to him.

My brain stopped for a moment. I was so happy and shocked all at once. My fingers had fisted his shirt, and I had to unlock them consciously.

I smiled, then whispered as each of my fingers released him, "Callum, what happened back there? You know, with you turning into flames?"

His gaze flicked down at me, then back to our surroundings, "I guess my abilities are progressing." I could hear his excitement as he spoke. I couldn't help but be excited with him.

"So, you now have an aptitude for fire? You're like the Fantastic Four guy?"

He chuckled, "Well, I'm pretty sure I can't fly, so I'm not completely like him." As he spoke, yelling broke out from outside.

Callum rushed the door and carefully pushed it open. I tried to see, but several others had pushed in front of me. Through a small hole in the gathering of people, Nightlins had sprung onto some of the Realmers that had run out of our building. Callum rushed out, pulling out his sword, igniting his shield as he ran. We followed him.

The instant we ran out, the leader of the Nightlins jumped down from one of the buildings. We tried to move out of his way, but one person got in his way. The creature caught him up with his sharp claws. The man yelled and tried to swing his blade down into the creature's face, but the thing took hold of one of his arms and legs. I could hear the wet crunching and popping sound of the man's ligaments and muscles tearing. It happened so quickly that my mind decided not to make sense of the scene before me. The man was there in the creature's grasp one moment, and then in the next, parts of him were thrown through the air.

We scattered and tried to take refuge behind some of the buildings. I lost sight of Callum. The Realmers were tearing into the Nightlins. The large Czars were joining forces and pouncing on a Nightlin ripping and clawing. Because the Czars were made from light and energy, they were nearly indestructible. They're only weakness was the Hunters, weak humans compared to everything else. The Nightlins did their best to take out each Hunter.

I had my sword in my hand hanging by my side. I was standing in the middle of the fight watching everything around me. I didn't see the Nightlin leader come for me.

I was suddenly on the ground, looking up into his empty eyes. Saliva fell on my cheek. He leaned down and breathed into my face. He smelled of rotting flesh. My heart thumped loudly in my chest, threatening to come out. I pushed with all my strength. My sword laid beside me. I reached out fruitlessly. My hand kept grabbing the dirt. I got my knees between our bodies, putting some distance between us. Masada rested in its holder against my thigh, and I grappled for it.

His claws dug into my shoulders, and I screamed in agony. I could feel him hit my bone. It felt like volts of electricity had been shot through my system.

My fingers grasped the handle of Masada, and I clumsily pulled him out. I shoved the blade into the creature's abdomen. The blade lit up with the white-blue light. Light from the blade spread across and through the creature's body. The Nightlin screamed, making my eardrums rattle. He leapt from me and ran through the foray.

I stayed lying on my back. Most of the smaller Nightlins had been killed or were in the process of being disposed of. Charred remains of Nightlins were scattered across the ground. People and animals were covered with the black oily blood of the Nightlins.

I propped up on my elbows and surveyed the damage. Three Realmers were gone. Dead. Several others were very much hurt and were going to need help soon. A handful were able to walk around and speak tangibly. I spotted Callum at the corner of one of the buildings. He had steam rising from him. He was helping someone to stand. He looked over at me. I gave a small wave and slowly sat up.

My shoulders were killing me. Blood oozed out of the openings. I gingerly tried to pull some of my shirt and armor away from the cuts, but it hurt like something awful. I was going to need stitches, morphine, and ice cream at some point.

"Here, let me help," Callum knelt beside me with some water. He poured the water over the wounds, and it stung. I hit him.

"I'm sorry. I'm sorry, but it'll help some."

"Yeah, sure." I glared at him. My sarcasm was ruined when I grimaced from pain.

"Come on. We've got to get moving." He placed his hands under my arms and lifted me close.

I slipped because my feet weren't cooperating fully. My head was also spinning from the pain that lanced through my shoulder. Images blurred.

"Slow down, wait a minute." I took a breath and tried to get centered. My breaths came out shaky and shallow. I could still feel Callum's hands on my waist and his chest against my back.

More screeching and screaming erupted through the night. This time the sounds seemed to be coming from the main building. Everyone tried to get the dead and injured into some of the buildings for shelter, while those that could walk and run started up the hill.

Callum stayed beside me.

"Alright, let's go." I grabbed my sword. I tucked Masada back into the holder. I started walking then, slowly jogged up the hill. Callum stuck by me the whole time, never saying a word. We stuck to the shadows and kept our eyes to the sky. I looked at every fallen person that we passed, hoping that it wasn't Ashlen or Harris or Raleigh.

Every now and then, Aeroes and other Nightlins flew or weaved through the sky. They dove toward the rooftop, sometimes with someone clutched in their claws.

Of course, we didn't stay on the main road, but it was difficult trying to find a way to get into the building without being seen. Callum found a small hidden door that was covered in shadows. He decided to try it first, in case he was going to have to kick it in or burn it with his new powers. He seemed pretty keen on burning.

He waited for a moment when the Nightlins were out of sight and raced for the door. He plastered himself against the building and edged toward the door. I guess it was locked because he started shoving heavily into it. He glanced over his shoulder at me and then pressed his palm to the door. His hand turned orange, with blue flames dancing across his skin, from the heat. I heard something pop, and he pushed once more. The door fell in, and Callum stumbled in after it. He disappeared because the room was pitch-black. He stuck his head back out and waved for me.

I stared up at the sky. Nightlins flew every which way. More Nightlins had arrived. The Nightlin, that we had almost run into on the street, had his black wings stretched out far, and he hovered right above the smaller Nightlins. Their focus was on something else, but I waited for more of them to disappear from my sight before I took off.

I ran straight for the door. Callum waited just inside. He caught me before I could stumble. Again, I was momentarily blinded, but Callum seemed to know where to go. He took my hand and led me through the dark. We came out into a hallway. A torch was set into the wall. The flame meagerly dipped high and low. The light it threw onto the walls was hazy and added to the fear that had built inside of me. Callum dropped my hand and jogged down the hall. I ran to keep up with him.

The hall had led us to the dining room. We took a hall that would lead us to Chuck and the Hunters. When we reached the room, it had been utterly destroyed. Instead of only part of the wall missing, now three walls and the majority of the ceiling were gone. Debris and bodies scattered the floor. I tried not to study them. Callum pulled me across the room to the other door. The Realmers were in the corner of the small room, firing arrows or wielding a sword.

The Nightlins swooped down and tried to grab the Realmers, but they were met with Czars of all different sizes, each with their counterpart riding on its back. The Hunters yelled battle cries and dove into the melee. Callum pulled me over to the Realmers. He stood in front of me with his arm pushing me hard against the wall.

We made it and hunkered down behind the others. We were under several heavy wood tables with rocks piled on top. We were cramped in the small space.

I looked at the dirtied and bloodied faces that surrounded me. They were worn and thin. They weren't going to last much longer. They had fight in their eyes, but I could tell their bodies were going to fail them first. Callum leaned out a few times and shot fireballs at the Nightlins, which surprised them thoroughly.

A small hole between two of the tables gave me a view of what was happening in the sky. I watched the same dark creature that I had nearly walked up to, soaring around the outside of the building. I needed to figure out something.

I needed to act, to stop the killing.

I made sure no one was looking and crawled to the corner of the room, where some of the rubble from the ceiling would make it easier to access the rooftop. I glanced behind me, but everyone was occupied with their own fight. I reached up, putting my weight on my arms and pushing myself up to the edge so that I could see over the rock roof. I pulled myself up onto the top of the building as fluidly as I could, hoping no one had seen me.

I stayed kneeling. I pulled my bow and arrows from my pack and fitted an arrow to the string then sighted down the shaft. I tightened my core and breathed through my nose, trying to gain control of my nerves. The black creature hadn't noticed me yet, so I was hoping to get the upper hand. Its back faced me, and its head was turned to watch below.

I pulled my arm back, aiming for between his shoulder blades. As the arrow came back, I pulled air in then let it out, letting the arrow fly simultaneously.

The arrow soared straight toward it, but it seemed to hear it at the last moment and turned swiftly, catching the arrow in his side. Black fluid sprayed out, and it screamed with anger. Its head whipped around, and its eyes landed on me.

It turned toward me and pinned its wings to his sides, making a dive straight for me. The creature was on top of me in seconds. Its claws tore through the skin on my arms and hands. With its claws, it grabbed my bow and arrows and crushed them. One large clawed hand tightened around my wrist. My feet left the rooftop. I lashed out, hitting it wherever I could. It dropped me. I rolled across the roof, holding my hurt hands against my chest. The wind around me shifted then, and it hit me again. This time its claws tore into my bicep and side.

I think I heard someone yell my name.

It was hard to breathe. I was sure I had broken one or more bones. I stayed lying on my back, staring up. My hearing didn't seem to work. The wind blew against my body and face, but that was all my senses relayed to me.

My head fell to the side. The rough surface of the roof pressed into my cheek. Silver metal gleamed in the moonlight. The sword had somehow fallen from my back. I rolled over to my stomach and slowly pulled myself toward the shiny handle. I glanced to see if I could find the creature, but he wasn't in my line of vision.

The creature screamed, and I jerked around to see arrows flying toward the monster. The black creature spun wildly through the air dodging the arrows perfectly. I spotted Callum's head and shoulders just above the roofline. His hands moved in a blur with him fitting arrows to the string. His dark hair swirled in the wind. Dirt and blood covered his face and ran in streaks down his arms. He yelled as he released each arrow.

My heart leapt with hope, and my crawling pace quickened. I heard a screech, and as my hand settled around the hilt of the sword, I rolled, facing the black sky. I swiftly yanked the sword from the scabbard and held the sword before me, trying to keep anything from attacking me. The creature had flown toward me from the side, but twisted past to avoid the sword. I pulled my knees under me and sat on my shins. I kept my eyes tuned to anything moving.

The wind blew my hair in my face, and my arms hurt from holding the sword. The gashes along my arms, hands, legs, side, and forehead throbbed, making it hard to concentrate. The cut on my right bicep leaked blood down my arm and collected in the bend of my arm.

The dark creature circled me. I was in the middle of the roof since the farside had collapsed. It swooped in close then flew out of reach again. It tried to push me to the edge of the crumbling ceiling, but I moved at the last second. I nearly fell and scraped my chin on the rough roof. Its massive wings spread out behind it, looming overhead.

The creature taunted me.

My anger made my headache worse. I gripped the sword and tried to keep my arms up. It could tell I was tired.

The top of Callum's head barely poked above the roofline. He yelled at people below him, trying to find more weapons. He kept looking fervently at me. His eyes frantic as he motioned the people below to hurry.

The creature flew on my right, and then, it was on top of me. It tore the sword from my hands and flung it over the side of the building. It laughed uproariously. I kneeled on the rooftop watching it. My mind rifled through every outcome, every possible action. I scanned the roof searching for any weapon I could use.

It lunged.

Callum screamed my name.

The creature's claws tore at my chest. Its razor-sharp talons sliced my skin open, reaching inside me. The pain was excruciating. Black spots filled my vision. I knew I didn't have much longer. Its mouth opened in a demonic smile.

Angry tears streamed down my face as I screamed. One of its arms wrapped around my body, keeping me pressed against it; the other hand greedily ripping inside my chest. My feet left the rooftop.

Cold enveloped me. Ice weighted my limbs.

The hollows of its eyes gazed into my soul. The black skin pulled tight as it laughed in my face.

Despair filled me. How could it laugh? How can this be real? Callum?

Its claws sank deeper and under my sternum and ribs. It seized my heart in its grasp and tightened its grip. My breath left my lungs, and my eyes squeezed shut. The pain lanced through my body. I gave in. Empty blackness swallowed me.

An alarm went off.

BEEP! BEEP! BEEP!

BEEP! BEEP! BEEP!

My eyes sprung open. Sunlight hit my face, blinding me for a moment. A golden room surrounded me. The navy bed sheets tangled around my body. The room seemed familiar. I gasped.

Home.

What the fuck?

EPILOGUE

Callum

MY HEARING CAME BACK FIRST.

High pitched screams, and other unidentifiable noises were excruciatingly loud to my sensitive hearing. So, I turned it off.

Serene stillness settled around me, though I knew it was anything but. My eyes wouldn't open, so I used my other senses.

Smoke, dirt, blood, and death permeated the air. Death. I could almost taste it, like iron and rotted meat.

Spreading my fingers out and moving my hands away from my body, chunks of the building had fallen away. My right hand brushed over something squishy and cold. I recoiled. More death.

Why couldn't I see?

I wiped my hands on my clothes then tried to wipe my eyes clean. I couldn't feel anything on my face except for dirt and blood, but no reason to cause blindness. I stayed kneeling on the ground and concentrated with every ounce of strength to open my eyes.

Blinding white light filled my vision.

I snapped my eyes shut. My fists clenched by my sides, and my nose flared from tension and anger. Something had felt different about that light. I slowly opened my eyes again.

The light never dimmed, but I could make out shapes. The outline of the room and the hole where the Nightlins had burst through stood out. The white light encompassed everything I looked at, even myself.

Slowly standing, I stretched my hand out in front of me and turned it over. The white light rolled around my hand. Little tendrils of light flickered and crawled through my fingers.

I dropped the mute from my hearing. Someone close by screamed. I spun to see Irene gaping. She took a couple steps towards me and stopped. Her eyes were big and round, her mouth in the shape of an O.

"You're, you're on fi-fire."

I looked down at my body, and this time my eyes made sense of what I could see. The flames licked up my legs and arms. The white light wasn't pure but shades of blue and orange, the colors defining different shapes and textures.

"Callum?"

Irene stood with her fingertips pressed to her lips. Her large, blue eyes were cautious.

"It's okay, Irene." My voice crunched out.

I looked once again at my body covered in white flames. Okay, how to... de-flame?

I closed my eyes and concentrated on turning it off. Opening my eyes, nothing had changed. I closed them again. My muscles contracted, and my hands tightened. Be calm; think of something soothing. For some reason, Sloane popped into my mind. That day standing by the crystalline pool filled my head. The way the light had reflected from the perfectly colored water onto her face and hair. The coolness of the cave was drowned out by her.

"It's gone," Irene murmured.

My eyes flashed open to a normal, dark world again. I gazed down at my body, and everything seemed normal. Normal as in covered in mud, red blood, and black goo. No evidence of the white fire was seen anywhere.

Except, when I took a step forward, I looked down and saw two black footprints had been scorched into the stone, where I previously stood.

"Where's Sloane?" I asked.

ABOUT THE AUTHOR

K.R. Bowman has been writing stories since she was a child, always with her head in the clouds, dreaming up different worlds. She has a Bachelor's in Interior Design that she uses for her day job. Her loves are traveling and discovering new pieces of the world. She currently lives in the south, where she drinks way too much sweet tea.

She loves all types of fiction but mostly writes fantasy, sci-fi, and mystery with a female lead. She loves action and adventure, and characters that a quirky underdog.

Printed in Great Britain
by Amazon

57432068R00156